D0262703

Dear Reader,

It has been a great pleasure for me to write a special story set in 1908. The Edwardian period has a strong nostalgia about it. It has been described as: "A leisurely time when women wore picture hats and did not vote, when the rich were not ashamed to live conspicuously and the sun never really set on the British flag." It was an era that contrasted with the periods that preceded and succeeded it—the long reign of Victoria and the harsh and terrible reality of the First World War.

Yet the Edwardian period has also been referred to as "the birth of now," a period that has far more in common with modern times than we might imagine. When I was writing this book I was constantly surprised at the parallels with modern life and that much of the technology in use today originated or was first developed in this period. Much of the London Underground had been built and was already referred to as "The Tube." The first aeroplanes were taking to the skies. The rich had installed telephones in their houses and the King would ring his friends up when he had decided to drop in for a visit.

I have set Jack and Sally's love story against the glittering backdrop of Edwardian high society and I hope that you enjoy this glimpse of that very special year, 1908.

Nicola

www.nicolacornick.co.uk

Nicola Cornick

DAUNTSEY PARK

The Last Rake in London

First published in Great Britain 2008, this edition 2012.
MIRA Books, an imprint of Harlequin (UK) Limited,
Eton House, 18-24 Paradise Road,
Richmond, Surrey, TW9 1SR

ISBN 978 1 848 45045 5

54-0112

MIRA's policy is to use papers that are natural, renewable and
recyclable products and made from wood grown in sustainable forests.
The logging and manufacturing processes conform to the legal
environmental regulations of the country of origin.

Printed and bound by
CPI Group (UK) Ltd, Croydon, CR0 4YY

The ancestral line of the Dukes of Kestrel had bred rakes
and rogues aplenty in the eighteenth and nineteenth
centuries. The family seat, Kestrel Court, is nestled in the
Midwinter Villages and you can read about the exploits
of the Kestrel family in Nicola Cornick's bestselling
series, the BLUESTOCKING BRIDES:

THE NOTORIOUS LORD
ONE NIGHT OF SCANDAL
THE RAKE'S MISTRESS

Available as eBooks.
Visit www.mirabooks.co.uk

Other novels by **Nicola Cornick**

WHISPER OF SCANDAL
ONE WICKED SIN
MISTRESS BY MIDNIGHT

To my wonderful grandmother, born Doris Mary Wood
in 1908, still an inspiration to me now.

Prologue

June 1908

Jack Kestrel was looking for a woman.

Not just any woman, but a female so unscrupulous, greedy and manipulative that she would blackmail a man who was dying.

He had been assured that she would be at the art exhibition at the Wallace Collection tonight, but he did not know what she looked like. Whilst he tried to locate the curator to arrange an introduction, Jack stood at the top of the staircase and scanned the crowd that had flocked to the exhibition of portraits and miniatures. Most people were standing in small groups in the conservatory and the hall, chattering, drinking champagne, their purpose not so much to view the paintings as to see and be seen. The gentlemen were in evening dress, the ladies vivid in rainbow-coloured gowns and picture hats, their diamonds rivalling the glitter of the chandeliers.

Jack turned and walked slowly along the corridor that led to the Grand Gallery. His cousin, the Duke of Kestrel, had loaned some portraits to the exhibition tonight including two very fine paintings by George Romney of Jack's great-grandparents, Justin Duke of Kestrel and his wife. Jack was curious to see them; the last time he had viewed them they had been tucked in a dark corner of the family seat, Kestrel Court in Suffolk, in dire need of a clean. Buffy the present duke was an unashamed philistine about the arts and saw his collection as nothing more than an asset to sell as the income he gained from his land dwindled. Only the previous week, Jack had loaned Buffy a thousand pounds to prevent him from sending his entire collection of Stubbs's racing paintings to Sotheby's.

There was only one person viewing the Kestrel portraits in the small drawing room. They were beautifully displayed and lit from below by a cunning arrangement of oil lamps. The same soft light that illuminated the portraits of Jack's ancestors also shone on the woman standing before them, giving radiance to her face beneath the wide brim of her hat, making her complexion glow like cream and roses and shadowing her eyes with mysterious darkness. She was wearing a beautiful peach silk evening gown that draped sinuously over her body and her huge black picture hat had matching peach ribbons and roses on the brim.

Jack stopped in the doorway, his eyes resting on her face. For a moment he felt an odd sensation in his chest, almost as though she had reached out and physically touched him. It was not a feeling he had ever experienced before. Apart from a disastrous entanglement in his youth, he had kept his relationships with women a simple and straightforward business of mutual physical convenience. Not one of them had made the breath catch in his throat or his heart miss a beat. He decided to ignore the sudden and disturbing stir of emotions within him and crossed the room to her side.

She did not turn. She seemed engrossed in the portrait of Justin Kestrel, with his dark Regency good looks, the rakish smile on his lips and the hint of humour in his dangerous eyes.

'Do you like the portrait?'

She turned at last at Jack's softly spoken question and her beautiful hazel eyes widened as they went from his face to the portrait and back again. He saw her mouth turn up in a reluctant smile.

'He was very handsome,' she said drily. 'The resemblance is striking, as no doubt you are aware.'

Jack bowed. 'He was my great-grandfather. Jack Kestrel, entirely at your service, madam.'

Her dark brows lifted slightly, but she did not give him a name in return and Jack knew it was deliberate. It was also unusual. Very few women refused Jack Kestrel's acquaintance. His looks generally gained him their interest even before they learned how rich he was.

'And this—' her attention had turned to the portrait of Justin's duchess, vivid and bejewelled in emerald satin and with the most glorious auburn hair '—must be your great-grandmother.'

'Indeed,' Jack said. 'Lady Sally Saltire. She was reputed to be as clever as she was beautiful. Half of London society was at her feet. In Regency times she was known as an Incomparable.'

'How marvelous.' His companion seemed amused. 'It is unusual to hear of a clever woman who did not trouble to hide her intelligence. I admire her for it.'

'I do not believe that she cared what others thought of her,' Jack said. 'And her husband adored her. He said that she was more than a match for him in every way.'

He laughed. 'She could certainly shoot straighter than he could.'

'A useful accomplishment,' she agreed. She leaned closer to the pictures to admire a small square portrait of a little girl in a white dress. The lamplight caught on the strands of tawny brown hair beneath her hat and burnished them to gold, setting the shadows dancing against her cheek.

'Is this their daughter?' She asked.

Jack nodded. 'My Great-Aunt Ottoline.'

'Is she still alive?'

'Very much so,' Jack said feelingly.

A spark of mischief lit her eyes. 'I imagine she must be quite a character.' She turned to face him and once again Jack felt the impact of that clear hazel gaze. Something shifted within him, something poignant and unexpected, like a hand squeezing his heart.

'Well,' she said, 'it has been a pleasure making the acquaintance of your dangerous ancestors, Mr Kestrel.'

She was leaving, and Jack was determined to stop her. He wanted to know much, much more about her. He was not going to let her go yet.

'Is art a passion of yours?' He asked.

She shook her head. 'No more than an interest, like music. My work is my passion.'

Jack slanted a look down at her. He was surprised. She did not look like a New Woman, the type of female who was independent and earned her own living as a shop assistant or factory worker. She looked too glossy, pampered and rich. He was about to ask her what she did for a living when she smiled at him, a luscious smile, but quite without promise of any sort.

'If you will excuse me, Mr Kestrel, I think I shall go and look at the Cosway miniatures now. They are accounted extremely pretty.'

'Then may I escort you to the Grand Gallery?' Jack asked.

After a brief second's hesitation, she shook her head. 'No, I thank you. I am here with a friend. I should go and find him.'

'What was he thinking of to leave you alone?' Jack asked.

She flashed him a smile. 'I am able to take care of myself. And he genuinely is no more than a friend.'

'I am pleased to hear it.'

She sighed. 'You should not be. I do not seek to further our acquaintance, Mr Kestrel. I am too old a hand to have my head turned by a handsome face.'

She did not look a day above five and twenty, but Jack thought she sounded world-weary. And he was too experienced to push her too hard. That way he would lose all that he had gained.

'At the least, tell me your name,' he said. He took her hand. She was wearing long black silk evening gloves that reached to her elbow. They felt deliciously smooth beneath his fingers and for a moment he thought he felt her hand tremble in his. Her long black lashes flickered down, hiding her expression.

'I am Sally Bowes,' she said. 'Good evening, Mr Kestrel.' She smiled, withdrew her hand from his, turned and walked away down the corridor towards the Grand Gallery. The light shimmered on her peach gown and the voluptuous curves beneath.

Sally Bowes. The shock and disbelief hit Jack squarely in the stomach like a blow. Unscrupulous, greedy, manipulative… A woman who would black-mail a dying man… He knew now what she did for a living. She was a nightclub hostess who used the weak-ness of men against them to extort money.

Yet the information was counter to every instinct he possessed about the woman he had been talking with. They had only spoken for a few moments and yet she had entranced him. He did not usually make errors of judgement of that magnitude. And along with the shock he felt something deeper, something that felt like disappointment.

He took an impulsive step after her, but then saw a gentleman join her, offering her his arm, and saw her smile up into his face. A pang of jealously pierced him, all the sharper for being so unexpected. He recognised the man; Gregory, Lord Holt, was a very old friend of his. He wondered if Holt was Miss Bowes's next intended victim.

Jack straightened. Tomorrow he would seek out Miss Bowes again and tell her in no uncertain terms that her attempts to extort money from his uncle had to cease. He would warn her that, in tangling with him, she was engaging a very dangerous enemy indeed.

Chapter One

'Miss Bowes?'

The voice was low, mellow and familiar. It spoke in Sally's ear and she came awake abruptly. For a moment she could not remember where she was. Her neck ached slightly and her cheek was pressed against something cold.

Paper.

She had fallen asleep in her office again. Her head was resting on the piles of invoices and orders that were on the desk. She half-opened her eyes. It was almost dark. The lamp glowed softly and from beyond the door drifted the faint sound of music, the babble of voices and the scent of cigar smoke and wine. That meant it must be late; the evening's entertainments at the Blue Parrot Club had already begun.

'Miss Bowes?'

This time the voice sounded considerably less agreeable and more than a little impatient. Sally sat up, wincing as her stiff muscles protested, and rubbed her eyes. She blinked them open, stopped, stared, then rubbed them again to ensure that she was not dreaming.

She was not. He was still there.

Jack Kestrel was leaning forward, both hands on the top of her desk, which brought his dark eyes level with hers and put him approximately six inches away from her. From such an intimate distance Sally could not focus on all his features at once, but she remembered them clearly enough from the previous night. He was not a man one would forget in a hurry, for his appearance was very striking. He had dark brown hair, very silky looking and a little ruffled from the summer breeze, a nose that was straight and verging on the aquiline and a sinfully sensuous mouth. Sally was not generally impressed by good looks alone. She was no foolish débutante to lose her head over a handsome man. But Jack Kestrel had had charm to burn and she had enjoyed talking to him the previous night. She had enjoyed his company too much, in fact. Spending time with him had been dangerously seductive. It would have been all too easy to accept his escort, and then, perhaps, to accept an invitation to dinner...

Sally had not been so tempted in a very long time and had known she could not afford to get to know Jack Kestrel any better. As soon as he had told her his name she had been wary, for all of Edwardian society knew who he was. The ancestral line of the Dukes of Kestrel had bred rakes and rogues aplenty in the eighteenth and nineteenth centuries and there were those who said that this man was the last Kestrel rake, cut from the same cloth as his ancestors. Cousin to the present Duke, eventual heir to the dukedom, he had been banished abroad in his youth as a result of an outrageous scandal involving a married woman and had returned ten years later having made an independent fortune.

Sally could see why he had gained the reputation he had. There was certainly something powerfully virile about him. Women were supposed to swoon at his feet and she had no intention of joining their ranks and littering his path.

She realised that she was still staring at him. Suddenly hot, she dragged her gaze away from Jack's mouth and met his eyes. His expression was distinctly unfriendly. She drew back immediately, instinctively, and saw his gaze narrow at her reaction. He straightened up and moved away from the desk.

He was not in evening dress tonight and Sally thought that looking as he did, he could not be mistaken for a member of the Blue Parrot's usual clientele. The club catered for the filthy rich members of King Edward's circle who were mainly fat, pampered and accustomed to soft living, and to the sophisticated American visitors whose money and influence increasingly held sway in London. Occasionally the club also hosted the soldier sons of the old aristocracy, roistering it up on leave. Jack Kestrel looked as though he might have been a soldier once—he had a long scar down one lean cheek—and he certainly looked as though he would be more at home on the North-west Frontier or in southern Africa than in a club off the Strand. He was very tall, broad and sunburnt and Sally guessed he was about thirty. Instead of evening dress he wore a long driving coat in dark brown leather over a suit that was as carelessly casual as only Savile Row could make, and he carried his height with a lounging grace that was compulsive to watch. He turned back towards her and Sally felt her breathing constrict. She could not deny that Jack Kestrel had a dangerously masculine appearance. His features were hard and uncompromising.

'I apologise for waking you,' he drawled. 'I suppose

that in your profession you must snatch your sleep where you can.'

Sally was not quite sure what to make of that. Although she enjoyed accounting, she did not normally find it so riveting that it kept her from her bed. She was tired that evening only because she had been out late at the Wallace Collection the night before and then up early supervising the final redecorations of the Crimson Salon, which was to open to the public in two weeks' time. The renovations had taken six months and the new developments were going to be the talk of London. Even the King himself had promised to attend the unveiling.

'You *are* Miss Bowes?' Jack added, for a third time, when Sally still did not speak. Now he sounded downright impatient.

'I… Yes, I am. I told you that last night.' Sally cleared her throat. She realised that she did not sound very sure. She certainly did not sound like the authoritative owner of the most successful and avant-garde club in London. Once, long ago, in the genteel drawing rooms of Oxford, she had indeed been Miss Bowes, the eldest daughter, sister to Miss Petronella and Miss Constance. But a great deal had happened since then.

Under Jack Kestrel's pitiless dark gaze she felt younger than her twenty-seven years, young and strangely vulnerable. She straightened in her chair, brushed the tangled hair out of her eyes and hoped desperately that the inkstains she could see on her fingers did not also adorn her face. It was infuriating that she had been caught like this. Normally she would change into an evening gown before the club opened, but because she had fallen asleep she had not had time, and no one had come to wake her.

'What can I do for you, Mr Kestrel?' She assumed her most businesslike voice. She had already realised that this could not be a social call to follow up their meeting the previous night. No matter how brief and sweet their encounter had seemed at the time, something fundamental had changed. Now he was angry.

'I think you must know perfectly well why I am here, Miss Bowes.' Jack's tone was clipped. 'Had I known who you were last night, I would have broached the matter then. As it was, I realised your identity too late. But you must surely have known I would seek you out.'

Sally got to her feet. It made her feel stronger and more capable. 'I am sorry,' she said politely, 'but I have no idea what you are talking about, Mr Kestrel, nor why you are here, unless it is to enjoy the famous hospitality of the Blue Parrot.'

She had heard that Jack Kestrel had once spent a

thousand pounds on champagne alone in one sitting at the gambling tables in Monte Carlo. Sally wished that he would do the same at the Blue Parrot. But it seemed unlikely, given the hostile expression on his face.

Jack's mouth twisted with sarcastic appreciation at her words. 'Legendary as I understand the Blue Parrot's hospitality to be, Miss Bowes,' he drawled, 'that is not what I came for.'

Sally shrugged. 'Then if you could perhaps enlighten me?' She gestured to the papers on the desk. 'Stimulating as your company is, Mr Kestrel, I do not have the time to play guessing games with you. As I mentioned last night, my work is my passion and I am keen to return to it.'

Some emotion flared behind his eyes, vivid as lightning. Sally could feel the anger and antagonism in him even more powerfully now, held under tight control, but almost tangible. She wished the lamps were turned up. In the semi-darkness she felt at a strong disadvantage.

'I can quite believe that you have a passion for what you do, Miss Bowes,' Jack said, through his teeth. 'You must possess a great deal of nerve to pretend that you are unaware of my business with you.'

Sally did not reply immediately. She moved out from

behind the shelter of the desk, turned up one of the gas lamps, struck a match and lit the second and the third. She was pleased to see that her hands were quite steady, betraying none of the nervousness she was feeling inside. She could feel Jack Kestrel watching her, his dark eyes fixed on her face. She wished the room were a little bigger. His physical presence felt almost overwhelming.

She turned to find that he was standing directly behind her. There was something close to a smile lurking in his eyes, but it was not a reassuring smile. Now that she was standing she found that her head reached only to his shoulder, and she was a tall woman. It was unusual for her to have to look up in order to look a man in the eyes.

'Well?' he said softly. 'Have you changed your mind about this unconvincing little game of pretence that we are indulging in?' His appraising dark gaze travelled over her. 'I must confess that you are not quite as I imagined,' he added slowly. He raised a hand and turned her face to the light. 'When we met last night I thought your looks unusual, but when I found out who you were I was surprised. I was expecting someone a great deal more conventionally pretty. After all, they call you the Beautiful Miss Bowes, do they not—'

Sally slapped his hand away. Despite her anger, his touch had made her skin prickle. His gaze made her acutely aware of her body beneath the plain brown shirt and skirt she was wearing. She felt very strange… She paused to think about the hot, melting feeling within her. She felt as though she was bursting out of her corset and coming *unlaced*. Not a single one of the gentlemen who frequented the Blue Parrot had ever made her feel that way, although plenty had tried.

'Mr Kestrel…' she kept her voice steady '…you speak in riddles. Worse, you are boring me. My good looks, or lack of them, are something about which I alone need be concerned. As for the rest, unless you explain yourself I shall have to call my staff to remove you.'

He laughed and his hand fell to his side. 'I'd like to see them try. But I will explain myself with pleasure, Miss Bowes.' He spoke with deceptive gentleness. 'I am here to take back the letters that my foolish cousin Bertie Basset wrote to you. The ones you are threatening to publish unless his dying father pays you off.'

His words made no sense to Sally. She knew Bertie Basset, of course. He was a young sprig of the nobility, charming but not over-endowed with brains, who came to the Blue Parrot to play high and drink with the girls. When last she had seen him, her sister Connie had been sitting on his knee as he played poker in the Green Room.

Connie... Of course...

Sally rubbed her brow. Jack had called her the Beautiful Miss Bowes, but it was Connie, her youngest sister, who was known by that title. If she had not been so distracted by Jack Kestrel's touch, she would have realised sooner that he must have confused her with Connie. Miss Constance Bowes was indeed so beautiful that the gentlemen wrote sonnets to her eyebrows and made extravagant promises that she was quick to capitalise upon. But Sally had never envied her sister's looks, not when she had the brains of the family.

Jack Kestrel was watching the expressions that chased across her face.

'So,' he said thoughtfully, 'when I first mentioned the matter you had no idea what I was talking about, did you, Miss Bowes? And then, suddenly, you realised.'

'How on earth do you know?' Sally snapped. She was annoyed with herself for having given so much away.

'You have a very expressive face.' Jack sat down on the edge of her desk and swung his foot idly. 'So you are not Bertie's mistress. I might have guessed. He would be too young and unsubtle to be a match for you, Miss Bowes.'

'Whereas you, Mr Kestrel,' Sally said, very drily, 'no doubt claim, quite truthfully, to be far more experienced.'

Jack shot her a sinfully wicked grin. For a second it reminded her forcibly of their meeting the previous night. Sally's knees weakened and her toes curled within her sensible shoes. 'Naturally,' he said. 'And please call me Jack. I doubt that this place operates on formality.'

It did not, of course, but Sally was not going to let Jack Kestrel tell her what to do in her own club.

'Mr Kestrel,' she said, 'we digress. As you so perceptively pointed out, I am not your cousin's mistress. I know nothing of this matter. I believe there must have been a misunderstanding.'

Jack sighed. His expression hardened again. 'There usually is in cases like this, Miss Bowes. The misunderstanding is that my uncle is going to part with a large sum of money.'

This time the angry colour stung Sally's face. 'I am not attempting to blackmail anyone!'

'Perhaps not.' Jack came to his feet in a fluid movement. 'But I also believe that you know who is.'

Sally stared at him, her mind working feverishly. If her guess was correct, then her sister Connie, the toast of London, had done a monumentally foolish thing and was trying to blackmail a peer of the realm. Unfortunately it was all too easy to believe because, though Connie might be incredibly pretty, she was not over-endowed with intelligence. And she was spoilt. If she did not get what she wanted, she would stamp her foot. If she had wanted Bertie and the love affair had turned sour, she might well try to take him for what she could and the result of that madness was Jack Kestrel, standing in Sally's office, looking both hostile and unyielding.

'Perhaps it is your sister who is the culprit,' Jack Kestrel said softly, and Sally jumped at how easily he read her mind. 'I have not met her, but I have heard about her. She also works here, does she not?'

Sally pressed her fingers to her temples in an effort to dispel the headache that was starting to pound there. She could not give Connie away—that felt too disloyal. She needed to speak with her sister first. Except that Connie never confided in her these days. They were not close—had not been since Connie's last disastrous, broken love affair. Her sister had withdrawn into herself after that and barely spoke to Sally any more. But now Sally was going to have to make Connie talk.

'Please leave the matter with me, Mr Kestrel,' she said. 'I will deal with it.' She looked up. 'I give you my word that your uncle will not be troubled further.'

Jack sighed again. 'I would like to trust you, Miss Bowes, but I do not. Do I look as though I came down in the last shower?' He shook his head slightly. 'You could easily be party to this affair and simply to accept your word would be very green of me.' His contemptuous gaze swept over her, leaving Sally hot with anger and mortification. 'You should know that my uncle is elderly and has been increasingly frail for some years,' Jack added. 'Recently we were told that he did not have long to live. A matter such as this will hasten his end. But perhaps you do not care about that.'

'Perhaps you should speak to your cousin,' Sally snapped back, 'and persuade him not to write ill-considered love letters. There are, after all, two sides to every affair!'

Jack smiled. 'Indeed there are, Miss Bowes, and I will be speaking to Bertie and suggesting that he does not involve himself in future with good-time girls on the make.'

'You are offensive, Mr Kestrel,' Sally said. Her voice shook with anger and the strain of remaining civil.

'I beg your pardon.' Jack did not sound remotely apologetic. 'I dislike blackmail and extortion, Miss Bowes. It tends to bring out the worst in me.'

Sally shook her head irritably. 'I do not believe that this is helping us progress the matter, Mr Kestrel.'

'No, you are quite right,' Jack said. 'And until I can tell my uncle that I have destroyed those letters with my own hand, I cannot rest easy. Surely you would not expect me to do otherwise, Miss Bowes?'

Sally would not have expected it. A forceful man like Jack Kestrel was not going to back down on a matter like this. Which left her with a huge problem. How could she protect Connie and yet ensure that the letters were either returned or destroyed? She had always defended Connie, it was a habit with her, even though she thought these days that her sister was as hard as nails and did not really need her protection.

'Miss Bowes?' Jack's voice broke into her thoughts. 'You seem to be having some difficulty making your decision. Perhaps it might concentrate your mind if I tell you that, if you do not hand over the letters, I shall call the police in.'

Sally spun around on him, her eyes flashing. 'You would not do that!'

'Yes, I would.' Although there was amusement in Jack Kestrel's eyes, his tone was cold. 'As I said, I don't like blackmailers, Miss Bowes. It is only out of deference to my uncle that I did not go directly to the authorities.' His expression hardened further. 'Oh, and I will do everything I may to ruin the reputation of the Blue Parrot and to put you out of business. And you may be certain that my influence is extensive.'

Sally stared at him, two bright spots of angry colour vivid in her cheeks. She had no doubt that he could put his threat into practice. He was rich and well connected, a member of King Edward's exclusive, excessive circle of friends, able to turn the fickle monarch's attention in other directions. At present the Blue Parrot was fashionable, but how long would that last if the gilded crowds who thronged its doors chose to take their business elsewhere? And she had just taken a huge loan from the bank in order to improve her business. She was dependent on her investors. It would be all too easy to ruin her financially...

She closed her eyes, took a deep breath and opened them again. Jack Kestrel was standing looking at her with the same quizzical expression in his eyes that she had seen there before. Her heart thumped once, then settled to its normal beat.

'You are harsh in your threats, Mr Kestrel,' she said,

as steadily as she could. 'This is nothing to do with me and yet you seek to make me pay for it. It is not the behaviour of a gentleman.'

Jack shrugged. 'I play the game by the rules that are set for me, Miss Bowes. It was your sister who raised the stakes.'

Sally pressed her hands together. She could see no point in arguing. She knew he would make no concessions. 'Very well,' she said. 'If you would give me a couple of hours to deal with this matter—'

'One hour. I will give you one hour only.'

'But I need longer that that! I don't know where Connie—' Sally caught herself a moment too late.

'So it is Connie who is the Beautiful Miss Bowes?' Jack raised his brows. 'Of course.' He took a letter from the pocket of his coat and unfolded it. 'I see that the initial in the signature is a C. How slow of me. I should have spotted that.'

'You should certainly be surer of your ground before you make wild accusations,' Sally said. 'You are extremely discourteous, Mr Kestrel.'

Jack laughed, refolded the letter and put it away. 'I am direct, Sally. It is a quality of mine.'

The warm tone in his voice, the way he said her name, made Sally's heart turn over even as she deplored his familiarity.

'I did not give you leave to use my name, Mr Kestrel,' she snapped.

'No?' Jack gave her a mocking glance. 'I must admit that you do seem given to formality. Do your clients have to address you as Miss Bowes as well?' He looked thoughtful. 'Actually, I suppose a touch of severity probably appeals to some of them, if it comes accompanied by a cane and some chastisement.'

Sally felt the bright red colour sting her cheeks again. Jack Kestrel was not alone in assuming that the Blue Parrot Club was a high-class brothel; indeed, Sally herself often suspected that some of the girls made their own arrangements with their clients. In the early days her concern for their safety had made her try to stop them selling their bodies as well as their company, but in the end she knew they would go their own way and only stipulated that they made no such arrangements on the premises. Nevertheless she worried about them and she knew that, though they were touched at her concern, they thought her naïve. Sally sometimes thought so herself. She lived in a world of glittering sophistication and racy excitement and her sister maintained she had the morals of a Victorian maiden aunt.

'You are labouring under several false assumptions, Mr Kestrel,' she said icily. 'On these premises the only expensive commodity that the customers can buy is the champagne. I have my licence to think of. I am the *owner* of the Blue Parrot, Mr Kestrel, which means that I am no more than a glorified office clerk.' Once again she gestured to the pile of bills and orders on her desk. 'As you see.'

Jack Kestrel laughed sardonically. 'I am more than happy to accept your protestations of virtue, Miss Bowes.'

'You misunderstand me,' Sally snapped. 'I do not feel the need to justify myself to you, Mr Kestrel, merely to explain matters.'

Jack inclined his head. 'And your sister, Miss Bowes? Surely she cannot also work in the office?'

'Connie is a hostess,' Sally said. 'Their task is to entertain the customers with their conversation, Mr Kestrel, and to help them to part with their money.'

'A task which your sister seems eminently qualified for, given the evidence of her letter to my uncle,' Jack said.

Sally gritted her teeth. She could not really argue with that.

'Is your sister working tonight?' Jack asked. 'I will go and speak with her immediately.' He started to move towards the door.

Panic flared within Sally. She knew he would go and

demand answers from Connie and he was high-handed enough not to care whether he disrupted the business of the entire club in doing so. A public row would cause the sort of scene she could not really afford.

'Wait!' she said, hurrying after him. To her relief, he stopped. 'I do not know,' she said. 'I don't know if Connie is working tonight or not. I will go and find out.'

She was very conscious of Jack at her shoulder as she walked up the stairs from the basement. One of the waiters passed them, a tray piled high with empty plates balanced on his arm. The Blue Parrot had a dining room to rival any gentleman's club and a French chef as temperamental as any employed in the great country houses. Tonight, however, *Monsieur* Claydon sounded to be relatively calm and Sally gave silent thanks for small mercies. She did not think she could bear a kitchen disaster on top of everything else.

Jack held the green baize door open for her with scrupulous courtesy and Sally went out into the hall. The entrance to the Blue Parrot had been designed to be like a private house and had a black-and-white marble floor with potted palms and tastefully draped statuary. By the main door were two men in livery who, at first glance, might have been taken for footmen. A second glance, however, showed that they had the physique of prizefighters and the expressions to match. The elder of the two was Sally's general manager, Dan O'Neill, who had in fact been an Irish champion boxer and now ran the Blue Parrot on a day-to-day basis and was in charge of the floor when the club was open. His pugilist qualifications were extremely useful. It was not unheard of for some of the clients at the Blue Parrot to have a little too much champagne, play a little too deep at *chemin de fer* and need to be encouraged to leave quietly.

On seeing Sally, both men straightened up automatically.

'Good evening, Miss Bowes,' Dan said respectfully.

'Good evening, Dan,' Sally said, smiling. 'Evening, Alfred.'

'Miss Sally.' The second man shuffled a little bashfully, blushing like a schoolboy with a crush.

'Do either of you know whether Miss Connie is working this evening?' Sally asked.

The men exchanged glances. 'She went out earlier,' Alfred volunteered. 'I called a hansom for her.'

'Said it was her night off,' Dan added.

'Do you know where she went?' Jack Kestrel asked. Sally was very aware of him beside her, could feel his tension and sense the way he was watching the other men very closely.

Dan looked at Sally for guidance and then cleared his throat as she nodded. 'I think she was dining with Mr Basset,' he said.

Sally heard Jack's swift, indrawn breath. 'Well, well,' he said pleasantly, 'how interesting. Perhaps she is hedging her bets in case her blackmail doesn't work?'

Sally bit her lip, trying to ignore his insinuation. 'My apologies, Mr Kestrel,' she said. 'It seems you will have to wait a while to speak with my sister—unless you are party to the places where your cousin would take a lady to dine.'

'I am quite happy to wait,' Jack drawled. He looked at her. 'As long as you are sure your sister will come home tonight, Miss Bowes.'

Sally flushed at this thinly veiled slur on Connie's virtue. She saw Dan take a step forward, his face flushed with anger, and Jack Kestrel square his shoulders as though preparing for a fight. She waved her manager back. She did not want a brawl, especially one that for once she was not sure that Dan would win. Jack Kestrel looked as though he might be a useful man in a fight. And, in truth, she could not be certain that Connie *would* come home. There had been times when her sister had been out all night, but after the first, terrible scene when Connie had screamed at her that she was not their mother, Sally had tried not to interfere. Her heart ached that she did not seem able to reach Connie, who went her own wayward path.

'Then perhaps,' Sally said, 'you would like to take dinner whilst you wait, Mr Kestrel? On the house, of course.'

Jack smiled a challenge. 'I will gladly take dinner if you will join me, Miss Bowes.'

Sally was shocked. If he had asked her the previous night, then she would not have been surprised, but now she could not imagine why Jack would want her company. Then she realised, with an odd little jolt of disappointment, that it was probably because he wanted to keep an eye on her and make sure that she did not slip away to warn Connie of what was going on. He did not trust her.

And she did not feel like indulging him.

'I do not dine with the guests, Mr Kestrel,' she said coldly.

Jack held her gaze. 'Humour me,' he said.

The air between them fizzed with confrontation. Sally hesitated. She never dined with the customers at the Blue Parrot in order that there should be no misunderstandings about her role at the club. It was the job of the hostesses to mix with the patrons and to entertain them. The owner might mingle with her guests, but she preserved a distance from them. But if Jack Kestrel did not get what he wanted, she knew he could cause a great deal of trouble for her, and one dinner seemed a small price to pay whilst they waited for Connie to return. Then, she hoped against hope, she would be able to deal with this matter and remove the unexpected and wholly unwelcome threat to her business that Jack Kestrel posed.

'Very well,' she said reluctantly. 'But you will need to give me time to change my gown.'

Jack bowed. 'I am happy to wait for you.'

Sally saw Alfred's brows shoot up towards his hairline. The staff had never seen her break her own rules before.

'Dan,' she said, 'please show Mr Kestrel to my table in the blue dining room.' She paused, her gaze sweeping over Jack. He might not be in evening dress, but she could not deny that he looked pretty good. Many men would kill for a physique like Jack Kestrel's and the elegance of his tailoring could not be faulted. 'We have a dress code, Mr Kestrel,' she said, 'but I suppose we can waive it on this occasion. Dan, make sure that Mr Kestrel has anything he asks for.'

Jack inclined his head. 'Thank you, Miss Bowes.'

'My pleasure.' Sally met his eyes and felt something pass between them, something hot and strong and heady as a draught of the finest champagne. She felt a little dizzy. Then Jack smiled and the breathless feeling inside her intensified. Damn and damn. She did not want to be reminded of the previous night and the fact that he possessed that fabled Kestrel charm. She had never felt quite like this before. She was never remotely attracted to any of the clients at the Blue Parrot. And why it had to happen now, with Jack Kestrel of all people, whose reputation was dangerous and intimidating and whose word could ruin her business, was not only deeply disturbing but also absolutely impossible.

'Excuse me,' she said, masking her awareness of him with the cool composure she had cultivated for her role of a woman of business. 'I shall not keep you waiting long.'

And she turned and hurried away from him before she gave away too much of her feelings.

Chapter Two

He wanted her.

He wanted the Blue Parrot's cool-as-ice owner in his arms and in his bed and Jack Kestrel was accustomed to getting the things that he wanted. It should have been impossible with her sister's blackmail standing between them, but Jack was determined to find a way to have Miss Sally Bowes.

It had been a relief in some ways to discover that his instincts about her the previous night had been sound after all. Jack did not like being made to doubt his own judgement. But whatever the sins of Miss Connie Bowes, he was sure that her sister was as honest as she claimed to be. Sally was no blackmailer.

He watched Sally as she mounted the fine silver-

and-brass staircase to the second floor. She was a tall woman and she held herself very upright, with the unconscious grace of someone who had learned deportment in her youth. Not for the first time, he wondered about her background. He had been away from London a long time, too long to know anything of the owner of the most popular club in the city. But he was determined to find out more.

Even though he knew the club servant was waiting to show him to his table, he waited and watched Sally out of sight. At the turn in the stair he saw her hesitate and look back, and he felt a powerful flash of masculine triumph that she had been aware of his scrutiny. Their eyes met for a long second and he felt the impact of that look through his whole body, then she disappeared into the shadows at the top of the stair and he became aware of the servant hesitating at his side.

'This way, if you please, sir.' The man said, his hostility barely concealed behind a display of immaculate deference. Jack smiled inwardly. He had sensed from the first that Sally Bowes's employees were extremely protective of her. They knew that he constituted some sort of threat and so they did not like him. He found their loyalty to her interesting, and wondered what she had done to inspire it.

The manager was leading him from the impressively arched entrance hall down a passageway with a thick red carpet underfoot, past doors leading to all the entertainments that the Blue Parrot had to offer. All the vices, Jack thought. The Smoking Room, the Blue Bar, the Gold Salon, where, no doubt, the gambling tables would be set up under a blaze of chandeliers, as they were at Monte Carlo. There was nothing so vulgar as the cabaret at the Moulin Rouge here, no dancing girls or painted devils serving the drinks. Jack thought that Sally had probably made a sound decision in not attempting to export the raffish style of Paris to London's Strand. The Blue Parrot had all the elegant comforts of a gentleman's club and country house combined, but it also had an indefinable edge of glamour and excitement that made it so much more attractive than the stuffy old clubs of St James's.

The servant was standing back to usher him through into the dining room, but then the door of the Gold Salon opened and Jack saw the glitter of the chandeliers within and the croupiers dealing the cards at the baccarat table. He paused.

'Sir...' there was a note of anxiety in the manager's voice now '...Miss Bowes said that I was to escort you to the dining room.'

Jack smiled. He was feeling lucky tonight. 'Do not concern yourself,' he said. 'I will play a few hands whilst I wait for Miss Bowes to join me.'

He took a seat at the baccarat table. A waiter materialised with some champagne. One of the smart-as-paint blonde hostesses also started to drift towards him, but Dan stopped her with a word and Jack saw her tilt her head and open her eyes wide at whatever it was the manager said to her. She drifted away again with a regretful backwards glance at Jack.

Jack took his cards, sat back in his seat and wondered how long it would take Sally Bowes to join him. Most of the women he had taken out whilst he had been in Monte Carlo, Biarritz and Paris had made him wait at least an hour for them. He had never found it worth the waiting. Brittle, fashionable, society women bored him these days; they all seemed to be cut from the same cloth, superficial copies of one another. He was not interested in affairs with society sophisticates and could not bear to find himself an innocent bride as his father demanded. He knew he was jaded. No one could tempt him.

No one interested him except Sally Bowes, with her cool hazel eyes and her understated elegance.

When he had first seen her that afternoon, he had

thought she looked colourless, prim and restrained, a far cry from what he would expect from one of the Blue Parrot's infamous hostesses. But the memory of the previous night was still in his mind and the stunningly sensuous figure Miss Sally Bowes had cut in her peach silk gown. He had enjoyed her company then and wanted to know her better. And the startled awareness he had seen just now in her eyes suggested that she was not indifferent to him either. The attraction that had flared between them so unexpectedly surprised and intrigued him. On discovering that she was actually the owner of the club, his interest in her had been piqued further. Here was a woman who must have considerable strength of character, intellect and a will to succeed, as well as a subtle appeal that was devastatingly attractive to him. She was a challenge, an enigma, cool and composed, yet revealing a fiery nature beneath. He had almost forgotten what it was to be strongly attracted to a woman, but now the hunger flooded him with shocking acuteness. He had to have her.

Women. In his youth they had been his weakness. He had been as feckless as his young cousin Bertie—worse than Bertie, if truth be told. His excesses had been extreme. And then he had fallen in love and it had been the single most destructive experience of his life, never to be repeated.

Jack shook his head to dispel the memories and took a mouthful of the cool champagne. Six months before, when he had returned to England from the continent, his father had taken him on one side and said gruffly, *'Now that you've made your money and done trying to get yourself killed, boy, try to make amends for your misbehaviour by making a sensible match.'*

His misbehaviour. Jack's mouth twisted wryly at his father's understatement. Only Lord Robert Kestrel could refer to the scandalous elopement and subsequent death of Jack's married mistress ten years before in terms that were more fitted to a schoolboy prank.

A decade previously, when the whole scandal had occurred, it had been quite a different matter. Jack had been twenty-one and fresh down from Cambridge, full of high ideals and extravagant plans, plans that had come crashing down around him when Merle had been killed. The matter had been hushed up, of course, but in private there had been the most terrible scenes: his father in a towering rage, his mother griefstricken and appalled. It had been the disappointment that he had seen in his mother's eyes that had been his undoing. He could probably have withstood any amount of his father's anger because he knew he deserved it, but his mother's silent reproach cut him to the core. He was the only son, but he had lost her regard along with his father's respect. The last time he had seen his mother, she had been standing on the steps of Kestrel Court watching him leave his home in disgrace. She had died whilst he was abroad.

For years he had avoided the company of women entirely, burying himself first in the fight against the Boers in South Africa and later fighting with the French Foreign Legion in Morocco. The nature of the conflict had not really mattered to him; the only thing he cared about was to die in a manner that would make his father proud. But his recklessness was rewarded with life, not death, and a glorious reputation he did not want. He left the Legion and went into the aviation business with one of his former comrades and he had prospered. But even now, after ten years, it did not seem right that he should be alive and rich when Merle was cold, dead and buried. The relationships he had had since had been fleeting, superficial affairs. His heart had been in no danger and that was the way he preferred it.

And now he had met Sally Bowes and he wanted her. The idea of seducing her aroused all his most predatory instincts. He remembered what she had said about the Blue Parrot not being that sort of club. Maybe it was, maybe it was not. He did not really care. He was only interested in her. He was only interested in winning— the woman, the game, the money.

He turned his attention to the cards.

'Matty! Matty!' Sally reached her bedchamber on the second floor, flung open the door and hurried inside. She was out of breath. It was not because she had climbed two flights of stairs but was all to do with the fact that Jack Kestrel had been watching her as she had walked away from him. She had never been so conscious of a man's eyes on her, had never felt so aware of a man in all her life. Plenty of men came through the door of the Blue Parrot, rich men, power-ful men, charismatic men, and on occasion a man who was all of those things. None of them had affected her in the way that Jack did. None of them was as danger-ous and laconic and damnably handsome and coolly charming as Jack Kestrel.

None of them had threatened to ruin her business and, with it, her life. *That* was what she had to try to re-member about Jack Kestrel when her emotions seemed in danger of sweeping her away.

'There you are, Matty,' Sally said breathlessly, seeing her maid and former nurse sitting before the fire knitting placidly. 'I need to get changed for dinner. There is a gentleman waiting for me. Please help me.'

Mrs Matson rolled up her ball of wool with what seemed agonising slowness, skewered it with her knitting needles and got creakily to her feet.

'What's all the fuss about?' she demanded. 'A gentleman waiting, you say? Let him wait!'

Sally hurried over to the wardrobe and pulled open the door. Matty had been with her family for ever, nursing all three of the Bowes girls in their youth, then acting as Sally's personal maid when she had left home to marry. She had been with Sally through thick and thin, ruin and riches. When Sally had decided to open the Blue Parrot and had tactfully suggested that Matty might prefer to retire rather than go to live in a shockingly decadent London club, Matty had stoutly declared that she wouldn't miss it for the world. She had bought herself a little house in Pinner, on the new Metropolitan Railway line, but she spent most of her time at the club.

'Steady now,' Matty said, as Sally started pulling gowns from their hangers and discarding them on the bed. 'What's got into you tonight?'

'Nothing,' Sally said. 'Everything.' She swung around and grabbed Matty by the hands. 'Do you know where Connie has gone, Matty? There's trouble. Bad trouble. She has tried to blackmail someone…'

The deep lines around Matty's mouth deepened further as she pursed her lips. She looked as though she was sucking on lemons. 'That girl's bad through and through. You know she is, Miss Sally, whatever you say to the contrary. Goodness knows, I nursed her myself and she was a sweet little child, but the business with John Pettifer changed her…' She shook her head. 'Nothing but trouble now.'

Sally let go of her hands and started to unfasten her patterned brown blouse, her fingers slipping with haste on the buttons. She had felt very dowdy in her working clothes under the bright lights of the hall and the even brighter appraisal of Jack Kestrel's eyes

'Connie's unhappy,' she said, stepping out of the brown-panelled skirt. 'She loved John and she has not been happy since. But it goes back before that, Matty. It goes back to when our father died. It's all my fault.'

'Don't speak like that.' Mrs Matson's mouth turned down at the corners. 'If I've told you once, I've told you a hundred times, Miss Sally. You are not to blame for your father's death.'

Sally did not reply. It was true that they had had this discussion many times and she knew in her head that she was not directly responsible for Sir Peter Bowes's death, yet every day she reproached herself because she might have prevented it. She might have saved him...

'I don't know what to do with Connie,' she said now. 'I can't reach her.'

'You've tried.' Matty bent creakily to retrieve the skirt. 'You never stop trying. Time you thought about yourself for a change, Miss Sally, if you'll pardon my saying so. Now, who is this gentleman you're dining with?'

Sally sighed. 'Mr Kestrel. He has come to retrieve the letters that Connie is apparently using to extort money from his uncle.'

Mrs Matson made a noise like an engine expelling steam. 'Mr Jack Kestrel? The one who ran off with someone and broke his mother's heart?'

'Very probably,' Sally said.

If ever a man had been born to cause a scandal over a woman, Jack Kestrel was that man.

Matty tutted loudly. 'I remember the case being in all the papers. His mistress was married when she ran off with Mr Kestrel. Her husband went after them. She was shot and there was a terrible scandal.'

'How dreadful,' Sally said, shivering. She wondered what effect such a dreadful tragedy would have had on Jack Kestrel at such a young age.

'Old aristocratic family, that one,' Matty said. 'Your Mr Kestrel is the last in a line that goes back hundreds of years. They say he has inherited all his rakish ancestors' vices, and I suppose the business of his mistress proves it.'

'Did the Kestrels have any virtues as well?' Sally asked.

Matty had to think hard about that one. 'A lot of them were soldiers,' she said, 'so they were probably very courageous. Mr Kestrel joined the army after he was banished. I hear he won medals for gallantry.'

'Trying to get himself killed, more like.' Sally said. 'How do you know all these things, Matty?'

'I know everything,' Mrs Matson said smugly. 'He's a dangerous one, and no mistake, Miss Sally. You watch him. Charm the birds from the trees and the ladies into his bed, so he does.'

'Matty!' Sally was scandalised. The colour flooded her face. 'He won't charm me.'

'Best not,' Matty said. 'You need a nice young man after that dreadful husband of yours, Miss Sally, not a scoundrel. Now, how about the gold Fortuny gown for tonight?'

'No, thank you,' Sally said, considering for a moment the tumble of evening dresses on her bed. 'I think I need the Poiret column gown tonight, Matty, to give me courage.'

'We'll have to change your corset, then,' Matty said, with disapproval. 'Don't like these newfangled modern contraptions, myself. They'll be doing away with the corset altogether at this rate and then where will we be? What's wrong with the old styles, I always say?'

'You can't breathe in them,' Sally said.

'I've breathed perfectly well for nigh on seventy years,' the old nurse proclaimed. 'Nothing wrong in a bit of tight lacing. Sit down and I'll do your hair.'

Sally sat obediently before the big mirror and Matty started to unpin her hair and brush it out. It was long and thick, a rich chestnut colour with lustrous golden strands. Matty always grumbled that it was a crime Sally wore her hair in such severe styles so that no one could see how beautiful it was. Sally claimed that it was not her job to look beautiful, but to keep the Blue Parrot running smoothly.

'I'll put the matching bandeau and the diamond pins in tonight, Miss Sally,' Matty said now. 'No arguing, mind.'

Sally was not going to argue. Jack Kestrel was, she was sure, a connoisseur of feminine beauty and whilst she could not compete in looks with some of the Blue Parrot's prettiest hostesses—or, indeed, with her own sister—she knew she scrubbed up quite well. The Poiret dress also added to her confidence. Long, silky, lusciously rich and expensive, it slithered over her head and skimmed her body like a straight column of bright fuchsia-pink colour.

'Don't look so bad, I suppose,' Matty said grudgingly. 'You've certainly got the figure for it, Miss Sally. Doubt your young man will be able to take his eyes off you.'

'He's here to talk about his cousin, not to court me,' Sally said, repressing a traitorous rush of excitement at the thought of Jack Kestrel's eyes on her. 'His cousin Mr Basset, I mean, not the Duke of Kestrel.'

Matty puffed out her thin cheeks. 'Mr Basset, Miss Connie's young man?'

'Yes,' Sally said. 'Do you know about that? Does Connie really like him?'

Matty looked a little grim. 'You never know with Miss Connie, do you? Think she's out with him tonight, though. Told me earlier that she was dining with him.'

Sally frowned as she reached for her fuchsia evening bag. Albert the doorman had said much the same thing, which made no sense if Connie was trying to extort money from Lord Basset over his son's indiscretion. Surely she would wait for the affair to end before she tried to blackmail Bertie Basset? There was something else going on here. Sally was sure of it. Connie was up to something and Sally did not like the sound of it.

Not that she was going to discuss her doubts with Jack Kestrel. She was taking dinner with him merely to pass the time until Connie returned. Not for a moment could she forget that, nor allow herself to be distracted by Jack's undeniable charm or the inconvenient attraction he held for her. She would be cool and composed. She would remember that he was dangerous to her on so many levels.

She glanced at her reflection in the mirror. The Poiret gown shimmered seductively over every curve. The diamonds sparkled in her hair. She drew herself up. This was business, not pleasure and she had best not forget that.

Dan met her as soon as she stepped off the bottom step and on to the marble floor of the entrance hall. She raised her brows at the look on his face.

'Trouble?'

'Yes.' A frown wrinkled Dan's broad forehead. 'Mr Kestrel is in the Gold Salon. Said he wanted to play a few hands of baccarat.'

'And?' Sally kept a smile plastered on her face as a noisy group of diners passed by and paused to compliment her on the quality of the Blue Parrot's service.

'And now the bank is down five thousand pounds.'

'Damnation!' Sally felt a twinge of real alarm. A little while ago Jack Kestrel had threatened to ruin her business, but she had not thought he would do so that very night by breaking the bank at her own gaming tables.

'There's worse,' Dan said in an undertone, taking her arm and hurrying her along the corridor towards the casino. 'The King is here.'

'What?' For a moment Sally felt faint. 'The King? King Edward?'

'Himself.' Dan nodded in gloomy agreement. 'Playing at the same table as Mr Kestrel. And losing to him like everyone else.'

'Hell and the devil.' Sally's heels clicked agitatedly on the marble floor as she quickened her pace. Damn Jack Kestrel. She thought she had contained the threat he posed, had imagined him sitting at table harmlessly drinking her champagne and here he was beating the King at baccarat and bankrupting her in the process. Matty was right. He was dangerous. She should never have let him out of her sight.

'I wouldn't like to say that he was cheating, now,' Dan said, in his rich Irish brogue, 'but...' there was puzzlement in his blue eyes '...I've been watching him and either he is extraordinarily lucky or...' He let the sentence hang.

Sally paused discreetly within the doorway so that she could watch Jack Kestrel at the baccarat table without being observed herself. He sprawled in his chair, a lock of dark hair falling across his forehead, his cards held in one careless hand. He had discarded his jacket and the pristine whiteness of his shirt looked stark against the darkness of his tanned skin. Seeing him there, Sally thought once again of his rakish forebears. There was something about him, something to do with his air of lazy arrogance, the perfection of his tailoring, the casual grace with which he wore it, that recalled the gamblers of a previous century, the rakes who made and lost their fortunes in the London of the Regency, a time like the present one that was full of the glitter and the lure of money and scandal.

'Miss Bowes?' Dan said with increased urgency, and Sally's attention snapped back.

'I'm thinking what best to do.'

'Better think quickly, then,' Dan said grimly. 'We're down ten thousand now.'

Sally allowed her gaze to wander over the other oc-cupants of the baccarat table. She was not going to be hurried because what she did next could make all the difference between keeping and losing her business. It was on a knife edge. If Jack Kestrel kept playing and winning…

She knew most of the other people in the room. The King frequented the Blue Parrot regularly these days and brought his cronies with him. Despite being on a losing streak, he looked to be in a good mood. There was a full champagne flute at his elbow. The smoke from his cigar spiralled upwards, wreathing about the chandelier. He was watching the game from beneath heavy-lidded eyes and every so often he would stroke thoughtfully at his sharply trimmed beard.

'You have the devil's own luck, Kestrel,' Sally heard him say now. 'Lucky at cards, unlucky in love, eh? Which makes you rich but with no one to spend it on, what!'

The group of hangers-on laughed obligingly and Sally saw the shadow of a smile touch Jack Kestrel's firm mouth. She doubted that he had a great deal of difficulty in finding a willing woman on whom to lavish his fortune, for he was without a doubt one of the most sinfully handsome men that she had ever seen in the Blue Parrot. Nor was she the only woman to have noticed. The King's mistress, Mrs Alice Keppel, looking as regal as the Queen in a golden gown with diamonds sparkling on her impressive *décolletage*, was watching Jack with more interest than the King would surely deem strictly necessary. A blonde woman in a tight red-silk gown and with matching red lipstick had draped herself across the chair next to Jack, but he seemed unaware of her presence, for his dark eyes were narrowed on the cards and his full attention was on the play. Her foot was tapping with impatience that she did not command his interest and she flicked the ash from her cigarette with a red-tipped finger.

'What shall I do, Miss Bowes?' Dan was waiting for her instructions. 'Shall I throw him out, perhaps?'

Sally laughed. It was tempting, but she was not sure that she could allow Dan to use strong tactics tonight. Not in front of the King.

'No,' she said. 'Send for more champagne and caviar and smoked salmon.'

'More!' Dan's brows shot upwards. 'Lord save us, they've already had half a dozen bottles and they have only been here a half-hour!'

'You sound like my old nurse,' Sally said. 'We're not here to look after their health, Daniel, only to tend to their pleasure and take their money. I am going to remind Mr Kestrel that he has an appointment to take dinner with me.'

Jack looked up as Sally started to walk towards the baccarat table. The woman in red put a hand on his arm and started to speak to him, but he shook her off and her scarlet mouth turned down with disappointment. His gaze, intense and black, rested on Sally's face. It made her feel a little breathless.

The King's eyes lit up when he saw her approaching.

'Hello, Sally, old thing! How are you? Ten thousand pounds poorer by my reckoning, thanks to this chap here!' He nodded at Jack. 'Damned inconvenient habit he has of breaking the bank. I've told him to stop now because this is my favourite club, what, and I want to be invited back!'

'Thank you, your Majesty,' Sally said, smiling.

Jack stretched, the muscle rippling beneath the white linen of his shirt. 'Did your manager think I was cheating?' he enquired lazily. 'Usually they only call the owner when they are about to throw me out.'

Sally met his eyes. 'On the contrary, Mr Kestrel, I am here because I thought that we had an appointment for dinner. If you would care to continue playing, however, that is your choice.'

Jack laughed. There was a spark of devilment in his eyes. 'I'll play bezique with you, Miss Bowes.' He held her gaze. 'All my winnings tonight against one night with you.'

The shock hit Sally hard, depriving her of breath. The wicked spark was still in Jack's eyes, but beneath it was something hard and challenging. Despite herself, Sally felt her body stir in response to that very masculine demand.

There was a gasp of outrage around the table, followed by a moment of profound silence. The eyes of the woman in red narrowed. She looked like an angry cat about to spit. Sally felt her venom. Several of the men exchanged a look.

'Bad form, Kestrel,' the King said testily. 'Miss Bowes doesn't cover that sort of stake.'

'I beg your pardon, your Majesty.' Jack spoke gently. His gaze was still resting on Sally and it was dark and moody, but still with something in the depths that made her shiver. It was as though the two of them were quite alone.

'When I see something that I want, I go after it,' Jack said. 'The gamble just makes the game more exciting.' He raised one dark brow. 'Miss Bowes?'

'Mr Kestrel.' Sally's voice was quiet, but as cutting

as a whip. 'His Majesty is in the right of it. I have already told you once this evening that I am not that sort of woman and this is not that sort of club.'

'Everything has a price, Miss Bowes,' Jack said. The counters clicked softly as he stacked them together.

'I am priceless,' Sally said sweetly, and the King laughed and the tension eased. 'Your price, on the other hand,' she said, 'is ten thousand pounds in winnings and dinner with me, should you choose to accept it.'

'I'd take it, Kestrel,' one of the other men said. 'It's more than the rest of us have ever been offered.'

Jack stood up and shrugged himself into his jacket. 'I'll accept dinner gladly,' he said, 'and leave the rest to chance.'

Dan had arrived with the champagne and the caviar and King Edward took Sally's hand and kissed the back of it with heavy gallantry and said she was a pearl amongst women. She felt a huge relief—Jack's winning streak had been halted, albeit at a high cost, and the King's favour retained.

Jack took her elbow as they walked out of the casino together.

'Are you angry with me?' he asked softly. His breath stirred her hair.

'Does it matter?' Sally said tightly. 'The disapproval

of others strikes me as something that is supremely irrelevant to you, Mr Kestrel.'

He laughed and she saw the brilliant amusement in his eyes. 'You read me very well,' he said. 'You can still win back that ten thousand pounds, you know.'

Sally flicked him a glance. 'And you read me very badly, Mr Kestrel, if you do not think I meant what I said earlier.' She turned to face him. For a moment they were alone in the corridor. 'You want revenge on me for Connie's behaviour,' she said, 'so you think to break the bank and ruin me. That is all that matters to you.'

'You are mistaken.' Jack raised his hand and the back of his fingers brushed the line of her jaw. 'It is you I want, Sally Bowes. I wanted you from the first moment I saw you last night.'

Suddenly the corridor felt airless. Sally took a step back and felt the smooth, cool plaster of the wall against her sticky palms. She knew that the fact they were in public would make no odds to him at all. If Jack Kestrel would proposition a woman in front of the King, he would be eminently capable of kissing her in a corridor and not give a damn who saw them. She felt dizzy and hot.

'You can't have—' she began, but he never gave her

the chance to finish her sentence. He leaned in close and kissed her, biting down gently on her lower lip, and the aching need flashed through her and she moaned, opening her lips beneath his. He took her mouth wholly and completely and her body caught ablaze like a lightning strike. She had never experienced anything like it.

They broke apart as a couple came down the corridor and cast them a curious look. Sally turned away from the light. She had no idea what feelings and emotions were showing there, but her face felt too naked, too revealing of the turmoil inside her. Her heart was beating in hard, heavy strokes. She knew she was shaking. Jack took her chin in his hand, as he had done earlier in the office, and turned her face towards the light. He ran his thumb over her full lower lip, where he had kissed her, and the lust slammed through her body and she almost groaned aloud.

'Sally—' his voice was rough '—where can we go?'

She understood what he meant, but the thought brought the first, cold thread of sanity back to her overheated mind.

'I can't,' she said. She frowned a little. It was hopeless to pretend that she did not respond to him, that she did not want him. Her behaviour had given the lie to that. She tried to be equally honest with her words.

'You go too fast for me,' she said. 'I am not accustomed to feeling like this. I can't believe we...'

She saw his tight expression ease a little.

'I am sorry,' he said. 'In the heat of the moment—'

'Yes.' Sally smoothed the pink gown down over her hips. Her movements were jerky. Her hands still shook. 'Excuse me,' she whispered. 'You must excuse me, Mr Kestrel.'

He caught her wrist. 'You promised me dinner,' he said. A smile touched the corner of his mouth. 'My price, remember. You cannot run out on me now.'

Sally stared at him for what felt like an age. 'That will have to be all,' she said.

He inclined his head. 'Of course.'

'And you will have to give me a few minutes.'

He nodded. 'Certainly you cannot go into the dining room looking like that.' A smile lit his eyes, a mixture of tenderness and satisfaction that made her heart jolt. 'You look...ravished.'

The helpless desire swept through her again and she saw his eyes darken almost black with lust as he recognised the need in her. He reached for her again, but she wrenched herself away and hurried down the corridor to the powder room. Fortunately it was empty. She shut the door carefully behind her and stood, breathing hard, her back pressed against the panels, eyes shut.

What on earth had possessed her? What possible excuse could there be for her forgetting that Jack Kestrel was a danger to both her virtue and her livelihood, for letting him kiss her with such devastating expertise and for responding in full measure to that kiss? She must have been mad. She had not even drunk a drop of champagne. Her wits must have gone begging.

She must have wanted him as much as he wanted her.

Sally opened her eyes. Even now she could feel the imprint of Jack's touch on her body and the impossible, melting, uncontrollable warmth that had raced through her blood when he had kissed her. She pressed one hand to her lips. She had been kissed so seldom, and never like that. When they had been engaged, Jonathan, her husband, had kissed her once or twice, a mere respectful peck on the lips that should have warned her of future difficulties if only she had had the experience to realise, but it had never been like Jack's kiss, full of passion and desire and heated demand. *That* was the thing that had betrayed her. She had never felt wanted before, never felt wholly desired in a way that made her entire body tremble with sensual heat. When it had happened with Jack she had forgotten everything else in the maelstrom of her emotions.

She sank down on to the little plush red stool and stared helplessly at her reflection in the mirror. Jack had been right. She did look ravished. She *wanted* to be ravished, seduced. Jack had swept into her life and destroyed all her carefully erected defences in the space of two brief meetings. To experience physical love for the first time at the hands of Jack Kestrel, who could make her feel wicked and wanton and desirable… Just the thought made her burn.

With a little sigh she started to tidy her hair, adjusting the bandeau, securing the pins. She straightened her dress. She looked tidy again, the immaculate owner of the Blue Parrot, as neat and composed as ever. Except something had changed in her face. Her lips were a little swollen from Jack's kisses and in her eyes she saw a startled awareness and a knowledge, and a wanting. Her needs, her emotions and her desires were awakened now and were clamouring for release.

She glanced at the little gold clock on the wall. A couple more hours and she would be free of Jack Kestrel's dangerous presence. She could talk to Connie, secure the letters, send them to Jack and the business would be closed. She need never see him again. She could forget this madness that possessed her. This urge to kick aside every careful precept by which she had lived her life for so long was too frightening. She was not at all sure where it might lead her.

She struggled to re-assert her commonsense. She took several deep breaths to compose herself. A few more hours of Jack's company…then it would be over.

Chapter Three

Damn the woman. How could she look so cool and unemotional when only ten minutes before he had been kissing her senseless? How *dared* she look so cool when *he* was burning up with the need to possess her?

Jack watched Sally as she walked slowly towards him. The waiter had installed him at the very best table in the dining room, up on a dais tucked away at the back of the room and surrounded by drooping green fronds of palm. Somewhere, out of sight, a string quartet was playing softly. It was a charming setting, relaxed but extremely stylish. The food smelled wonderful.

But Jack had lost his appetite for food and he did not feel remotely relaxed. Every nerve ending in his body seemed tense and alert, wound up intolerably, waiting. He watched as Sally smiled and paused to answer the greetings of the other diners. She looked regal, untouchable and very, very seductive in the bright fuchsia-pink silk gown. He had noticed it when she had first walked into the card room. Of course he had. Every man in the room had looked at her. The gown fell long and straight to her ankles and flaunted every single one of her curves. Jack felt his mouth go dry and his breathing constrict as he remembered caressing those curves through the slippery silk. Damn it, there was only one end he wanted to this evening, and it involved him stripping that provocative silk from Sally Bowes's body and taking her to bed. He had never felt so impatient to have a woman in all his life.

Jack stood up as Sally approached the table and she gave him a very measured, very cool smile that acted like a complete aphrodisiac and sent his blood pressure soaring dangerously. He had only just got himself under control from the interlude in the corridor. His body was still in a state of semi-arousal.

'I am sorry to have kept you waiting,' Sally said, sounding as though she was not particularly sorry at all.

'You were not very long,' Jack said. 'I do hope,' he

added, determined to shake her out of her apparent calm, 'that you are quite recovered?'

A shade of colour touched her cheek. She avoided his eyes and made a business of unfolding her napkin. 'I am very well, thank you,' she said.

Good. Jack felt a flash of satisfaction to see that blush. She was not as cool as she pretended. He could feel the tension in her. It would take very little to stoke their mutual attraction back to the point it had been before—and beyond. He had every intention of doing precisely that later in the evening, but for now he was going to tread very carefully indeed to avoid frightening her away.

'I have been admiring the club,' he continued. 'You own all this?'

A small, distracting dimple appeared at the side of her mouth when she smiled. 'I own part of it,' she said, 'and the investors own the rest.'

Jack was surprised at her candour. 'You're mortgaged to the hilt?'

She shrugged and a shade of reserve came into her eyes and he wondered if she was remembering his earlier threat to ruin her business. She would not want to show any financial vulnerability to him.

'I own the building,' she said. 'That is the important thing.'

Jack waved the waiter aside and filled her champagne glass himself. 'And how did you come by it? It seems an unusual venue for a lady to own.'

'My grandmother left it to me,' Sally said. 'It was a private house then, of course, but I had no money to maintain it, so I turned it into a business.'

She had, Jack thought, a tough financial head on her shoulders to have made a success of it.

'Do you think your grandmother would have approved?' he asked.

'I doubt it.' Sally laughed. 'She was a very conventional Victorian lady, Mr Kestrel, and she disapproved of everything about me, from my liberal upbringing to my political persuasions.' She looked him in the eye. 'I belong to the National Union of Women's Suffrage Societies, Mr Kestrel. My sister Petronella is a militant suffragist.'

'Of course.' Jack remembered the name of Petronella Bowes from the newspapers. 'She was one of the women who chained themselves to the railings in Downing Street earlier this year.'

'Yes.' Sally ran her fingers reflectively up the side of her champagne glass. 'Nell supports the cause vigorously. After her husband died her support turned more active. I think that it filled a void for her and she is very passionate in her beliefs.' She looked at him. 'Do you dislike political opinions in a woman, Mr Kestrel? Many men do.'

Jack smiled at her. 'I believe I have sufficient self-confidence to deal with it, Miss Bowes.'

Sally gave a spontaneous peal of laughter. 'Yes, I suppose it is only men who feel threatened by intelligent women who object to such matters.'

'And as such their good opinion is not really worth a great deal,' Jack said. He leaned forward. 'Tell me, Miss Bowes, what do you look for in a man?'

He saw the bright light fade from her eyes. 'Despite what happened just now,' she said, 'I would say that I do not look for a man at all, Mr Kestrel.' Her voice was strained.

Jack touched the back of her hand lightly. 'Because of your politics? But surely not all suffragists are opposed to the opposite sex?'

'No.' She withdrew her hand from beneath his. Her gaze, as it met his, was direct and very candid. 'It is not because of my political persuasions, Mr Kestrel. I was married once and I am afraid that it did not encourage me to view affairs of the heart in any positive light.'

'If that is so,' Jack said, 'how do you explain what happened between us?'

'Oh…' She shifted a little, shrugged. 'That was… what would one call it? Chemistry? Physical attraction?'

'Lust?' Jack said helpfully.

'Lust. Yes, I suppose so.' Once again she ran her fingers thoughtfully down the stem of the wineglass and this time it was Jack who shifted on his seat.

'I heard,' Sally added, 'that you, too, have little inclination towards romance, Mr Kestrel.' She gave him a slight smile.

Jack raised his brows. 'I see that someone has been talking about me,' he said. He was not particularly surprised. Everyone in London seemed to be talking about him. He wondered what they might have said.

Sally smiled. 'Surely you are accustomed to that—a man like you?'

'A man like me?' He looked a challenge. 'What sort of man is that, Miss Bowes?'

She did not appear discomfited by his bluntness and took her time replying. 'A man who is rich and powerful, and successful in business and with women, I suppose.'

Jack laughed. 'You account me that?'

'Are you not?'

The waiter brought asparagus for them at that moment, wrapped in damask napkins and served on a silver platter. It saved Jack the trouble of replying. He had no intention of raking over his past affairs with Sally Bowes. He was only interested in their mutual future. And he never spoke of his unhappy romantic past and his relationship with Merle. Not to anyone.

He found that he wanted to ask Sally about her marriage, but he sensed it was too soon and she would rebuff him. She was consciously keeping him at arm's length. He did not intend to stay there for the whole evening. He might not believe in romance, but he definitely believed in physical attraction and the attraction he had for Sally was going to be satisfied.

He watched as she speared a stalk, dipped it in butter, and ate it with delicate relish.

'I hope you do not mind that I ordered for both of us,' she said, 'as I know what is the very best from the kitchens.'

Jack tilted his head thoughtfully. 'So do you also consider me a man who allows a woman to take charge?'

Their eyes met and locked. Sally licked butter thoughtfully from her fingers and Jack felt the lust spear through his entire body again. Perhaps, he thought ruefully, they should get back to talking about politics. Generally it was something of a passion killer, although with Sally Bowes it seemed that any topic of conversation could incite an almost ungovernable rush of desire in him. So far he had managed to keep it battened down, restrained, but it was the devil's own job.

'I doubt that you are a man to relinquish control in general,' she said. 'The way that you behaved earlier does not suggest a very...tractable nature.'

A mocking smile twisted Jack's mouth. 'I believe you understand me very well, Miss Bowes.'

'I believe I do,' Sally said composedly.

Her coolness, her frankness, her authority, sent Jack's blood pressure rocketing further. The dining room seemed extremely hot.

'And are you not going to ask what I think of you in return?' he asked.

Once again the dimple showed in Sally's cheek as she smiled. 'No, I do not think so, Mr Kestrel. You see, I am confident enough to have no need for your approval. Nor your censure.' Her tone changed. 'Indeed, as I said, I get plenty of that elsewhere.'

Jack raised his brows. 'Because of the politics?'

'And many other things.' Sally waved a careless

hand. 'A single woman running a club like this? And a widow to boot?' She looked at him. 'You may not be aware, Mr Kestrel, that I was on the point of divorcing my husband when he died suddenly. The police were called in to make sure that I had not murdered him to save myself the cost and disgrace of the divorce courts. I do not think one can get any more scandalous than that.'

'Only if you *had* murdered him,' Jack agreed smoothly. He was not shocked at her disclosures—he had seen far too much of the world to be shocked by most things—but he was curious as to what sort of man her husband had been. What had Sally Bowes looked for in a man, before her dreams of romance and marriage had turned sour and ended in death and disgrace? It was no wonder, he thought, that she was more careful of giving herself than most women in the glittering, amoral world of high society.

Sally gave a little snort of laughter. 'I assure you I did not murder Jonathan. Not that the idea was not tempting at times. He died of influenza. It was a most virulent outbreak that year. I was sick, too, but I survived.'

'What was he like?' Jack asked.

The amusement fled Sally's face and her lashes

came down to veil her eyes. 'He was weak and dissolute and he gave me grounds enough for divorce with his flagrant cruelty and his infidelity,' she said. For a second Jack saw a bleak chill of loneliness reflected in her eyes and then she shrugged and picked up her champagne glass again. 'Forgive me. I was forgetting that you have been abroad and so know nothing of my scandalous affairs.' She looked up at him. 'It was something of a *cause célèbre* at the time, as all divorces are, I fear.'

Jack could imagine that it might have been. Whether or not she was the injured party, divorce ruined a woman's reputation and deprived her of her place in polite society. To have gone as far as the courts, even if her husband's timely death had saved her the final disgrace of going through with the divorce action, would have been the end of Sally's good reputation. It was no wonder that she had had to carve out a new role for herself here at the Blue Parrot and she had done it with great style.

'I am sorry,' he said. 'Sorry that you had to endure that.'

She shrugged lightly. 'Fortunately I had my inheritance. It could have been worse. But you will understand now why the club is so important to me.'

There was a warning there, Jack thought. She had not forgotten his threat to take away from her everything she valued. She did not trust him. He doubted that she trusted anyone after everything she had experienced. She might have been as stunned as he by the physical attraction that had flared between them so violently, but it did not mean that she was entirely swept away. Once again the challenge she presented, the excitement of the chase, lit his blood.

'What I told you about Connie was true,' she said suddenly. Her eyes met his and his heart jolted at the impact of her look. 'I knew nothing about her plan to blackmail your uncle.'

Jack nodded. 'I know.' He had a cynical soul, but he thought his instincts were sound and they told him Miss Sally Bowes was honest.

She nodded, and he saw a smile of relief touch her lips. 'Thank you.'

The waiter took their plates and replaced them with dressed pheasant and tiny, sweet vegetables. Another bottle of champagne was delivered. Jack deliberately turned the conversation to Biarritz and Monte Carlo, to society and culture and the new Liberal government. At Sally's prompting he spoke a little about the aviation business he had set up after leaving the army. He was very conscious of Sally sitting so close to him, of her smile and her low, smoky voice and the brush of her fingers against his sleeve. The temptation to lean across and kiss her was becoming overwhelming, but he contained his impatience. Soon...

The lights seemed dimmer now and the music had changed to the soft caress of the piano. The waiter brought cream gateau with curls of bitter chocolate and candied violets. The champagne bottle was empty.

And Jack waited and calculated and planned more carefully than he had ever plotted a seduction before.

'Would you care for coffee, Mr Kestrel?' Sally finished the last of her dessert and put down her spoon. There was a smudge of cream on her cheek. 'Brandy? Cigars?'

'No, thank you.' By now Jack was conscious of nothing other than Sally and did not want to indulge in drinks or cigars. He reached forward and gently rubbed the cream away from her cheek. Her skin felt incredibly soft. He wanted to cup her cheek in his hand, explore the smoothness of her skin. The strength of the urge shocked him. His desire for her was coiled intolerably tightly within him, barely under his control. Fleetingly he wondered what on earth had happened to him. This was not how the game was usually played.

'You had cream on your cheek,' he said. His voice was a little hoarse.

'Oh!' For a second Sally looked adorably confused and vulnerable. She drew back, a wary look in her eyes, but he caught her hand and held it.

'I would like you to show me the gardens,' he said. 'May we go outside?'

The tension spun out between them like gossamer. Sally caught her lip between her teeth.

'Mr Kestrel, that really would not be a good idea at all.'

Jack thought it was the finest idea he had had in an age. To find a dark arbour, to hold her, to kiss her again…

'I promise not to touch you unless you wish me to,' he said, and knew he was lying.

He could see the uncertainty reflected in her eyes and sensed that she was torn. She knew as well as he what would happen when they were alone in the dark, and although she was tempted she was wary as well. He took her hand, rubbing his thumb gently over the back of it, and felt her tremble a little.

'I hear your gardens are modelled on the Moulin Rouge,' he said, 'and that you planned the design yourself. I should like to see them.'

Sally laughed reluctantly and the tension between them eased a little. 'We do not have the mock-elephant and the faux-Gothic castle, but they are very pretty.'

'So show me...'

He held his breath and after a moment she nodded. Her expression was veiled. 'Very well,' she said.

They went out of the restaurant and down the red-carpeted corridor towards the big garden doors. Jack watched the sway of her body sheathed tightly within the pink column dress and felt his own body harden in response. He had never felt so powerful and possessive a desire for a woman in his entire life. The strength of his need drove him. If he could have her in his bed, just the once, it would surely cure this hunger that threatened his very self-control. They were both experienced sophisticates who could take their pleasures when and where they found them. She would know the rules as well as he—and be prepared to indulge their mutual passion. He forced his hands into his pockets and ruthlessly reined in the feelings that threatened to drive him to madness and prompted him to take her, here and now, against the wall.

Out in the garden the path wound its way between rose bushes decorated with paper lanterns that swung gently in the summer breeze. Even though the night was warm, Sally shivered.

'You're cold,' Jack said. He slipped off his jacket and put it about her shoulders.

'No, I—' Sally clutched the lapels of the jacket close. In the shadowed darkness her eyes were very wide and dark. 'I think that we should go back inside.' She sounded hesitant, as though the strength of his desire had communicated itself to her and was making her nervous. 'This was a mistake. Besides, Connie may have returned, and—'

'Damn Connie.' The abrupt reminder angered Jack and he spoke more roughly than he had intended. He put a hand on Sally's arm. 'I don't want to talk about her. In fact, I don't want to talk at all. Sally?'

In response she tilted her face enquiringly up to his, which was exactly what he wanted. Her breath feathered across his cheek in a gentle caress. He could smell her perfume, as light and fragrant as the summer flowers that surrounded them.

He bent his head and kissed her. As an exercise in calculated seduction it was practically perfect, a textbook example of rakish behaviour of which, under other circumstances, Jack might have been justifiably proud. What was completely unexpected was his reaction. He had thought that this time he would be prepared, in control, but as soon as his lips touched hers, all logical thought processes vanished, drowned out in an excitement and a need so violent that it almost floored him.

Sally caught her breath and for a moment she went rigid in his arms, then she relaxed and her lips parted beneath his. Jack caught her to him then in an embrace as possessive as it was demanding, wrapping his arms about her, absorbing the taste and touch of her, each kiss both intense and seductive. Her palms were pressed against his chest and she responded to him without resistance, without artifice. She tasted faintly of chocolate and sweet innocence and it was so intoxicating Jack almost lost the final shreds of his self-control and plundered her mouth without reservation. But he was an experienced man, not a boy; he held on to his restraint by a thread, forcing himself to take it slowly, exploring her with a thoroughness that was gentle, yet ruthlessly determined beneath. This time he knew he had to court her response, not demand it. This time he needed to get her to the point where neither of them wanted to stop.

The suit jacket slid from her shoulders to the ground and he felt her shiver and drew her closer. The pink gown was smooth and silky beneath his hands, but it was not what he wanted to feel. He wanted her, her nakedness beneath him, her bare skin against his own. He wanted to uncover all the curves outlined by the dress, to trace them and learn them and give her exquisite pleasure.

'I want to make love to you.'

He said the words against her mouth and she drew back with a little gasp. He sensed it was purely instinctive and it was not the reaction of a sophisticated woman. He felt a tremble rack her body and then she had stepped back, out of his arms.

'Jack, I…'

'You want me too.' He knew it was true and he was arrogant enough to want to make her admit it.

'Yes—' she did not hesitate, but her tone held him at arm's length '—I do. But we cannot, Jack. Have you forgotten Connie, and your cousin, and that about three hours ago you threatened to destroy my business?'

He *had* forgotten, forgotten everything in the blazing heat of holding her and kissing her and wanting her. He thought about it for a split second and discounted it all. He reached for her again, not bothering to reply, seeking to persuade her through the touch of his hands and his mouth on her trembling, quiescent body.

He kissed her until he felt all the strength leave her body, felt her knees tremble and threaten to give way and felt the sweet taste of surrender in her mouth. She would be his now. He knew it. The flare of triumph the thought evoked in him almost pushed him over the edge. He swung her up into his arms and strode towards the door of the club. Her head was against his shoulder. Her hair brushed his cheek.

'The service stairs,' she whispered. 'I can't let anyone see...'

Briefly, Jack considered walking straight through the hall of the club with Sally clasped in his arms and carrying her up the main staircase to her bedroom. He rejected the thought with reluctance. He didn't give a damn on his own behalf, but he supposed that she did have a certain professional reputation to maintain and he respected that. When they reached the terrace doors he put her down gently, steering her into the corridor and straight through the plain doors that led down to her office and the kitchens and up to bedchambers above. In the light he could see that Sally's face was bemused and blank with passion, her lips parted, her breath coming quickly with the strength of her desire. Even so, he did not want to give her a single moment to reconsider what they were doing. He waited for a turn in the stair, a dark corner, and then he pulled her into his arms, pressing her back against the banisters with the pressure of his body against hers, for another soul-searing kiss. She made a noise of surprise and pleasure deep in her throat and his erection swelled in response. He held her trapped against the wall with his hips and kissed her long and deep until they were both gasping for breath.

Taking him by surprise, she caught his hand and ran up the remaining steps with him, pulling him through the door on to the landing and along the corridor to her room.

Jack turned the key in the lock behind him and stood looking at her. Only one lamp was burning and in its light she looked glorious—her breasts rising and fall-ing with her panting breath, her hair tumbling free of the bandeau, her lips soft and stung from his kisses.

Jack did not move. Like a true rake he had planned not to give her the chance to change her mind, to seduce her ruthlessly. But now he hesitated.

'Are you sure,' he said slowly, 'that you want to do this?'

Her beautiful eyes opened very wide and for a second he felt an absolute dread that she was going to refuse him. Why it should matter so much to him he had no idea; all he knew was that it did. And then she smiled and the relief slammed through him.

'Yes,' she said. 'I am sure.'

Sally had never been so sure of anything in her life. She knew it was foolhardy, out of character, probably downright irresponsible to make love with Jack Kestrel, but she did not care. She felt utterly reckless.

She had told Jack a little of her circumstances over dinner, but nothing of her feelings: her confusion and distress over Jonathan's repudiation of her, the fear and pain she had felt when he had so cruelly vented his frustrations on her, the absolute belief that she was plain, unattractive, unlovable as a person, not just because she was not beautiful on the outside, but also because there was something inherently wrong with her. She had been so sheltered when she had married, moving straight from her father's comfortable home to a similar house provided by her husband. She had been a conventional product of her class and upbringing. And then it had all gone horribly, disastrously wrong. Two terrible tragedies had rocked her life. Her father had died and her marriage had proved tobe a sham.

For five years she had worked to put that disaster behind her, accepting that it was Connie who was the pretty one and she was the one with the intelligence if not the looks. And then Jack Kestrel had walked into the Blue Parrot and his desire for her had been like rain falling on parched ground and she had decided that, no matter how rash and impulsive it was, she was going to find out at last what physical love was all about.

Except that she had assumed that Jack would take charge, and now he was hesitating and his delay was making her nervous. Grabbing her courage in both hands, she walked straight up to him.

'You will have to unfasten my gown,' she said. 'I am sorry, but I cannot manage it without a maid.'

Jack smiled then, a smile that made her toes curl and her stomach hollow with longing. He turned her around and started to unbutton the Poiret dress, bending his lips to the curve of her neck, kissing the skin that he uncovered, the flick of his tongue over her making the goose pimples rise all over her body. The gown fell to the floor with an expensive slither and Sally stepped out of it. She kicked off her shoes, her toes in their silk stockings sinking into the thick carpet. Standing there, armoured in her corset, she suddenly felt the same conviction that had always plagued her. She looked ugly and unattractive, Jack would change his mind, make an excuse, leave her. The thought made her feel suddenly sick and cold and she crossed her arms for comfort.

Jack turned her back to face him and their eyes met, and Sally's heart skittered with nervousness and excitement at the look on his face, for he was looking at her as though she was the most exquisite thing he had ever seen. His hand was on one of her shoulders, warm on her bare skin, and now he slid it down to her wrist and held her gently.

'Sally Bowes,' he said, 'you are the most beautiful girl.'

Shock and disbelief held her still, staring at him. He took a step towards her and pulled the end of her bandeau so that her hair tumbled down about her shoulders. The pins fell silently on to the soft carpet, but he ignored them, tangling a hand in her hair, bringing her lips to his to kiss her again. The world spun, tilted, and Sally would have fallen with the sheer sensual demand of his mouth on hers, but he scooped her up in his arms and tossed her into the middle of her big double bed.

'I am sorry,' he said. 'I just don't have the patience for this.'

She looked at him, uncomprehending. Surely he was not simply going to *stop*? There was a danger that, if he did, she might just kill him out of sheer frustration. She felt the mattress shift as he moved away, and she struggled to sit up. She heard the click as he took Matty's sewing scissors from the table and saw the lamplight glint on the silver. Her throat dried as she realised his intention. These were proper, big dressmaker's scissors, not some harmless toy.

'But... They're sharp!'

He put a hand on her bare shoulder, pushing her back down to lie on the yielding bedcovers.

'Keep still, then.' The words were laced with wickedness. 'I'm sorry about the corset,' he said again. 'I'll buy you a new one.'

He placed the scissors on the neckline of her chemise, between her breasts. She felt the cold kiss of the metal against her skin and shuddered with nervousness and hungry desire. Her nipples chafed against the cotton, waiting for the cut that would free her breasts from constraint. The heat pooled low in her belly. She wanted to squirm but the fear held her still.

The first snap of the scissor blades made her shiver uncontrollably. He cut downwards, straight, his hand steady. The material eased. Her breasts felt full, straining for his touch, but his concentration did not waver. When the tip of the blade touched her belly button he stopped for a moment and Sally shifted, fisting her hands into the bedcovers.

'Don't stop, damn you,' she said, and heard him laugh.

The cutting continued. She watched his face, intent and dark in the faint lamplight, watched the flash of the scissors and the pale exposure of her skin as the material of her corset and chemise and bloomers parted. The blade slid over the curve of her belly and paused at her pubic bone and she caught her breath on a sound that was part-sob, part-moan and moved her hands to cover herself. Jack laid the scissors down and forced her wrists back to her side, then took the remaining cloth in both hands and ripped it straight down the middle, pushing it aside to expose her body to the light and to his gaze.

Air touched her bare skin, hardening her nipples to tight peaks, caressing the tight, secret place between her thighs that ached for fulfilment. Driven beyond frustration, Sally kicked off her stockings, then rolled over and grabbed Jack's shirt, pulling him violently down to her. Something tore. She felt his skin, warm and hard and a little rough against the palms of her hands. His mouth was on hers, bold, possessive. His hand went to her breast, his lips and tongue following to nip and lick and taste her there. Sally writhed on the bed, arching under him. He tossed the shreds of her underwear aside, shrugged out of his own clothes and straddled her hips, pinning her down.

She was so utterly lost and adrift in a world of unfamiliar sensation that when the moment came she had forgotten that there was something she had not told him. He was not being careful because he did not know he had to. He took her with one, hard thrust and she felt the resistance from her body, felt him push past it so that he was buried deep inside her and then, when his mind caught up with his body, she felt him go very still.

It hurt. It hurt quite a lot, enough to pull her out of the deliciously warm and sensuous world she had been wrapped up in. She winced and he shifted slightly and that was painful too. She felt anxious, disappointed, and unsure how her pleasure could have melted away so quickly. He raised one hand and pushed the tumbled hair back from her face and his fingers were gentle against her cheek.

'Sally?'

Sally closed her eyes for a moment of pure mortification. All those wonderful, mindlessly exciting sensations had died completely now, leaving her feeling nothing other than embarrassment and extreme discomfort. How could she still be entwined in such an intimate embrace with this man—*a man who was a virtual stranger*—and feel nothing but awkwardness?

'Must we talk about this now?' she said beseechingly.

A smile touched the corner of his mouth. 'No,' he said, 'we don't need to talk now.'

'Good.' She tried to move away from him, intending to get up and find her clothes—any clothes—anything with which to cover herself, but he followed her movement, still keeping himself inside her. It made her nerves prickle with an echo of the excitement that had possessed her so recently. Despite herself, she shivered.

'Jack—' she said.

'You didn't want to talk.' He shifted her more closely beneath him, sliding deeper into her. To her shock, her body responded, rocking against him. He made a sound of satisfaction in his throat and bent his head to her breasts, sucking her nipples, sliding within her with slow, deliberate strokes, his skin slick against hers until she started to feel heat pooling low inside her again and her body twitched and shook with a need that was a shocking, dazzling, exquisitely unbearable revelation to her. He was so high and hard within her, the demand of his body on hers was absolute, and she felt overwhelmed with the sensation and she screamed aloud and felt her mind reel and shatter into tiny pieces. She felt Jack shudder and collapse beside her and she lay still, breathing hard, in awe and astonishment.

Jack rolled over and turned up the lamp. His face was dark, the expression hard, and her heart missed a beat.

'And now,' he said politely, 'we talk.'

Jack propped himself on one elbow and looked at Sally Bowes. On the floor beside the bed were the scraps of her underclothes that he had cut from her body. The scissors glittered on the side table. The sheets were tangled and Sally was tumbled amongst them, her hair about her shoulders, her skin flushed with latent arousal. The expression in her eyes was bemused and heavy with satiation. She looked like a fallen angel.

She also looked very, very desirable. Jack felt his body stir and ruthlessly clamped down on the urge to make love to her again. So much for his misguided belief that once he had had her the fever would be gone from his blood. It burned all the hotter now, now that he had tasted how delicious she was, now that he wanted more.

Now that he knew she was his alone.

He felt a huge, primal surge of masculine satisfaction, something that he had never experienced before. It was disconcerting to discover that he could feel this way. It hinted at emotions he did not wish to explore.

'So,' he said, when she seemed disinclined to start the conversation, 'you were a virgin.'

He looked at her. She was avoiding his eyes, fidgeting with the covers, looking both tempting and defiant. Something like indignation stirred in him. 'You,' he said, 'are a widow, damn near a divorcée, you're the owner of the most sophisticated club in London…' He stopped. 'How the hell,' he finished slowly, 'did that happen?'

She smiled ruefully. 'It…didn't happen.'

'No,' Jack said. 'I appreciate that now.'

Sally looked down. She had wound the sheet about herself so that it wrapped her lovely, voluptuous body up in a column of white. He wanted to unwind it again, take her again.

'Jonathan was unable to consummate our marriage,' she said, after a moment.

'Clearly.'

'He…did not find me attractive.' She looked defensive, blushing. 'I thought that there was something wrong with me.'

'So you thought to use me to prove that there was not?' The words came out more harshly than Jack had intended. He saw her flinch and cursed himself.

'I thought,' she corrected him, 'that it was extraordinary that you seemed to want me.'

It did not seem extraordinary to him. Resisting her was his only difficulty. Her husband had evidently been a fool. Unless…

'Did he prefer the company of men?' he asked.

Sally shook her head. 'I do not think so. I think he preferred street women. He said that he had no difficulties with them, but that I was too…' she hesitated, her tone flat '…too dull to interest him. He tried to make love to me, but it was no good. After we had tried— and failed—several times, he never came to my bed again. It was mortifying. I thought that it was my fault.'

Jack made an involuntary move towards her, then let his hand fall. He wanted to reassure her, to prove to her—again—that he found her incredibly attractive, but they needed to finish the conversation first.

'Listen to me,' he said. He caught her hand. The

sheet slipped a little. She made a grab for it, but he held her still.

'It must be apparent to you now,' he said, 'that you are an exceptionally attractive woman. Your husband's lack of interest in you was in no way your fault.'

She bit her lip. 'Thank you.' She sounded as polite as though he had handed her a plate at a tea party. Jack wanted, suddenly and violently, to kiss her.

'And there was never anyone else?' he said.

She shook her head slowly.

'So why me?' Jack said. 'Why now?'

She looked at him with those beautiful hazel eyes and hesitated.

'Sally?' he prompted.

'Perhaps I should not say it,' she said, 'but it was because I wanted to.' She gave a little shrug. 'Maybe it is immodest in me to admit it…'

Jack gave her a look. 'A little late for that now.'

She smiled a little. 'Yes.' She looked at him very directly. 'I wanted to find out what it was like. And…' suddenly she blushed very vividly '…I wanted to find out with you.'

'You could have warned me,' Jack said mildly. 'It would have been nicer.' He smiled. 'Nicer for you.'

She evaded his gaze. 'It wasn't exactly bad for me,

Jack.' She traced a pattern on the sheet with her fingers. 'Would it have made a difference to you, had you known? Would you have refused me?'

Jack thought about it. He remembered the absolute, driving need that he had felt to possess her, the sweetness of her surrender, the desire he had, even now, to slake his hunger for her again. He shook his head.

'No,' he said. He put a hand out and caught hold of the sheet that wrapped her up. 'But then, I am a rake.'

Her eyes widened. He realised she was shocked.

'I thought—' She cleared her throat. 'I thought that you would leave now.'

He laughed and tugged suddenly on the end of the sheet. It unfurled, leaving her naked to the waist.

'What a lot you have to learn, my sweet,' he said.

Chapter Four

Sally woke up as the morning sun crept across the floor of the bedroom and touched her face with its warmth. She opened her eyes slowly. She could tell that it was very early, for the light still had its dawn pallor. Out in the street she could hear the rumble of carriage wheels and the scrape and crash of the vendors setting up their stalls, but behind that noise were the calls of the birds in the garden at the back of the house and the splash of water in the fountain. It sounded peaceful.

She yawned, stretched and reached out a hand. The bed was empty. Somehow she had known that it would be. Jack had gone whilst she was asleep.

He had made love to her twice more through the long, hot darkness of the night, teaching her things she could never have imagined, taking her to places she had never even thought could exist, showing her things about herself and her responses that had dazzled and overwhelmed her. He had held her in his arms and shown her tenderness, but despite her inexperience she had not confused that with love. She knew he did not love her. There was something within Jack she was already all too aware that she could not reach, something dark that he had locked away.

He had left a note. On the table beside the bed was a crisp white piece of paper.

'Dinner tonight at eight.' The arrogant black scrawl suggested that he had not for a moment considered that she might refuse him. Despite herself, Sally smiled a little. So it was not over yet. Her body suffused with heat at the thought.

With a sigh she sat up, reached for a robe and thrust her feet into the little swansdown slippers that were one of her few concessions to frivolity. She frowned a little to see the pink dress crumpled on the floor, but the pieces of the corset made her blush. She would never, ever be able to view Matty's needlework scissors in the same light again.

She opened the door of her room and walked along the landing to the stairs. Her body ached a little. It felt unfamiliar, heavy, lush in its satiation. Sally examined her feelings. There was no guilt. She felt more astonished at herself than anything else. Astonished and pleased... But beneath the pleasure she was a little afraid. She was afraid that she might have fallen in love with Jack Kestrel last night. Everything had happened so fast, like a whirlwind. If she opened the door a crack and acknowledged her feelings, she was afraid that the love would swamp her. Her parched soul, which had welcomed Jack's desire for her, would give freely of its love as well. And he would not want that.

She had not mistaken lust for love the previous night. She might be inexperienced—less so now, admittedly—but she was no impressionable girl. She knew that Jack had wanted her desperately, violently, in the same way that she had wanted him, but equally she knew that it was just an affair to him. Yet she could not help herself. She could feel all the danger signs: the swooping sensation in the region of her heart at the thought of seeing Jack again, the breathlessness that was not merely from anticipation of his lovemaking, the pleasure she took in his company.

She would have to be careful and sensible, for Jack would surely not want her love and she did not wish her heart to be broken...

Yawning, she went down the staircase and into the hall. She loved the early morning when the building was quiet and felt as though it belonged to her alone. This morning all her senses seemed to be more acute; she could smell the rich beeswax and lavender furniture polish, see the way in which the early sunlight gleamed on the wood and hear the sounds of the carts outside in the street. The Strand never slept. Even this early there was the rumble of wheels and the sounds of raised voices. But here in the club there was no noise but the splash of the little waterfall in the atrium as it played amidst the spiky palm fronds and cool marble statuary.

There was a letter on the mat by the door. It had been hand delivered and must have arrived at some point in the night. Sally recognised her sister Petronella's scribble on the envelope. She picked it up and sat down on the stairs to read it.

Please, dear Sal, please, please help me! Clarrie and Anne are in Holloway Prison because they refused to pay their fines and their families are without support and have nowhere to turn. I need money for food and lodging and medicines. My own little ones are sick with the fever. If you could but loan me two hundred pounds...

The feeling of well being drained abruptly from Sally's body and she read the letter again carefully. Two hundred pounds… A cold, cold shiver touched her spine. She let the letter drift from her fingers. Two hundred pounds was a fortune, enough to buy a house, more than enough comfortably to keep a family for a whole year. But she knew medicine was prohibitively expensive and fever could sweep through crowded tenements like a fire, destroying all in its path. She also knew that Nell would not ask for money unless she was absolutely desperate. Like Sally herself, Nell was too proud for charity and was determined to earn her own money.

Sally leaned her head against the banister and closed her eyes. She did not have two hundred pounds to spare. She had overreached herself with the refurbishment of the Blue Parrot and was already in debt. Yet she had always looked after Nell and Connie, trying to help them if she possibly could. It was part of the pact she had made with herself because of her guilt about their father's death. She thought of Nell struggling to look after her own and other women's children when their men folk were dead or had deserted them and they were in prison. Her throat locked with pity and distress.

I do not know how I may manage if you cannot help me, Nell had written. *I have my own fines to pay for breach of the peace and sometimes I feel it is not worth the struggle, and yet I cannot abandon the principle of universal suffrage. But if the choice is between that and Lucy and George starving, then I do not know what I can do. Please help me, Sally. You are my only hope.*

Sally sighed. She did not support the suffrage movement through militant action as Nell did and felt a terrible guilt that she professed the politics and yet did so little to help her sister. And now there were children suffering and dying of the fever for want of the money to buy medicines. Sally could not bear for anything to happen to them.

She picked up the letter and went back upstairs, her mind running over ways in which she might raise the money to help. She could not borrow further from the bank unless she mortgaged the house, a course of action she was loath to take. There were perhaps a few people whom she could approach for a loan—Gregory Holt, an investor in the club and an old friend of her family, had always offered himself as a shoulder to cry on, but Sally knew he wanted more than friendship from her and did not wish to take advantage of him and put herself in his debt. She could not ask Jack. She barely knew him and that would put their relationship on quite a different footing. She was determined to maintain her independence.

She knocked on Connie's door as she passed along the landing, but there was no answer; peeping around the door, she saw that the bed had not been slept in. With another sigh she went back to her room and rang the bell for the maid to bring her morning tea. The day did not seem quite so bright with promise now. She knew she had to find a solution to Nell's problems and find it fast. She had no idea what to do.

'What do you think?' Jack said. He was watching Sally's face as he waited for her reaction. They had dined at White City, in the Grand Restaurant at the Franco-British Exhibition, and now they were poised two hundred feet above the ground in the fairground amusement called the Flip Flap. Beneath them the white-stuccoed buildings of the exhibition were spread out like a magical world that gleamed in the moonlight. The cascade was lit by a thousand coloured lanterns that were reflected in rainbow colours in the waters of the lagoon. Sally gave a sigh of pure enjoyment and Jack felt a surprising rush of pleasure to see her happiness.

'It is quite, quite beautiful.' She turned to him, smiling. 'And quite absurd of you to pay for us to have the entire carriage to ourselves.'

Jack shrugged. 'I didn't want to have to share the experience with anyone but you,' he said.

Sally turned away, resting her elbows on the side of the carriage and looking out across the lights of the capital.

'They say you can see as far as Windsor on a fine day,' she said. 'We came when the exhibition first opened. It was a terrible crush. I brought my sister Nell and her children.' She laughed. 'Connie refused to come because she said that, although it was fashionable to be seen here, there were too many ordinary people. Her loss, I suppose. We had a splendid time.'

Jack was not surprised at this insight into Connie Bowes. The more he got to know her sister, the more different they appeared. He'd had someone out looking for both Connie and his cousin Bertie Basset all day, ever since he had received a message from Sally that morning informing him that Connie had not returned home the previous night. He was not sure which of them irritated him the more, Bertie for causing his family so much distress at a time when his father was dangerously ill, or Connie for undoubtedly having an eye to the main chance.

It had been an unsatisfactory day. Jack was not accustomed to finding his attention wandering in business meetings, a fact directly attributable to the woman now standing beside him enraptured by the view. His concentration had been severely affected all day. He had a pile of work requiring his consideration, several urgent decisions to be made and a diary full of appointments to keep, yet he had chosen to take Sally Bowes to the exhibition rather than using the evening for the business dinner he had originally planned. His sanity must be in question.

He had been shaken when he had awoken that morning to realise that he did not want to leave Sally's bed. He had wanted to stay with her so strongly that the impulse had completely perplexed him. He had never wanted to stay with a woman any longer than it took to say goodbye. But Sally had been warm and soft curled up beside him in the big bed, her body satiated from the passion of their lovemaking. He had found himself holding her as though he never wanted to let her go.

Somehow he had found the strength to leave, but then he had lost the advantage by spending the entire day thinking about her anyway. He smiled ruefully to himself. He had thought that to take her to bed would drive this need for her from body and his mind, only to find that his desire was more acute than ever.

Just as disturbing as his unquenched lust was the guilt he felt on seducing an innocent. Jack played the game by the rules and ravishing virgins was not his style. He knew that Sally would say she was as much seducer as seduced, that his scruples were unnecessary, and that she could take care of herself, but he still felt that what he had done was wrong. Perhaps he was more old fashioned and conventional than he had imagined, for despite the fact that he had known her three days, and despite his deep-rooted rejection of marriage, he wanted to do the right thing. His instinct to propose to Sally was very strong and he assured himself it was nothing to do with the pleasure he took in her company, but simply because he had been brought up a gentleman.

'Jack?' Sally was standing looking at him, her face tilted up towards him, eyes bright with excitement. Tonight she was wearing a gown of deep green silk that seemed to flow fluidly over her body. It was embroidered with flowers and decorated with lace at the neck, a concealment that only served to emphasise the lush curve of her breasts. The night was warm and so she had only a diaphanous shawl about her shoulders. Beneath it her skin gleamed pale and tempting.

'I wondered,' she said, as the Flip Flap started to descend to the ground again, 'if you would care to take a swan boat on the lagoon with me before we go back?'

Jack's preference would have been to go directly back to the club and take up where they had left off the previous night, but Sally looked so excited and happy, and she caught his hand and pulled him towards the lake. They paused on the white ornamental bridge that crossed the water.

'Such a beautiful night!' Sally said. She glanced sideways at him. 'With anyone else I would say that it is a night made for romance, but I remember you telling me yesterday that you do not believe in such fanciful stuff.'

'I do not believe in love,' Jack said. 'It is a convenient fiction invented to dress up physical desire.'

Sally sighed, her gaze on the rippling water. 'And yet you must have been in love once?'

'It is true that I thought I loved Merle.' Jack spoke harshly. Her words echoed too closely the painful memories he had been thinking of only moments before. 'I did love her. It was the single most destructive experience of my life.'

Sally's eyes were wide and dark on his face. 'Why?'

'Because I lost all control and all judgement.' Jack shrugged. 'I don't want to talk about it.' Suddenly he made a sharp gesture. 'You thought you were in love with your husband when you married, didn't you? And that could hardly be said to have turned out happily.'

Sally was silent for a moment. 'I was young,' she said. 'I thought I was doing the right thing. I expect you did too when you eloped. Everyone makes mistakes.'

Jack laughed harshly. 'Not everyone makes mistakes that were as unforgivable as mine.'

Even though he was turned away from her, he could feel Sally's gaze on him. She put a gentle hand on his arm.

'Do you ever talk about Merle?'

'No.'

'It was a long time ago. Do you still love her?'

Jack did not answer, did not know the answer. He had loved Merle passionately and then he had wanted to forget her equally as passionately, but had never been able to escape her memory and her legacy. He was haunted by his guilt over her death and his self-loathing at his own weakness. But he did not want to think about that now. He wanted to wipe out the memory in the passion of Sally's embrace.

Sally shivered and drew her shawl more closely about her shoulders as though she could sense his disquiet. 'Never mind the boat ride,' she said. 'Let's go back,' and although she did not utter a word of reproach, Jack knew that his abruptness had broken the spell between them.

He caught her wrist, pulling her into his arms. He kissed her hard, the thrust of his tongue invading her mouth mercilessly, feeling her yield. He felt angry, but was not sure why. All he knew was that he wanted to slake all that anger and pain in Sally's warmth. His hands held her tightly against him, and he slid one of them from her waist to her breast, feeling the nipple harden against his palm. He eased the pressure of the kiss and heard her catch her breath.

'We cannot do this here...' Her whisper was shocked and with a rush of awareness Jack realised they were still standing on a bridge in the middle of the lagoon, illuminated on all sides by the brightly coloured lights of the cascade. Anyone could see them.

He took her hand and pulled her towards the archway that led out into Wood Lane. For the first time he was glad that they had driven there rather than taking the underground. At least the car would afford them some privacy, although it would probably feel like hours until they got back.

He held the car door for her, started the engine, then slid in beside her into the intimate darkness. He could hear her breathing and feel the powerful awareness that shimmered between them. The complicated anger was still in him, but overlaid with desire. He gripped the wheel of the Lanchester tightly, concentrating solely on getting back to the Strand. If he started to think about making love to Sally he would probably stop and do precisely that in the middle of a London street.

'I don't understand,' Sally said. Her voice was soft. 'I don't understand how I can feel like this when I barely know you and I don't understand the devils that drive you.'

Jack took one hand briefly from the wheel and covered her clasped ones. 'Don't think about it,' he said. There was a rough undertone to his voice. He could sense her gaze on him in the darkness, but he did not dare look at her. If he did so, he would kiss her and then…

They said nothing more as the car drew up outside the Blue Parrot, but the silence between them was electric. The tension had spun tighter and tighter as the journey progressed and now that they had finally got to their destination the anticipation was almost choking him. This time Jack picked Sally up and carried her through the main doorway and up the stairs, under the astounded gaze of Alfred the doorman and various assorted and scandalised guests who were milling around in the entrance hall. Sally struggled, one of her pretty little sequin-encrusted evening slippers coming off and bouncing down the steps.

'Put me down!' she hissed. Her face was pink with indignation. 'Everyone can see!'

Jack smiled down into her face. 'So?'

'You are doing this to the benefit of your own reputation and think nothing of mine,' Sally said.

Jack put her on her feet gently on the soft carpet at the top of the stairs. 'Too late, my sweet,' he said. 'Everyone already believes you to be a racy and outrageous nightclub owner—so why not live up to the role?'

He dropped a kiss on her parted lips, smiling again as he took in the startled, upturned faces of their audience down in the hall. Loosening his tie, he said, 'Come along. I am taking you to bed.'

'Jack!' Sally blushed a vivid scarlet.

'It's no more than I have wanted to do all day,' Jack

said. He could barely wait to get her as far as the bedroom as it was. With one arm about her, he hustled her
down the corridor, past the appalled, upright figure of
Mrs Matson, thrust open the bedroom door and pulled
her inside.

'I can't afford to lose another corset,' Sally said.

Jack laughed. 'You won't even notice it's gone,' he
promised, lowering his mouth to hers again. The shimmering, devastating pleasure took him again as soon as
their lips touched and he allowed his mind to go dark
until he was aware of nothing but their spiralling need
and the urgent demand to claim her again as his and
his only.

This time when Sally awoke it was still dark outside and there was only one candle burning low in the
room. The building was quiet. Jack was lying beside
her, one arm lying across her bare stomach in a casual
gesture of possession. She moved slightly and his arms
tightened about her, drawing her closer to him. He felt
warm and a lock of his hair tickled her cheek.

Sally lay still for a moment. Her mind felt sleepy
and heavy, but her body was starting to stir, aroused
by the proximity of Jack's nakedness. For a second the
sensation troubled her. She had always thought that

a woman's physical needs were supposed to be less powerful than those of a man and yet she had matched Jack's need for her every step of the way. And surely she should feel guilt over her behaviour. She had not known him long, did not know him well, but felt so powerful a desire for him that it was completely immodest.

Jack moved, murmuring in his sleep, and pressed his lips to the soft curve of her neck, and something shifted within her that felt unfamiliar and sweet and a lot like love was meant to be. For a moment Sally fought it, denied it, tried to tell herself that it was too soon to love him, impossible, pointless, hopeless and heartbreaking. But she could not resist the feelings that flooded her mind and her body.

With a sigh she turned over to face Jack. She did not want to be in love with him. She knew it was one of the most stupid things that she could do. He was a rake with a dark past and there could never be anything other than a casual affair for them. But it was too late. Against all sense and reason her feelings were engaged and she acknowledged that she felt such a deep and burgeoning love for him that it filled her with a helpless wash of emotion.

She needed to distract herself. Smiling a little, she

ran her hands over Jack's chest, feeling the hard muscle beneath the smooth skin. He was warm and he smelled deliciously of cedar wood cologne. She bent over and lowered her lips to his chest, kissing him softly, touching her tongue to his bare skin and tasting him with a sensual curiosity that was both exploratory and provocative. Her hand slid lower, down the line of his belly and thigh, her mouth dipping to follow its trail. He stirred and groaned her name, already aroused, his erection straining.

'Does this feel good?' She whispered, astonished at her own daring, excited at what she could do to him.

'Minx.' He caught her to him, tumbling her beneath him, rolling her over so that she was lying on her stomach on the pillows. 'You learn too quickly.'

Confused, she tried to turn around to ask him what he was doing, but he held her hips down and she gave a shattered cry as she felt the moist flick of his tongue between her thighs. She felt intensely vulnerable as he opened her to the skilled, intimate stroke of his tongue. The sensations gathered and exploded around her like exquisite torture and then she felt the tip of his erection tease her and he entered her in a series of thrusts that immediately sent her tumbling over the edge into cataclysmic orgasm. Trembling, quiescent, she tried to slump on the pillows but he held her steady, maintaining the power of his thrusts, one moment buried within her, the next withdrawing in a rhythm as strong and primal as time. She felt his hands tighten on her hips and then he thrust deep and hard, emptying himself into her.

For a moment there was nothing but the harshness of their breathing and then he lifted her unresisting body in his arms and turned her to face him, laying her down on the pillows. His kiss was as deep and searing as his possession had been and when he let her go there was a fierce expression in his face as though he were angry with her in some way. She stared up at him, feeling again the sense that there was a part of him that was tormented and dark, a part that he kept locked away where she could not reach him.

'I will conquer this,' he ground out, and then his mouth came down on hers again with absolute demand and his hand came up to cup her breast as though through his utter dominance of her body he might somehow control his own desires. Feeling the helpless need that coursed through her at the renewed claim in his touch, Sally freed her mouth and gasped, 'Jack, please, I can't...'

But she saw the wicked glint in his eyes and knew it was pointless to protest.

'You can,' he whispered, his lips drifting over the curve of her breast. 'You will,' and she gave herself up to sheer sensation. Yet beneath the desire ran the deep and strong current of her love and, now that she had acknowledged it, Sally knew she could never be free of it.

'Miss Sally!'

Sally awoke in a panic to the sound of Mrs Matson's voice. For one dreadful moment she was afraid that her old nurse had come in and found her in bed with Jack. Then she moved and once again the bed felt empty and cold and she realised with a lurch of the heart that Jack had gone.

'Miss Sally.' Mrs Matson was staring fixedly at the dent in the pillow where Jack's head had lain. 'I thought I told you to find a nice young man?'

'Mmm.' Sally rolled over to prop herself on her elbow. Her memories of the previous night suggested that Jack Kestrel might be many things, but he was not Matty's idea of a nice young man.

'And instead,' Mrs Matson continued, still staring

with apparent fascinated disapproval at the tumbled bed, 'you choose a scoundrel.'

'Yes,' Sally said. She yawned. 'Was there anything else, Matty? I am a little tired this morning.'

'I'm not surprised,' Matty said astringently. 'And, yes, there was something, Miss Sally. I wanted to let you know that Miss Connie has come back. I saw her getting out of a motor car outside only a moment ago.'

With a muffled curse Sally leapt from the bed, remembering, as Mrs Matson gave a loud shriek, that she was entirely naked. She grabbed a robe, knotting it about her waist, and hurried out on to the landing.

As she leaned on the wrought-iron banister at the top of the stairs she saw the front door open surreptitiously and her sister Connie come in. She had her shoes in her hand and was tiptoeing across the marble floor to the stairs.

'Good morning,' Sally said.

Connie jumped and dropped the shoes with a clatter. She was wearing what Sally recognised to be an evening gown, presumably from the previous night, a sky-blue confection that should have looked divine, but actually looked a little dishevelled now. Her sleek blonde hair was ruffled and she wore no stockings. Connie had a classically pretty face with a pink-and-white complexion and china blue eyes that was almost too perfect in its symmetry. The only thing that marred her expression was the downward droop of her mouth, which seemed to imply perpetual disappointment.

'What on earth are you doing up at this hour?' Connie demanded, her blue eyes narrowed. She looked less than friendly.

'I always get up at this time,' Sally said calmly. She watched her sister as Connie started to climb the stairs, wincing in her bare feet. 'Usually you don't see me,' she continued, 'as you never wake until eleven.'

'Don't ask me where I've been,' Connie said crossly.

'All right.'

'I was with Bertie Basset,' Connie said. She reached the landing and stopped defiantly in front of her sister. 'I have been with him for the last couple of days.'

'I see,' Sally said. Bertie Basset. She felt a cold dousing of shock as she remembered Jack's original suspicions about Connie trying to fleece the Bassets one way or another and her own conviction that her sister was up to something. She had hoped against hope it might not be true.

Connie was frowning at her. 'You look different,' she said. 'More…pretty.' She scowled. 'Anyway, don't scold me. I'm too tired.'

Sally touched her sister's elbow. 'I need to speak with you, Connie. Urgently.'

Connie pouted. 'Must you? I'm too tired to talk now! We dined at Grange's last night and then we went dancing.' Connie smiled mistily. 'Then we went to Bartram's Hotel. It's very expensive.'

'I see,' Sally said drily, wondering if Connie would have been less free with her favours had Bertie proposed to take her somewhere cheaper.

'I dined with Mr Kestrel last night,' she added.

Connie's eyes opened very wide. 'Mr *Jack* Kestrel? He wanted to dine with *you*?' Her face crumpled with disappointment and jealousy. 'Oh, I would have liked to meet him!'

'He would like to meet you too,' Sally said grimly.

Connie smiled, good humour restored. 'Naturally he would. Everyone who is anyone in London wishes to meet me.'

'In order to take back the letters Mr Basset wrote to you, which I believe you have been trying to use to blackmail Mr Basset's father.'

Connie bit her lip. A shade of colour had crept into her cheeks and she looked defensive. 'That was a mistake.'

'It certainly was.' Sally tapped her fingers on the

banister. 'What are you up to, Connie?' she said softly. 'I know there is something going on. You have been with Mr Basset all night and yet you were trying to extort money from his father.'

Connie sighed exaggeratedly. 'Oh, Sal, you are so naïve!' Her hair swung forward, hiding her expression. 'Bertie and I had a falling out. I thought it was all over.'

Sally's heart sank at this confirmation of her sister's guilt. 'So you tried to make some money out of the affair.'

'Why not?' Connie straightened up. 'He owed me something.'

'And now that you and Mr Basset are reconciled, what are you planning to do?' Sally asked sarcastically. 'Write Lord Basset a letter of apology?'

Connie brightened. 'Oh, that is a splendid idea! We may pretend that the whole matter never happened.'

'I was joking,' Sally said. 'Mr Kestrel is hardly the man to let the matter go, even if Lord Basset is. And does Mr Basset know that you threatened his father, Connie?'

The colour deepened in Connie's cheeks. 'No! But he would forgive me if he did. We love each other.'

This unlikely declaration made Sally raise her eyebrows, but she managed to repress the expressions of disbelief that jostled on her lips. 'Best to make a clean breast of it, then,' she said, 'and tell him everything before his cousin does. Mr Kestrel will no doubt come back later. You could try to convince him of your good faith, although I think,' she added drily, 'that he will be less easy to persuade than Mr Basset.'

'Oh, I will win him around,' Connie said airily. 'He is supposed to have an eye for a pretty face.' She yawned. 'I must go to bed, Sally darling, or my complexion will look dismal tonight.'

With a vague wave of the hand she scampered along the corridor, and Sally heard the decisive click of the door behind her. Sighing, she walked back to her own room and started, rather listlessly, to hunt for something to wear. Talking to Connie about her attempted extortion had depressed her spirits. Even if Connie and Bertie were reconciled, it seemed likely that Lord Basset would think the connection highly unsuitable and try to separate the pair, using Jack as his messenger. And Connie's feelings for Bertie did not appear to go very deep.

Anxiety gnawed at her. In the heat of the night with Jack she had forgotten all about Connie and her extortion and blackmail. She had given herself to him with a passion and a hunger that had driven everything else from her mind. Now, however, she remembered that they would not have met at all had Jack not come to the Blue Parrot to find Connie. And he would not have forgotten his original intention, no matter how hot the desire that burned between them. She thought of Jack, and their fledgling affair, and the fact that her bed was cold and empty in the morning. She thought of her newly discovered love for him, how fragile and foolish it was, and then she felt afraid, and she could not quite shake the superstitious conviction that something was going to go terribly wrong.

'Mr Churchward has called to see you, Mr Kestrel,' Hudson, the butler, intoned. 'I told him that you were still at breakfast and he is awaiting you in the library.'

Jack threw down his napkin and got to his feet. He had taken breakfast alone as his uncle's poor health left him bedridden and Lady Basset never rose before midday even though she was as fit as a fiddle. The house in Eaton Square was gloomy and quiet as a tomb now that his uncle was so ill and the Bassets no longer went out or entertained. Jack felt a strong urge to move out again to his club for the rest of his stay in London.

Bertie had made no appearance at the table that morning and Jack had assumed, a little grimly, that he had not come back the previous night. Not that he could talk. These days the milk was being delivered when he arrived home. Once again he had forced himself to leave Sally sleeping and had crept out like a thief. This time the impulse to stay with her had been even stronger than the night before. Their intense lovemaking had not quenched the need he had for her. The reverse was true. He had tried to satisfy his desire by slaking his body, but it only seemed to make matters worse. He wanted to possess Sally Bowes's soul as well as her body, bind her to him as his alone. He had thought it no more than a physical urge. He had been profoundly wrong. The urge to propose marriage to her after a whirlwind three days was growing ever stronger. But that was madness. He had wanted to marry Merle, but there had never been another woman since whom he wished to wed. He could not love Sally as he had loved Merle. He did not want to expose himself to that sort of pain again. Surely this instinct he had to claim her was no more than a combination of old-fashioned guilt and primitive possessiveness.

Frowning, he crossed the hall and went into the library. He had forgotten about Churchward's visit. Several days ago, when his uncle had first told him about Bertie's indiscretion and Connie Bowes's blackmail, he had asked the lawyer to look into her history. Now he felt vaguely uncomfortable about this, as though he was in some way being disloyal to Sally. He thought of Sally's candid eyes, of the honesty that she had shown him. Whatever her sister's duplicity, Sally had surely been telling the truth when she had said she knew nothing of it. All he could do now was to try to deal with the matter as best he could without hurting her.

Mr John Churchward, of the firm Churchward, Churchward and Boyce of High Holborn, was perched on a chair in the library, his briefcase on his knee, looking slightly nervous. John Churchward was only the latest in a line of the Churchward family who had served the Kestrels as lawyers for decades. The Boyce mentioned in the company name was a recent partner, but Jack had never met him. All his business, including the sorrowful meeting before Jack had been banished ten years before, had been concluded with this man, a thin, stooping figure who had a nervous habit of constantly adjusting the glasses that habitually slid down his nose and whose age was indeterminate. Ten years before, Mr Churchward had been in the unhappy position of confirming that Jack's father did not intend to pay him any type of allowance at all during his exile. On Jack's return as a rich, self-made man,

Mr Churchward, who had not looked a day older, had seemed genuinely pleased to see him and to discover the independent success Jack had made of his business ventures.

'I came as soon as I could gather the information you required, sir,' Mr Churchward said now. 'I have made some enquiries into the background of Miss Bowes and her relationship with Mr Basset.' He shook his head sorrowfully. 'A most flighty young lady, if I may say so, sir, and…' he cleared his throat, blushing slightly '…somewhat indiscriminate with her affections as well.'

'You do not surprise me, Churchward,' Jack said, grimly. 'Tell me your worst.'

'Well, sir…' Churchward made a fuss of opening the case and removing a sheaf of papers '…Miss Constance Bowes is the youngest daughter of Sir Peter Bowes, an architect of some renown who unfortunately lost all his money in unwise speculation at the end of the last century. She has two elder sisters, the notorious suffragette Petronella Bowes—' here Churchward's voice dipped with distinct disapproval '—and the equally infamous Mrs Jonathan Hayward, who owns a *nightclub* in the Strand.'

'Miss Sally Bowes,' Jack said, his lips twitching. 'I

believe she prefers not to be known by her married name, Churchward.'

'I dare say,' Mr Churchward said frostily. 'A woman of that stamp—'

'To return to Miss Constance,' Jack said, cutting in ruthlessly as Churchward's description of Sally roused a violently protective feeling in him, 'what of her subsequent career?'

'Well, sir...' Churchward cast Jack a startled look at his inflexibility of tone. 'Miss Constance was twelve when her father lost all his money and fifteen when he died. She lived for a number of years with a maiden aunt. There was...' he consulted his notes '...some scandal over a flirtation with a piano teacher and later a thwarted elopement with a young gentleman called Geoffrey Chavenage.' He cleared his throat. 'When her sister, Mrs Hayward—Miss Bowes, that is—was widowed Miss Constance went to live and work with her at the Blue Parrot Club.' Churchward stopped. 'Two years ago, both women were involved in a rather unsavoury lawsuit for breach of promise.'

Jack, who had got up and strolled over to the window whilst this recital was continuing, now turned around sharply. '*Both* women?' he questioned. He felt a chill down his spine, a premonition that something was about to go awry. 'Are you sure?'

'Yes, sir.' Churchward extracted a couple of sheets from his pile of papers. 'Miss Constance Bowes sued a Mr John Pettifer over breach of promise to marry. Her elder sister stood as a witness and supported her throughout the case. They won,' Mr Churchward said, with gloomy dissatisfaction, 'and were awarded substantial damages.' He paused, pushing his glasses back up his nose. 'It was also Mrs Hayward who dealt with the matter of her sister's unfortunate elopement. The Chavenage family allegedly paid out to keep the matter from the courts because Miss Connie was under age at the time.' He cleared his throat. 'So one might conclude, sir, that this case involving Miss Constance and your unfortunate cousin is part of a pattern to entrap young gentlemen into indiscretion and subsequently extract payment from them.'

Jack's dark eyes had narrowed and a muscle tightened in his cheek. 'And you are certain,' he demanded, '*absolutely* certain, that Miss Sally Bowes—Mrs Hayward—supported her sister in bringing both these cases?'

He saw Churchward's surprise at the vehemence of his tone. The lawyer's eyes blinked myopically behind the thick lenses of his glasses. 'Yes, sir.' He held out the papers. 'I have the court transcripts here. Miss Bowes was her younger sister's most staunch supporter in the case against Mr Pettifer and my sources also informed me of her role in the Chavenage case.'

Jack took the papers. He would not, he told himself sternly, believe a word against Sally until he had seen the evidence with his own eyes. And yet even as the thought went through his mind he was scanning the papers before him. In Churchward's neat annotations he read that the Chavenage family had apparently paid Mrs Hayward seven thousand pounds to keep the matter of her sister's elopement with Mr Geoffrey Chavenage out of the courts. Chavenage senior was a Member of Parliament and Jack could see how badly the elopement of his son with an underage girl might affect his political standing. With increasing anger and disbelief he turned to the court transcripts for the Pettifer breach of promise case. Again, Sally had been very active in supporting her sister's claim and had presented Connie Bowes as an innocent who had been cruelly betrayed by an experienced older man. Jack raised his brows with incredulity that the judge could have been so taken in.

'Of course,' Mr Churchward was saying, in his precise manner, 'we must consider the possibility that

Miss Constance Bowes was indeed the injured party in both of these instances—'

He broke off as Jack slammed one fist into the palm of his other hand. 'I think,' Jack said, 'that is as likely as hell freezing over.'

'Sir?' Churchward looked confused.

'Apologies, Churchward—' Jack straightened up, casting the papers aside '—but I do not for one moment think that is likely. Miss Constance's attempt to blackmail my uncle fits too neatly with the pattern for it to be a coincidence.' He strode over to mantelpiece and rested an arm along the top whilst he tried to think coolly and calculatedly about Sally Bowes's deception. She had told him that she knew nothing of Connie's extortion threats and that she would do all she could to return the letters.

And he had believed her.

Fool that he was—he had been taken in by her apparent frankness, intrigued by her intelligent mind, led astray by his lust for the luscious body she hid beneath those deliciously silky gowns. There was evidence here, chapter and verse, of two occasions on which the Bowes sisters together had entrapped a young man and walked away with a fortune, but in his hunger for Sally Bowes he had almost fallen for her lies. He had exonerated the elder sister from the greed and cupidity of the younger, when in fact she was probably the one who arranged all the details of these unscrupulous affairs. Sally provided the brains, Connie the looks, to fleece the gentlemen of their choosing.

Something twisted inside him that felt almost like pain. Jack was not accustomed to feeling pain in any of his love affairs. It was something that had not happened to him for ten years. Then he felt anger, so intense and searing that for a moment his mind went blank.

'Mr Kestrel?' He became aware that Churchward was addressing him. 'What would you like me to do now, sir?'

'Churchward,' Jack said slowly, 'thank you for gathering this information for me. What I would like you to do now is to find out who the investors are in Miss Sally Bowes's club, the Blue Parrot. Find out, and then approach them to see if any would be prepared to sell their stake.'

Churchward's brows shot up. 'Are you looking to invest in a nightclub, sir?'

'No,' Jack said grimly. 'I am looking to ruin Miss Sally Bowes's business, Churchward. Find the investors and buy them up. I want that club. I want Miss Bowes in my power.'

* * *

'Mr Kestrel is here to see you, ma'am—' Sally's secretary had barely managed to get the words out when Jack Kestrel shouldered through the doorway into the office.

'I'll announce myself,' he said. 'Miss Bowes…' He gave her an unsmiling nod.

Sally had been unable to concentrate all morning, a fact that she knew her secretary had noticed with curiosity. She had made half a dozen errors in her arithmetic and had started and abandoned three letters to the club's suppliers. Her attention had been torn in half between worrying about Nell's situation and thinking about Jack, and neither had been conducive to work. When Jack's name was announced she had felt her heart do a little flip and the heat had rushed through her body in an irresistible tide, but then she had seen his face, his hard, uncompromising expression, and the smile had faded from her eyes as she had known at once that something was dreadfully wrong. Her superstitious dread had been well founded.

He did not look in the least glad to see *her*. In fact, he looked thunderous.

'Thank you, Mary,' Sally said, rising to her feet and nodding to the secretary to close the door behind her.

Her heart was beating uncomfortably fast now. Already the abruptness of Jack's tone and the dislike that she could see in his eyes reminded her all too clearly of their first meeting, before they had taken dinner together, before he had kissed her, before that tempestuous and passionate lovemaking that even now stole her breath to remember it. She felt confused, as though time had slipped back and all the things that she knew had happened between them over the past few days had never been.

'This,' she said, as calmly as she was able, mindful of the staff in the outer office, 'is distressingly similar to your arrival two days ago, Mr Kestrel.'

Jack slapped a pile of papers down on the desk in front of her. 'Do you deny that you supported your sister in a claim for damages after an elopement and also in a breach of promise case in 1906, Miss Bowes?' he demanded.

Sally's stomach lurched. She felt a little sick. So Jack had been digging into Connie's past affairs. She might have guessed that he would. He must have started his enquiries before they had met, but even so she felt horribly betrayed. She remembered the previous night, the things she had done, the heated, intimate, perfect things she had allowed him to do to her, and she could not bear to think that all the time he'd had no trust in her. Even now the memories could make her melt with longing and she hated the fact that he could still do that to her when he was standing there like a cold-faced stranger. That was humiliating. But what was blisteringly painful was the fact that she had loved him then and, despite everything, loved him still.

'You have been quick to make enquiries into our business, sir,' she said stiffly.

'Naturally,' Jack said. His expression was stony. 'Did you think I would simply trust your word, Miss Bowes? How surprisingly naïve for a woman like you!'

He allowed his gaze to appraise her insolently from her plain brown shoes to her neatly pinned hair. 'I have to say that you have been very convincing over the past couple of days. I almost believed you honest. You are evidently both practised and clever.'

The pain of his contempt sliced through Sally like a knife. 'You have this utterly wrong!' she said. 'Yes, I was involved in supporting Connie through the breach of promise case two years ago, but she had been cruelly let down and I wanted to help her—'

'Oh, spare me the false protestations of innocence.' The derision in Jack's voice was searing. 'Your sister's attempt to extort money from my uncle is part of a pattern of blackmail that both of you have perpetrated for years.'

Sally's outrage swamped all other emotions. 'How dare you? It is not!'

Jack tapped the sheaf of papers. 'The detail is all here, Miss Bowes.' He straightened up. 'Chavenage, Pettifer, and now you seek to add my cousin to the list.'

Sally's mind was spinning. She knew that the cases looked damning, but her heart was sore that Jack had come to accuse, not to ask her for the truth. They had only known each other a brief time but even so, she had hoped that it would have been enough for him to trust her. Evidently not. He could make love to her with no emotional commitment whatsoever. He had no respect for her. She felt despair at the contrast with her own feelings.

'I know that the breach of promise suit looks bad,' she said desperately, 'but if you would only let me explain! Connie loved John Pettifer. His desertion caused her immense distress.' She stopped at the look of utter disbelief on Jack's face.

'You are breaking my heart, Miss Bowes,' he said cynically. 'The truth is that your sister is nothing but a gold-digger and you are as good as a procuress!' He looked at her thoughtfully and under his scrutiny the colour burned into her face because she knew he was thinking about their nights together.

'I am surprised,' he drawled, 'that you held on to your virginity for as long as you did when it was something that you could sell for money. Did you see me, Miss Bowes, and think that I was rich enough to be made to pay? How long before I receive a visit from your lawyer bringing a court case for deflowering an innocent girl?' He laughed, and the contempt in it shrivelled Sally's soul. 'Damn it, even if I have to pay up, it was almost worth it. You tasted very sweet.'

The fury and misery swamped Sally. She found she was shaking. She thought of Nell struggling to find two hundred pounds to save her own children and buy medicine and food and she thought of Jack's hateful callousness. If he already had such a low opinion of her, what did it matter what else he thought about her? She would never be able to change his opinion. Their sweet affair was over before it had barely begun and her love with it.

She took a deep breath.

'I would settle for two hundred pounds,' she said.

As soon as the words were out she thought she was going to faint at her own audacity. She felt sick and shaky. Jack had turned away for a moment and now he spun around to look at her and his eyes widened as though, even with the poor opinion he held of her, she had surprised him. Perhaps she had. Perhaps he had not expected her to be so shameless. Sally concentrated fiercely on thinking of her family and waited.

His gaze was hard and appraising as it scoured her from head to toe and left her trembling. Then he smiled, a cynical smile. His put his hand, very slowly, into his pocket and withdrew a leather wallet.

'My advice,' he drawled, 'would be to negotiate your fee in advance in future, Miss Bowes.'

Sally swallowed hard. Her throat was dry and her heart was beating so hard she thought he would be able to see how she shook.

'Two hundred pounds for two nights,' Jack said, extracting some fifty-pound notes from his wallet. 'You could have asked for much more.' He came up to her and put a hand against her cheek. His touch was gentle, but the expression in his eyes was hard. 'How much do you want to be my mistress?'

Sally closed her eyes. She knew that with her demand for money she had confirmed every belief he had about her mercenary soul. And yet despite the hostility between them he still wanted to sleep with her because the searing, sensual passion between them had not yet been sated. Having purchased her virginity, he thought he could buy her to be his mistress.

She had sold her virginity for two hundred pounds.

The reality hit her like a rip tide, making her tremble with despair and self-disgust. And straight on the heels of that thought she felt Jack lean down and his mouth take hers with ruthless intensity.

The kiss was a statement of possession and though it was over almost before it began, it shook Sally to the core. He let her go and she rocked back on her heels, catching her breath. Once again his gaze appraised her with insolent thoroughness, as though stripping every one of her clothes from her.

'How much?' he repeated. He put the banknotes in her hand.

'Nothing,' Sally said. She cleared her throat. 'That is…I have no interest in being your mistress, Mr Kestrel.'

A cynical smile tugged at Jack's lips. 'I am sure you could be persuaded, Miss Bowes, for the right price.' He straightened. 'We will discuss this later. In the meantime I want to talk to your sister. She is here?'

'I… Yes…' Sally tried to pull herself together. 'Connie is indeed here—I spoke with her this morning.' She glanced ostentatiously at the clock. 'Connie will still be abed, Mr Kestrel. You are somewhat early this morning, and I am afraid that my sister seldom rises before midday.'

'Then we will go and wake her,' Jack said grimly.

'Very well.' Sally stalked towards the door. She was still shaking. She needed some time alone. The banknotes seemed to burn her palm. 'Please would you wait here?' she said.

'I am hardly going to sit idly by whilst Miss Constance escapes out of a back window,' Jack drawled. He raised a brow. 'Surely you are not concerned about a gentleman entering her bedroom? There must have been plenty over the years, judging by the detail in these papers.'

Sally gritted her teeth. Having just proved herself perfidious and money-grabbing in his eyes, she was not in a particularly good position to defend anyone else. She tried to focus on Nell's children. Now they could have a roof over their heads and the medicines they needed. And Nell would be able to help the other families too…

'Constance,' Jack was saying thoughtfully. 'What a damnably inappropriate name for your sister, Miss Bowes. Unless it is constancy in the pursuit of a fortune, of course.'

Sally ignored him. She thrust open the office door and stormed into the outer office, where Mary and the girl who did the typing were sitting trying to pretend that they had not been eavesdropping on every word. This time Jack had to hurry to keep up with Sally as she marched up the two flights of stairs and charged down the corridor to Connie's room, flinging the door open.

The room was in darkness.

Sally picked her way across to the window and flung back the curtains so that the daylight flooded into the room.

It looked as though a tornado had swept through, or a very untidy burglar had ransacked the place. The bed was empty and unmade, the sheets and blankets in a tangle at the bottom. The wardrobe door was open and there were piles of clothes strewn on the floor with random shoes littered amongst them.

'What on earth—?' Jack began.

'Connie is very untidy,' Sally said abruptly, picking her way through the puddles of clothes to the dressing table.

'She is also very absent,' Jack pointed out.

Sally picked up the single sheet of paper that was on the dresser. It was only four hours since she had left

Connie to sleep off her excesses, but now a cast-iron certainty hit Sally hard in the stomach. Her sister had never intended to stay. She had sneaked in to get some clothes and then she had run away. With Bertie Basset. She looked at the note.

Darling Sally, by the time you read this I shall be gone! Bertie and I are to be married and we went away secretly, immediately after I saw you this morning.

Sally sat down very suddenly on the dressing-table stool. In the mirror she could see her shocked, pale reflection staring back at her. She thought of Connie and Bertie Basset and a lifetime of misery and infidelity and the divorce courts. Connie had never loved anyone but John Pettifer and Sally knew she did not love Bertie in the all-consuming way that a woman should love the man she chose to marry. Connie was using Bertie, and it could only end in heartache.

We knew that Bertie's father would never accept our love and would make poor Bertie give me up, so the only way for us to be together was to elope. We had resolved on it even before we heard that Bertie's horrid cousin Jack was on the warpath. I am sorry to have deceived you, but I love Bertie so much that the fact he now has no money simply cannot be allowed to weigh with me and I must be united with him...

Little liar, Sally thought. She knew her sister's feelings were as shallow as a puddle. She could see the whole swindle now: Bertie, immature and easily led, genuinely wanted to marry Connie and she wanted his title, money and status. They had cooked up an elopement together but Connie had also hatched a daring plan to have her cake and eat it. They had guessed, quite rightly, that Lord Basset would cut Bertie off without a penny, so Connie had tried to both blackmail Lord Basset and trick him into thinking the affair was all over. Had he paid up to keep her quiet, she would have got both the money and the man...

Emotion dried Sally's throat to cardboard. There was no denying that her sister was a cunning little piece. When Connie had heard of Jack's involvement she had realised that the money would not be forthcoming and had decided to cut her losses and run away with Bertie anyway. No doubt they would hope that, given time, the family would accept their nuptials.

Jack came across and took the piece of paper from Sally's hand. 'Not some new piece of fiction from your sister, Miss Bowes?' he said. A frown darkened his brow as he scanned the letter. 'In love with Bertie? What utter sentimental nonsense! I will say this for you and your sister—you are very inventive! I hardly need ask if you were party to this!'

'Of course I was not,' Sally said. She slewed around on the seat in order to glare at him. 'Can you not read, Mr Kestrel? Connie apologises for deceiving me. Or are you so suspicious by nature that you think that we are in this together and that she put that in the letter merely to mislead you?'

Jack's eyes narrowed as he reread the lines. 'It matters little one way or the other, I suppose,' he said dismissively, 'since you are both as greedy and materialistic as each other.' He gave a short laugh. 'So your sister thought to get my uncle to pay her off and thus finance her to run away with my cousin? A cunning plan!'

Sally got slowly to her feet.

'It's a damnable disaster,' she said.

Jack stared at her. 'But surely you must be pleased, Miss Bowes?' he said sarcastically. 'Your sister has managed to catch herself a baron's heir this time, no mere gentleman like Geoffrey Chavenage or John Pettifer. And even though my uncle may cut Bertie off without a penny, he cannot cancel the entail, and of course, my uncle is very sick and might die at any moment…' Once again Sally felt the stinging contempt in his gaze. 'It is a neatly executed swindle, I will give you that.'

'It's nothing of the sort,' Sally said. 'It is madness. My own experience teaches me that no one should marry unless they truly love one another—' She broke off at the look of bored cynicism in Jack's eyes.

'You really are a piece of work, are you not, Miss Bowes?' he said. 'Such high-flown sentiments, such grasping avarice!'

'Neither Mr Basset nor my sister should be contemplating matrimony with anyone,' Sally snapped. '*He* is weak, immature and easily led and *she* is not in love with him, whatever she says! Your uncle will probably recover his health and live to be one hundred and in the meantime they will have no money and will fight like cat and dog and the whole marriage will be a complete fiasco and end in misery or the divorce courts within six months!' She looked at him. 'I suggest that you take yourself off to Gretna Green to try to prevent the marriage, Mr Kestrel, and let us hope you are not too late! They can only have had a few hours' start.'

Jack did not move immediately, as she would have wished. Instead he stood still, watching her with a quizzical expression that disquieted her.

'It is an excellent idea of yours to stop the wedding,'

he murmured, 'and I fully intend to go to after the happy couple. There is just one small aspect of the plan that I would change, Miss Bowes.'

'Well?' Sally demanded impatiently. 'What is it?'

'You,' Jack said. 'You are coming with me.'

'No, I am not!' Sally was so horrified that she took a hasty step backwards and almost tripped over her skirts. Jack immediately put out a hand to steady her, but she snatched her arm from his grip.

'You are not in a strong position to argue, Miss Bowes,' Jack said smoothly. 'You have just taken two hundred pounds from me.' He paused. 'I think that gives me the right to demand what I like from you.'

Sally shook her head. 'No, it does not. I did not intend—'

'What, to sell yourself to me?' Jack raised a brow. 'Forgive me, but I thought that that was exactly what you intended.' He slid a hand around the nape of her neck, drawing her closer. 'Did you think that a couple of nights was all that I wanted?' he asked, his lips so close to hers that she could feel his breath. 'Oh, no, Miss Bowes. I want you with me, in my bed, until I tell you otherwise.' He rubbed his thumb experimentally over her lower lip and his eyes darkened with desire and satisfaction at the gasp she could not quite stifle.

'I think,' he added conversationally, 'that I might decide to claim the ten thousand that your casino owes me, as well. That should take you a long time to pay off.'

Sally gasped and he took advantage to cover her lips with his own in a savage kiss.

'I'll be waiting in the car,' he said, as he let her go. 'Don't take too long.'

After he had gone out Sally stalked across the room and slammed the door of Connie's wardrobe for no more reason than it gave vent to her feelings. She had never been a violent person before she met Jack Kestrel, she thought bitterly. In two short nights he had turned her life upside down. And now, if she cared what happened to Connie, she had little choice other than to go with him. She could imagine what would happen to Connie once Jack caught up with her and Bertie Basset. He would drag Bertie back to London and leave Connie to fend for herself.

You have just taken two hundred pounds from me. I think that gives me the right to demand what I like from you.

For a brief moment, Sally put her head in her hands. Damn him, how she wanted to give the money straight back to him. But she could not, not if she did not want

Nell to suffer. The deed was done now and what did it matter? Jack had believed the worst of her before, had thought she and Connie had deliberately set out to fleece Chavenage and Pettifer. His scorn had seared her to the soul so what did it matter now if he thought she was a greedy adventuress who sought to make profit out of their nights of passion? At least she had the money for Nell's children and that made her fiercely glad.

She went into her own bedroom, drew aside the curtain, and looked down on to the street. The Lanchester was standing outside the main entrance to the club, its silver bodywork gleaming in the sunshine. Sally sighed. She had barely noticed the motor car the previous night, being conscious only of Jack and the need to get back to the club as quickly as possible. Now, as she saw the small crowd that was gathering to admire it, she thought bitterly how typical it was of Jack Kestrel to have the longest, lowest, sleekest, most ostentatious and expensive car in London—and to flaunt it outside her front door.

She pulled a small portmanteau out of the cupboard and started to pack a few necessities, trying to work out how long they might be away for. She knew she had an excellent manager in Dan, who could look after the business of the club on a day-to-day basis. And if they were to take the railway to Scotland, she supposed she would not need to be away for more than a few days. She would be back in plenty of time to put the final touches in place for the grand opening of the Crimson Salon.

'I want you with me, in my bed, until I tell you otherwise,' Jack had said. Sally shivered with a mixture of nervousness and sensual awareness. She could not deny that she found Jack devastatingly attractive, but she had never imagined, never dreamed, that it would be like this. That very morning she had acknowledged that she had tumbled helplessly in love with him. His poor opinion of her and callous disregard for her feelings had bruised her, but it had not destroyed the blazing awareness there was between them. She trembled to think of being once again in his bed, but she knew that she would not, could not, succumb to him again.

Resolutely putting the thought from her mind, she took an envelope from the desk, stuffed Jack's money into it and scribbled Nell's direction on it. Then she went to join Jack in the car.

Chapter Five

Jack glanced sideways at Sally Bowes as she sat beside him on the deep-red leather seat of the Lanchester. She looked cool, composed and very, very desirable. It took all his self-possession not to lift the saucy black veil she was wearing and kiss her luscious red mouth. She was pin neat in a black-and-white travelling outfit and picture hat that framed her face and Jack admitted to himself that he wanted to rip it all off her and make love to her on the bonnet of the Lanchester. But Alfred, the Blue Parrot doorman, probably would not care for that. He was currently polishing one of the car's gleaming panels with the sleeve of his uniform and looking as excited as a child with a new toy.

Jack waited whilst Sally handed Alfred an envelope,

with a low-voiced instruction that he could not hear. The doorman nodded, stood back and raised a hand in farewell.

'I do not think we need to go as far as the border,' Jack said, as the car moved off into the Strand. 'Bertie has always been a great friend of my sister Charlotte. I suspect they will have gone to Oxfordshire to enlist her support for their marriage.'

'So are we driving to Oxfordshire rather than travelling by rail?' Sally asked. 'That will be a novelty.' She looked around the car with what Jack could only consider to be disfavour. 'It is fortunate that we are *not* aiming for Gretna or Mr Basset and my sister would surely be celebrating their first wedding anniversary before we had even arrived.'

'The Lanchester does a top speed of forty miles an hour,' Jack said. He smiled drily. 'At least you did not weigh her down with baggage.'

Sally turned her head away so that all he could see was her profile. 'I can imagine that the sort of women you know would be encumbered with vast piles of luggage, Mr Kestrel, but I do not require a great deal.'

'No,' Jack said. 'Only whatever two hundred pounds can buy.' He waited a moment, but Sally did not rise to the bait, although he saw a hint of colour steal into her face. 'Where did you send the money?' he asked.

She jumped. Her hands fluttered nervously before she stilled them in her lap. 'What do you mean?'

Jack sighed. He knew she was playing for time. 'I saw you, Sally,' he said. 'My guess is that you took the two hundred pounds I gave you, put it in an envelope and gave it directly to your doorman to deliver. Who was it for?'

'You're mistaken.' Sally's voice was nervous now. 'That is, I did give Alfred a letter to deliver, but it was not...' Her voice trailed away. 'I did not think,' she added, with bitterness, 'that the terms of our *agreement* required me to account to you everything that I do.'

Jack shrugged. He was not even sure why he was asking about the money. On the night after they had met she had indicated that she had pressing debts associated with the club. Perhaps she had sent the cash to pay off the most urgent ones. And it did not matter much anyway, since he would shortly purchase a controlling stake in the Blue Parrot and take her business away from her. He felt a savage satisfaction at the thought.

He looked at her, so pristine and orderly in her smart

black-and-white travelling clothes. Her face was as serene and innocent as it had been when he had met her three nights ago. What an immense asset it must be to her to be able to hide so conniving a mind behind so artless an appearance. No wonder he had been taken in by her apparent honesty. Even though he had already been disillusioned with her as a result of the information Churchward had imparted to him, he had still been shocked by her brazen demand for the money.

He felt a wash of anger through his body that his judgement had been so flawed. He would not trust her; would not make the same mistakes again.

And yet he had what he wanted. He should be pleased, because her amorality meant that he could negotiate and gain the one thing he wanted—Sally Bowes as his mistress for as long as he wanted her, until his passion for her was slaked. He was certain that he would be able to persuade her if the price was right. His hands tightened on the steering wheel as he tried not to think about taking her to his bed. He was behaving like an ardent youth rather than a man of experience. Later, when the matter of his troublesome cousin and Sally's scheming sister was settled, he would take Sally to the nearest inn and make love to her until they were both exhausted. Until then he was going to have to contain his desire. It was going to be a long day.

It was late in the afternoon when Jack nosed the Lanchester through the imposing stone gateway of his sister's home at Dauntsey Park, near Abingdon, and drew to a halt on the gravel sweep in front of the house. Sally looked about her with interest. The place was huge and somewhat Gothic in style, with towers that would not have looked out of place on a Bavarian castle built on a crag, rather than a stately home reclining in the green fields of Oxfordshire. Seeing her incredulity, Jack broke the silence that had existed between them for most of the journey.

'It is a monstrosity,' he agreed. 'Stephen Harrington's grandfather built it in the middle of last century to incorporate all his favourite architectural styles.' He sighed. 'He had rather a lot of different favourites, as you'll see inside.'

Sally managed a cold smile. She was tired and out of temper. She and Jack had barely spoken for four hours, including an extremely tense stop for lunch at an inn on the river at Windsor. During the latter part of the journey Sally had tried to sleep, but she was too conscious of Jack's presence in the enclosed space of the car. Besides, the brim of her outrageous hat made no concessions to comfort and she could not rest her head comfortably. She'd had to make do with keeping her face turned away from Jack and now she had a crick in her neck.

She cast a quick look at him from beneath the hat's brim. His face was set, stern and dark, and, seeing his expression, she felt her pulse trip a beat. His hands moved on the wheel, tanned and strong, and Sally felt a shiver go through her. Despite all that had happened, she could not be indifferent to him. The passion between them had been explosive. Now she did not know what she felt for him, but it was strong and emotional and it filled her throat. She could feel the tension in the car filling the space between them.

As they had drawn closer to Abingdon so Sally's nerves had started to tighten. Supposing Connie and Bertie were not to be found at Dauntsey Park after all? Then she and Jack would be obliged to head off to Gretna Green, and who knew whether or not that too would be a wild goose chase? She could end up travelling with Jack the length and breadth on the entire country, and all to no avail. And if they did find the eloping pair, Jack would no doubt haul Bertie back to London and leave her with Connie to make shift for themselves as best they could. In her hurried preparations before their departure, Sally had at least remembered to bring sufficient money to ensure she could afford to pay their fare back to town, but she had visions of walking with an inconsolably sobbing Connie along the muddy lanes of Oxfordshire, trying to find the nearest railway station.

Jack opened the driver's door, then came around to open her door too and Sally wrenched her thoughts away from impending disaster and gave him her hand so he could help her out onto the gravel. His touch was impersonal and as cold as the look he gave her. Sally's heart shrivelled a little more to think of herself here in a strange place, with a man whose only real feeling for her was a contemptuous desire.

A butler had already thrown open the front door of the house and now a little auburn-haired girl of about four tumbled down the steps and clutched Jack's trouser leg with a shriek of glee.

'Uncle Jack! Uncle Jack!'

A young woman of about twenty-five or six ran down the broad steps behind her, threw herself into Jack's arms and planted a smacking kiss on his cheek.

'Jack! It *is* you! How absolutely marvellous!'

Sally watched as Jack's face broke into a broad

smile. He bent and picked up the child and spun her around whilst she screamed with excitement and pleasure. There was a strange hollow feeling in Sally's heart as she looked at the tableau. Seeing Jack looking like that was like looking at an entirely different man. His affection for his sister and niece was so open and uncomplicated. He looked relaxed and happy.

A nursemaid appeared and tried to take the excited child from Jack. She clung on tenaciously, her little fat arms clasped tightly about his neck until Jack tickled her and ruffled her hair, saying that they would play later when she had had nursery tea. Only then would his niece—Sally had by now gathered that her name was Lucy—condescend to let him go and only then with many a backwards glance.

As the child was reluctantly carted off to tea, Sally turned her attention to the young woman who was hanging on Jack's arm and laughing. So this was Jack's sister. They both had the same intensely dark eyes and high cheekbones, but the good looks that were so hard and masculine in Jack were softened in Charlotte by the roundness of her face and an open, friendly expression. If this was indeed the cousin in whom Bertie Basset confided, Sally could see why he might choose her. She exuded a warmth that soothed Sally's battered soul.

'Hello, Charley!' Jack said. 'How are you?'

'All the better for seeing you,' Charlotte Harrington said, beaming. 'Oh, this is too, too splendid, Jack darling! I was so sure that you would have forgotten!'

There was a moment of absolute silence, during which Sally registered the surprise and uncertainty on Jack's face and the fact that he was too slow to hide it, and then Charlotte said accusingly,

'You *did* forget, didn't you?'

'Charley—' Jack began, but his sister was already smiling again.

'Never mind!' she said. 'You are here anyway. We are having a Saturday-to-Monday party in honour of Great-Aunt Ottoline's birthday—'

'*Great-Aunt Ottoline!* She is here too?' Now there was something approaching fear in Jack's voice and Sally bit her lip to stop the smile that was coming. It seemed that in his haste to track Bertie down, Jack had walked straight into a family party he had been invited to join, but had forgotten about entirely. To see his discomfiture was interesting when he had appeared to be a man who could take most things in his stride. His

Great-Aunt Ottoline must be fearsome indeed, Sally thought.

'Aunt Otto has not arrived yet. We expect her in time for dinner.' Charley was frowning at her brother's slowness. 'I told you—it is *her* party! Papa and Cousin Buffy may also be attending—I am not sure yet.'

'Papa! Buffy?' Jack's tone was failing. Sally's enjoyment of his discomposure was growing in commensurate leaps and bounds. She had never seen Jack so at a disadvantage in their short acquaintance and it was rather gratifying.

'Hello!' Charley said suddenly, sticking out her hand and shaking Sally's own with great enthusiasm. 'I do apologise—I have been very remiss in greeting you. I was so excited to see Jack, you see, as was Lucy. I am sorry!' She paused expectantly and after a moment Jack said, with cold courtesy, 'Charley, this is Miss Sally Bowes. Miss Bowes, my sister Mrs Harrington.'

'Splendid to meet you!' Jack's sister said, beaming. 'Only fancy Jack bringing you to a family party, Miss Bowes! I assure you, that has *never* happened before.'

'How do you do, Mrs Harrington?' Sally said, lips twitching. 'I think,' she added, 'that Mr Kestrel would not have considered bringing me here for a moment had he remembered that he was engaged for a family gathering.' She glanced at Jack's stony face. 'I am little more than an acquaintance.'

'Exactly so,' Jack said drily. His sideways glance at her reminded her of the precise nature of their acquaintance and made her skin prickle with awareness.

Charlotte looked from one to the other, a frown puckering her brow. 'Then if you forgot all about my invitation and did not bring Miss Bowes here to meet us, why *are* you here, Jack?' She demanded.

'We are here to look for Miss Bowes's sister,' Jack said. His gaze was enigmatic as it rested on Sally. 'We have reason to believe that Miss Connie Bowes has eloped with Bertie Basset and we were wondering whether they had come here, Charley. I know Bertie always turns to you first in moments of crisis.'

'Oh!' Charlotte looked taken aback. 'Well, no, I—' She looked at Sally and her expression softened into genuine concern. 'My dear Miss Bowes, I am so sorry! What a worry for you. But I am afraid I haven't seen Bertie for over a month. It is true that he does rather treat me as an elder sister and confide in me.' She smiled. 'Lady Basset is not the type one can speak to—far too interested in her own affairs, you understand—and poor Bertie is an only child—'

'Charley, you are a terrible rattle,' Jack interrupted. 'The only point of importance is that Bertie is not here.'

There was a rather awkward silence.

'Never mind,' Sally said. 'I am sorry to have troubled you, Mrs Harrington.' She tried to keep her disappointment from her voice. Jack had been so sure that Charlotte would be the first person that Bertie would turn to and it was only now, when their search had drawn a blank, that Sally realised how much hope she had been placing on finding Connie at Dauntsey Park. Now, let down and weary, she felt absolutely flat.

'We shall have to look elsewhere,' she said, and turned back to the car.

'Wait!' Charlotte caught her arm. 'You cannot travel on today! Where would you go? Stay with us and rest, and then we may all put our heads together and decide what is to be done.'

She turned to her brother with an engaging smile. 'Jack? Miss Bowes is exhausted. Surely you can stay here tonight?'

Jack was slapping his driving gloves thoughtfully in the palm of his hand. It was clear to Sally that Charlotte's suggestion found very little favour with him and she suspected that it was because the last thing he wanted was to have to introduce her to the rest of his family, or explain to them the story of Bertie and Connie's elopement. He could not have made more clear to her the contempt in which he held her.

'I could not possibly impose on you, Mrs Harrington,' she said. 'I suggest that Mr Kestrel takes me to the nearest town, where I may find some lodgings, and then he may return here to join your family party. We can always continue our search in the morning.'

Charley looked horrified. 'Oh, that would be far too shabby, Miss Bowes! Jack would not dream of treating you thus, I am sure.'

Jack, Sally thought, looked eminently capable of treating her far worse than that, but whatever he was about to say was forestalled by the appearance of a couple of gentlemen from around the side of the house. They were dressed in tennis whites and carrying rackets and were deep in conversation, but when they saw the three of them—and, more specifically, the Lanchester—they hurried over.

'I say,' the taller and fairer of the two exclaimed, 'what a corking piece of machinery, Kestrel! Makes my Model T Ford seem positively sedentary!' He smiled at Sally and shook her hand. 'Hello! You must be Jack's latest. He always did have excellent taste in women as well as motor cars.'

'Stephen!' Charley Harrington said reprovingly. 'This is Miss Sally Bowes.'

Sally smiled, but her attention had almost immediately gone to the man who had been playing tennis with Stephen. She had had no idea that her old family friend Gregory Holt was a connection of the Harringtons, but if this was a family party, then he must be.

Greg was smiling at her, but his cool blue eyes were thoughtful as he looked from her to Jack and back again. 'How do you do, Miss Bowes?' he said formally. 'It is a delightful surprise to see you again and so unexpectedly.'

Sally's heart was thudding. She could feel Jack's gaze on her face. If he had looked tense before, now he was looking positively thunderous.

'Miss Bowes,' he said, even more coldly than before, 'I believe you are already acquainted with Stephen's cousin, Gregory Holt?'

Holt took Sally's hand and held it for far longer than form dictated. 'Miss Bowes and I have known each other a long time, Kestrel.'

'Indeed,' Jack said icily. Sally could feel the anger and tension in him. She felt even more awkward imposing on this family party now that Greg Holt was here. She had known Holt for years—he had been a pupil of her father's at Oxford—and many years before, when she had been so unhappy with Jonathan, Greg had offered more than just friendship. He was looking at her now with the same warm admiration that he had always shown her and he had also picked up on Jack's antagonism. Not that it seemed to bother him. He merely cocked a quizzical eyebrow and tightened his grip on Sally's hand.

'Well, this is splendid!' Charlotte was saying, beaming at them. 'You see, you are already amongst friends, Miss Bowes! Stephen!' she added, seizing her husband's arm and dragging him away from his appreciation of the car, 'Do tell Jack that he simply cannot be so ill mannered as to disappear when he has only just arrived. He has some cork-brained idea of not stopping here because he is looking for Bertie, and Bertie is not here.' She caught Jack's meaningful glare and stopped abruptly before the whole story of Bertie's elopement tumbled out. 'Anyway,' she added indignantly, 'poor Miss Bowes is very tired and cannot be expected to be dragged off on some wild goose chase this evening.' She spread her hands appealingly. 'Oh, Stephen, *do* something! Make them stay!'

It seemed to Sally that Stephen Harrington was well able to cope with his wife's melodrama, for now he merely thrust a hand through his tousled fair hair, smiled at Sally and remarked placidly that if Jack had decided to leave he doubted there was anything anyone else could do to change his mind.

'For you know he is as damnably obstinate as you are, my love,' he said to Charlotte, 'and once you have set your mind to something, there is no arguing with you.'

'And I,' Charlotte said with spirit, 'have *quite* set my mind to the fact that they must stay.' She turned back to Sally. 'At the least you must come inside and take some tea before you go dashing off again.' She slipped her hand through Sally's arm. 'This way, Miss Bowes. I am sure you will appreciate the chance to have a rest. Travelling by automobile is all very fashionable, but it can be wearisome, especially when accompanied by a bad-tempered brute!' She shot Jack a look of reproach. 'Stephen darling, Gregory, do take Jack away and give him a big drink of something in the hope of improving his temper, or, if that does not work, in the hope of making him incapable of driving that car!'

In Charlotte's opulently decorated blue-damask drawing room, Sally removed her hat and veil and sank with relief into a seat. She felt exhausted. Charlotte rang for tea and came across to sit beside her on the satinwood sofa.

'I am most dreadfully sorry about this, Mrs Harrington,' Sally said, as Charlotte turned, smiling, to face her. 'Mr Kestrel was certain that Mr Basset would have brought Connie here.' Her face fell. 'I was so disappointed to find that we had not guessed right.'

Charlotte patted Sally's hand comfortingly. 'I am sorry for your distress, Miss Bowes. It must be very difficult for you trying to do the right thing by your sister. Do you have any other relatives or are you alone in the world?'

'I have another younger sister,' Sally said, thinking of Nell, 'but our parents are dead.'

'And I suppose that you have always been the one to look after the others,' Charlotte said, nodding. 'It must have been lonely for you. Being the eldest can be a burden sometimes, can it not, Miss Bowes?'

'It can be,' Sally said, realising with a rush just how lonely she had been sometimes. She looked up to meet Charlotte's compassionate gaze. 'I do feel a sense of responsibility. Nell—my sister Petronella—is a great supporter of women's suffrage. She is a widow without two pennies to rub together.' She just managed to stop herself before she blurted out the whole tale of

Nell's debts and her own despair. Charley's warmth of manner was so soothing after Jack's contempt that Sally was terribly afraid she might tell her everything on the strength of ten minutes' acquaintance.

'And your sister Connie,' Charley prompted, 'the one who has eloped with my cousin…'

'Yes, Connie.' Sally shook her head. 'Well, I suppose one could say that Connie goes her own way. She works in my nightclub in the Strand, Mrs Harrington.' She looked a little defiant. 'You can see now why both Lord Basset and your brother consider her an unsuitable match for Bertie and think me a bad influence into the bargain.'

'Oh, Uncle Toby always was a stuffed shirt,' Charlotte said, waving a hand around. 'But I would have thought better of Jack.' She frowned. 'He is no snob.'

'Perhaps,' Sally said with a sigh, 'if he believed Connie's regard was sincere he might be more sympathetic. But…' she met Charley's eyes very honestly '…I think he believes her a fortune hunter. Certainly her behaviour has painted her in that light so it is no great wonder.'

'Well,' Charley said indignantly, 'that is no reason to judge *you* in the same way, Miss Bowes, and I will tell Jack so! He can be odiously callous and cutting at times. It is one of his worst faults—though there are plenty of others to choose from!' She smiled at Sally. 'Please do call me Charley, Miss Bowes, and I hope I may call you Sally? I am not one to stand on formality.'

'Of course,' Sally said, feeling slightly overwhelmed. Jack's sister was rather like a force of nature and quite unstoppable. 'I would be delighted.'

'That is settled, then,' Charley said. She gave the butler a bright smile as he entered with the tea tray. 'Thank you, Patterson. And would you please be so good as to ask Mrs Bell to prepare two further bedrooms? Mr Kestrel and Miss Bowes will be staying tonight.'

'I admire your confidence,' Sally said.

Charley laughed. She stirred the tea vigorously, splashing a fair quantity on to the tray and the plate of shortbread biscuits. The butler looked pained but resigned, as though such incidents occurred each day. One of the black Labradors came over to tidy up the damp biscuits.

'Tell me more about your sister Connie,' Charley said, as Patterson went out. 'If she is strong-minded, she could be just what Bertie needs. I think that he would benefit greatly from marrying a strong and clever woman. He is quite weak and easily led and needs firm guidance, like so many men.'

Sally smiled to think of Stephen Harrington being receptive to firm guidance. He hardly struck her as that sort of man.

'You are very generous, Charley,' she said, 'but I do not think that Connie is the right woman for Mr Basset.' She thought about the blackmail and sighed. 'Your brother is no doubt right in his judgement. I myself suspect that Connie is merely hunting a fortune.'

'Well, we shall see,' Charley said. Her chin jutted pugnaciously. 'If Bertie and Connie are genuinely in love, then I for one shall support them all I can! At the least they should be left to sort the matter out themselves. I cannot understand why Jack has dragged you into this farrago, Sally.'

'I did rather drag myself,' Sally admitted. 'I wanted to make sure that Connie was safe and well.'

'I suppose that Jack is acting as Uncle Toby's agent in all this,' Charley said, passing Sally her teacup, 'and has become all haughty about the family honour.' Her face broke into a mischievous smile. 'How rich is that, and Jack with the reputation he has! I shall tell him not to be so pompous!' She peered closely at Sally. 'I do hope that he has not upset you too much, Miss Bowes? He can be frightfully rude.'

'Indeed he can,' Sally said. She fidgeted with her teaspoon. 'But I can look after myself.'

'Well, I am not sure that you can, with Jack,' Charley exclaimed. 'He is so very high-handed. Sometimes I think he was born in the wrong century. He behaves like some sort of eighteenth-century rake—' She stopped, eyes widening, as the hot colour burned Sally's cheeks. 'Oh! Have I said something tactless? I do apologise!'

'No,' Sally said, 'no, of course not.' New friend or not, she thought, there was no possible way she could discuss Jack's rakish tendencies with his sister.

Charley handed her a plate of tiny cucumber sandwiches and apple and walnut cake. Sally ate hungrily, suddenly becoming aware just how tired and ravenous she was. She had not been able to eat much at lunch. Jack's presence had made her too nervous.

'Now,' Charley said, 'I have a plan. It is foolish for you and Jack to go charging off to Gretna Green tonight—' a dimple dented her cheek '—particularly in the Lanchester, which may be a splendid vehicle, for all I know, but would take days to reach Birmingham, let alone Gretna! I suggest that I send a footman to bring your cases in and then an overnight stay will be a *fait accompli*. I will tell Jack it is all decided.'

As Sally started to protest, she waved her comments aside. 'I can lend you something to wear for dinner if you require it, Sally, so you need not regard that as a problem. And I will talk Jack around. See if I don't!'

Sally looked down at her hands. 'You are very kind, Charley, but I do not think Mr Kestrel wishes me...' She paused, trying to find the right words. 'I do not wish to impose on your family party. Mr Kestrel and I are the slightest of acquaintances—'

'So you said earlier.' Charlotte raised a disbelieving brow. 'I thought quite otherwise when I saw the way that Jack was watching you. And as for the way he looked at Gregory Holt when Greg was holding your hand... Why, I half-expected him to challenge Greg to a duel over you, and they have known one another for years. I was never more astonished in my life!'

A wave of colour washed into Sally's face. 'Lord Holt is an old friend of my family,' she said carefully, 'and so no doubt he feels he has some licence as an old acquaintance.'

'Well, I don't think Jack thought so,' Charley said blithely. 'I thought he was going to punch him!'

'I assure you, you are quite mistaken,' Sally said hurriedly. 'Mr Kestrel and I have clashed very badly over this matter of the elopement and there truly is very little between us but hostility. It can only be a matter of indifference to him that Lord Holt is a friend of mine.'

'If you say so,' Charlotte said, with patent disbelief. 'And if you truly do not like Jack very much, then I cannot blame you. He is dreadfully arrogant and over-bearing. I will make sure to sit you a long way away from each other at dinner.' She grabbed Sally's hand. 'Oh, do stay, Sally! The weekend will be so much more fun if you do! I like you so much!'

In the face of such artless friendship Sally felt unable to refuse. 'I am happy to stay overnight, Charley,' she said smiling, 'but then Mr Kestrel and I must work out what best to do to retrieve Bertie and Connie. And,' she added on a note of warning, 'I think you might have a difficult job persuading Mr Kestrel to stay. As soon as you mentioned the words Great-Aunt Ottoline, I saw him turn pale.'

Charley giggled. 'Oh, Aunt Otto dotes on Jack. Mind you, she does have a determination to marry him off and she is *frightfully* strong-minded.'

'Show me a member of your family who isn't,' Sally murmured.

They went out into the hall. Jack and Stephen Harrington were emerging from the library. Sally thought that Jack looked slightly less angry than when she had last seen him, but as soon as his gaze fell on her he frowned.

'Jack,' Charlotte began, 'it is all decided. You are to stay here tonight.'

'No,' Jack said.

That, Sally thought, was quite unequivocal. He did not want her mingling with his family and friends. Equally she was sure that he wanted to keep the matter of Bertie's indiscretion with Connie from becoming common knowledge, especially if the situation could yet be salvaged.

'If you are quite restored, Miss Bowes,' Jack added coldly, 'we will continue our journey.'

'Jack—' Charley said again, but surprisingly fell silent as Stephen shook his head slightly. There was an awkward pause, broken by the sound of an imperious knocking at the front door. A footman hurried to open it. Patterson, who had evidently been distracted eavesdropping on the scene in the hall, adjusted his gloves and rushed forward to announce the new arrival.

'Lady Ottoline Kestrel!' he announced.

Sally saw Jack go rigid. There was a look of perfect horror on his face. 'I thought that you told me Great-

Aunt Otto was arriving later,' he hissed at Charlotte, out of the corner of his mouth.

'This *is* later!' Charlotte hissed back. 'It's not my fault! Don't upset her, Jack. She is very frail these days!'

'She doesn't look very frail to me,' Jack said grimly.

Sally looked at the tiny, bejewelled figure of Lady Ottoline Kestrel as her personal maid helped her into the hall. Although she was as thin and delicate as a little bird, and stiff in her movements, there was something strong and indomitable about her. Her eyes, the same dark brown as Jack and his sister, were sharp and piercingly alive. Her face was sunk in wrinkles, but beneath them Sally thought that she could see the same elegant bone structure that Charlotte possessed. Lady Ottoline must have been a beauty in her youth. Now she was simply terrifying and it was impossible to recognise the winsome girl Sally had seen in the portrait at the Wallace Collection. A huge hat adorned with ostrich and pheasant feathers nodded on Lady Ottoline's brow and her coat was trimmed with matching plumes.

'Good gracious, how many birds must have died in Aunt Otto's service!' Charley whispered irreverently.

She hurried forward, raising her voice. 'Great-Aunt Otto! How lovely to see you!'

'Humph,' Lady Ottoline said, inclining her cheek regally for her great-niece's kiss, 'how are you, Charlotte? And is that your dreadful modern contraption on the gravel outside, Jack? Didn't realise you were going to be here, though I suppose it is good to see you again, boy. Couldn't get the carriage up to the door though, with that machine there—it scared the horses!'

'I do apologise,' Jack said, following his sister's lead in bending to kiss their great-aunt. 'I will move it at once.'

'See you do,' Lady Ottoline said. 'You can bring my bags in whilst you're at it. Severs is too old to carry my luggage.'

Sally thought that if the coachman was as ancient as the maid, it was surprising they managed to totter anywhere at all. But Lady Ottoline, for all her physical frailty, was as sharp as a needle. Her piercing dark gaze was even now pinning Sally herself to the spot.

'And this is?' Her tone was icy.

Jack and Charlotte exchanged a look.

'Good afternoon, your ladyship,' Sally said. 'My name is Sally Bowes—'

'And she is my fiancée,' Jack finished. He grabbed Sally's hand and gripped it hard, speaking over the outraged squeak of pain and denial that she made.

'I do apologise for not introducing you properly, Aunt Otto,' he said. 'In the excitement of your arrival I quite forgot. Sally *darling*—' his tone forbade all argument '—this is my great-aunt, Lady Ottoline Kestrel.'

'Forgot your own fiancée, eh?' Lady Ottoline said. Her eyes appraised Sally's flushed face and softened slightly. 'Well, well, Jack. You do surprise me. For a moment I thought you'd brought one of your fancy women to a family party at your sister's house.'

'God forbid,' Jack said silkily. He slid an arm about Sally's waist, drawing her unyielding body close to him. His glance commanded her silence. She looked up at him and he gave her a smile so full of charm that she felt her knees weaken.

'We must have a chat later, my dear,' Lady Ottoline continued, giving Sally a wintry smile that was somehow more fearsome than her hauteur. 'I am anxious to learn all about you.' She looked sharply at Jack. 'Does your papa know?'

'Not yet,' Jack said. 'It is but a recent development.'

Lady Ottoline smiled again. 'Indeed. How charming. I shall send the news to Robert myself as soon as I have rested and partaken of tea. I only use the telephone in emergencies, but I feel this qualifies.' She nodded to Sally and beckoned to Charlotte. 'Come along, Charlotte! I want to see whether you took my advice and had the chairs in the Green Bedchamber re-upholstered after my last visit. They were shockingly uncomfortable...' Still talking, she hobbled off with the maid in her wake, and Charlotte shot Sally an agonised look before hurrying after her.

There was silence in the hall. Jack's gaze was locked on Sally's face.

'I'll go and help with the baggage,' Stephen Harrington said hastily, looking from one of them to the other. 'And move the car.'

'So,' Sally said, as the front door closed behind him and Patterson retreated discreetly down the passage to the servants' quarters, 'I am your fiancée now, am I, Mr Kestrel?'

Jack drove his hands into his trouser pockets. 'My aunt is both old-fashioned and increasingly frail in her health,' he said. 'I had no wish to distress her by introducing you as my mistress at a family party. That would have been quite inappropriate.'

Sally winced. 'At least we agree on one thing,' she said coldly, 'though why you had to introduce me as anyone other than an acquaintance who would shortly be leaving, I have no notion.' She glared at him. 'How could you possibly convince her that you actually have some affection for me—enough to wish to *marry* me?'

A disturbing smile tugged at Jack's lips as he scrutinised her face. 'I think we could both convince her of our passionate regard for one another,' he murmured. 'At the very least, we will have to try because I am afraid we shall be staying for a little while.'

Sally was infuriated. 'So you have changed your mind and decided we are to stay now? How high-handed of you!'

Jack sighed. 'We must. I have no desire to upset Aunt Ottoline and as Charley said, she is increasingly frail these days.'

'Your great-aunt is about as frail as an old boot,' Sally snapped. 'You are simply afraid of her. Either that, or you have another reason.'

Jack grimaced. 'Very well. I admit that I have no desire to tell Aunt Otto of Bertie's latest indiscretion. He is her godson and her heir. I am sure it would cause her concern to hear he was throwing himself away on a fortune-hunting night-club hostess.'

'You mean that she would disinherit him,' Sally said. She understood Jack's reasoning now. Keep the old lady sweet, keep the truth about Bertie and Connie's elopement from her, and with luck the whole matter might be sorted out and Lady Ottoline be none the wiser. Once again Jack's cynicism made her feel utterly disillusioned.

'And if I refuse to play along with your masquerade?' she asked.

Jack shrugged. 'I am sure you will find a way to oblige me. After all, I thought that we were both getting what we wanted from our association?'

'You mean the money,' Sally said. Her throat was tight. How had she made such an error of judgement? She wished so profoundly that she had never asked him for the two hundred pounds. She had been terribly distressed over Nell's situation, and equally furious and upset by Jack's poor opinion of her, but it had led her to make a fatal error. She could see that now, now that she had confirmed every last one of his prejudices against her.

'I will give you the money back,' she whispered. 'I made a mistake asking for it. It is not worth it.'

He caught her arm, his grip fierce. 'Too late, my sweet. You took the money. You spent it.'

Sally wrenched herself out of his grasp. 'I'll pay it back,' she said. 'I'll find a way, sell something…'

'You already did,' Jack said. His face was hard as granite. 'You sold yourself for it, if you recall. And I am sure I can persuade you to do the same again.'

Their gazes locked and he drew her, unresisting, towards him and dropped a kiss on her lips. A shiver racked Sally's body. How was it possible to feel so distant from this man and yet to feel his touch with a pleasure that she could not hide? It confused and distressed her.

'You will be my fiancée if I require it.' He bent his lips to brush the curve of her neck and the quivers of cool sensation skittered along her nerves. 'You see,' Jack said, turning her face up to his, 'it is not so difficult to pretend.'

'Save your displays of affection for the privacy of your own room, nephew, preferably after you are married!' Lady Ottoline Kestrel boomed from the top of the staircase. She started to descend the steps towards them.

'Well?' Jack whispered. He raised one black brow. 'Do you agree?'

Sally thought quickly. 'For this one night only I will pose as your fiancée,' she said, 'but not to oblige you, Mr Kestrel. Just as you do not wish Mr Basset's folly to be exposed to your great-aunt, so do I not want Connie to be subject to her censure. I wish to save this situation as much as you do.'

'Of course.' Jack gave her an ironic bow.

Without another word, Sally turned on her heel and walked out of the front door and down the steps. She needed fresh air and time to think. Behind her in the hall she could hear the sound of Lucy's excited chatter as the nursemaid brought her back downstairs to see her uncle again, as promised. Sally thought of the happy family circle into which she had thrust herself and felt mortified. But then, it was Jack who had insisted on bringing her here and Connie who had forced this whole affair with her elopement. She should not take the blame herself. All she could do was to find Connie as quickly as possible and extract both of them from the situation with minimum fuss.

Sally walked across the cool shaded courtyard, with its fountains and statuary, towards the moat. The later afternoon sunlight shone on the water and dazzled her eyes for a moment. She raised a hand to shield them.

'Are you all right, Sally, old girl?'

She had not heard Gregory Holt approaching, although now that he was beside her she reflected that she should have been aware of his proximity from the fug of pipe smoke that always enveloped him.

Even when he had been a pupil of her father's, he had smoked a pipe. Sally smiled to remember how she and Nell had teased him about appearing like an old man at the age of only twenty-one.

'Oh, Greg,' she said, 'I did not see you there.'

Greg took her arm and steered her along the path towards a stone bench placed to look out across the moat to the deer park beyond.

'Wanted to talk to you, old girl,' he said. 'I just heard that you are engaged to Jack Kestrel.' He cleared his throat. 'Don't do it, Sal. I know you have shocking judgement when it comes to men, but this is a terrible mistake. Almost as bad as your last one.'

Despite herself, Sally laughed. 'Must you always be on hand to warn me of the dangers of my romantic choices, Greg?' She sobered. 'I should have listened to you about Jonathan, I admit. I am sorry.'

Greg took her hand and gave it a tight squeeze. 'Should listen to me now,' he said. 'Don't get me wrong, I've been a friend of Jack's since we were in short trousers. He's a sound man in business and even better if you're in a tight corner, but he'd make the devil of a husband.'

'Then rest easy,' Sally said, 'for I have no intention of marrying him.'

Greg stared. 'Then why—?'

'It is a convenient fiction to explain my presence here to Lady Ottoline,' Sally said with a shade of bitterness. 'The truth is that Connie has eloped with Jack's cousin Bertie and Jack and I are intent on tracking them down. Jack does not wish Lady Ottoline to know the truth as I understand Mr Basset is her heir.'

Greg did not answer immediately. He knocked the bowl of his pipe against the edge of the stone seat and fumbled in his waistcoat pocket for a pouch of fresh tobacco. Only when he had relit the pipe did he reply.

'Jack's a fool to think the old lady can be taken in,' he said reflectively. 'She's as sharp as a new pin. And I'm surprised you went along with it, Sal. Not like you.'

Sally sighed. 'I don't like it,' she admitted, 'I am only doing it for Connie's sake.'

Greg sighed as well. 'You take too much responsibility for that girl. You should leave her to make her own mistakes and face the consequences, Sal.'

'I know,' Sally said. She remembered Mrs Matson saying much the same thing. 'But I have a duty to both Connie and Nell, Greg—'

'Nonsense,' Greg said rudely. 'You always did have some bee in your bonnet about Sir Peter's death being your fault and how you had deprived your sisters of their father's protection.'

Sally blushed defensively. 'It's true.'

'No, it isn't.' Greg spoke roughly, but his tone softened as he glanced at her face. 'There was nothing that you could have done, Sally.'

For a moment the memories threatened to swamp Sally's mind. She stared at the smooth green waters of the moat and remembered the river closing over her father's head and her frantic efforts to give him her hand and pull him to safety. She gave a violent shudder and pushed the memory firmly away.

'And what about yourself and Jack?' Greg was saying.

Sally could feel herself colouring up. 'I barely know him.'

'Which,' Greg said drily, 'hardly answers the question.'

'All right,' Sally conceded. Greg had always been shrewd and there was no point in trying to deceive him. 'I admit that there was something between us, but it was based on a misunderstanding. That's all.'

She felt his thoughtful gaze on her face. 'If he hurt you—' he began.

'He didn't,' Sally said quickly. She could not bear

to expose her feelings, even to Greg. She gave him a rueful smile. 'Bless you, Greg, for always standing as the brother I never had.'

Greg pulled a face. 'Not the relationship that I want with you, Sally, as you know.' He answered her smile with an equally rueful one of his own. 'You have always seen me as a brother and I have never seen you as a sister. That's the tragedy.'

Sally was silent. She knew that was the nub of the matter. It had been so tempting to run away with Greg when she had been desperately unhappy with Jonathan, but even in the depths of her misery she had known she would have been selling Greg short because she was not in love with him. To take his love and use it for her own ends seemed shabby then and it would be shabby now.

'Your reputation suggests you do not pine for me,' she said lightly.

'My reputation,' Greg said feelingly, 'was gained as a result of my attempts to forget you!'

'Don't try to pin that on me,' Sally said warmly. 'I was not responsible for turning you into a rake and a gambler. And if you say that I could have saved you, I will box your ears!'

'You could have saved me,' Greg said, with a straight

face. He sighed. 'I know that you never needed me,' he added, his blue gaze steady on her face. 'I understand that.'

'I do need you,' Sally said. 'I need you as a friend.' Fleetingly she thought of the two hundred pounds that she had sent to Nell. If only she had asked Greg to give her a loan, not Jack. But then she had always been damnably independent. It was one of her besetting sins. She would not have wanted to go cap in hand to Greg and ask for money. She had only thrown the request for two hundred pounds in Jack's face because he had incensed her.

'That must be the kiss of death on a romance,' Greg said cheerfully, taking her hand and pulling her to her feet. 'Come along. Time to dress for dinner.'

A shadow fell across them and Sally put up a hand to shade her eyes from the low afternoon sun. It was inevitable, she thought, that Jack should be standing there with a face like thunder as he took in the sight of her hand clasped once again in that of Gregory Holt's.

'Hello, Jack, old man,' Greg said easily, a smile tugging the corners of his mouth as he registered Jack's stony expression, 'your lovely fiancée and I were just discussing romance.'

'I see,' Jack said coldly. He turned pointedly to Sally.

'Charley sent me to show you around the place,' he said, 'but it seems that you are already quite at home.'

'Sally is certainly among friends,' Greg said, and Sally felt the unspoken but unmistakable threat in his words and saw Jack square up to the challenge.

'Excuse me,' she said hastily to Greg, freeing her hand from his and slipping past both men. 'I shall go and prepare for dinner.' And she walked away without a backwards glance to either of them. Let them sort out their differences without her. She could already feel the unresolved tension in Jack that could surely escalate into violence with one deliberately careless word from Greg. And it made no sense to her at all, for how could Jack be so possessive when she was no more than his temporary fiancée and he certainly did not love her?

Chapter Six

Jack fiddled irritably with his cufflinks whilst the long-suffering valet he had borrowed from his brother-in-law put the final touches to his wing collar.

'If you could just keep still a moment longer, sir,' the man said resignedly. Jack sighed and tried not to tap his foot. The dinner suit, shirt and tie were all borrowed as well as the servant. It was fortunate that he and Stephen were of a height. He was a little broader across the shoulder and could feel the material straining a little, but it was not a bad fit. He hoped he did not split the jacket. It was no wonder his brother-in-law had given him a tuxedo rather than his best tailcoat to wear, but he thought that Lady Ottoline would probably cut up rough when she saw that he was not in formal evening dress.

He wondered what Charley would find for Sally to wear to dinner. Whatever it was, it would not be able to eclipse that luscious pink gown she had worn two nights before. He rubbed a hand across his forehead. He felt a sudden, bitter flash of emotion that their previous nights together had been so different. He had thought her honest then. Now all that was left was the devastating passion that had flared between them.

And for tonight, at least, she was also his fiancée. A smile that was more satisfied than rueful lifted his mouth. He liked the idea of being engaged to Sally very much, far more than he had expected when he had made the impulsive announcement. He knew it was a gesture of somewhat primitive possession. Her sexual capitulation to him had the unforeseen consequence of making him want to claim her formally and show her to be his own. He realised that his need for her had been one of the reasons why he had been so angry with her for her duplicity. His feelings were engaged—desire and wanting, if not love—and so her betrayal was so much more acute.

His previous affairs had had the reverse effect on him to this; all he had wanted to do was walk away from them. Now he was determined not to let Sally walk away from him until he was ready to let her go. He acknowledged that it was a very basic reaction. He had wanted Sally from the very first and now he wanted everyone else to know she belonged to him, especially Gregory Holt, who had made his interest in her so plain.

'There you are, sir,' the valet said, stepping back to admire his handiwork. 'Not bad, if I say so myself.'

'Thank you, Jeavons,' Jack said.

As he emerged from his bedchamber he saw his sister and Sally descending the stairs in front of him. Charley had evidently gone to fetch Sally from her bedroom and take her down to dinner in case she was nervous. Jack shook his head cynically over Charley's naïvety. Could she not see that Sally Bowes was supremely capable of taking care of herself? But perhaps not—after all, he had made a serious error of judgement about Sally himself.

He hurried down the stairs to catch up with them and as they reached the hallway Sally turned towards him.

He stopped dead.

She looked utterly divine.

Tonight Sally was wearing a gown the colour of rich

autumn leaves, with layers of taffeta and silk chiffon embroidered with tiny little sequins around the square neck. Charley had lent her a ruby drop necklace and it glowed richly in the hollow of Sally's throat, a vivid counterpoint to the creamy pallor of her skin.

And she *rustled*. Whenever she moved, the layers of petticoats beneath the taffeta and chiffon whispered together sensuously, setting all of Jack's senses on edge. He could imagine the ruffles and lace beneath the sparkling gown and Sally's warm, smooth skin beneath that.

He seriously considered carrying her straight back up the stairs and into the nearest bedroom.

'Are you quite well, Jack?' Charley enquired, laughing. 'I have never seen you struck dumb before.'

'I…ah…' Jack pulled himself together quickly.

'Sally has been explaining to me that the two of you are always at odds, so I have put you at opposite ends of the table,' Charley said, fixing him with a blithe smile. 'Aunt Otto asked particularly that she should be placed next to you, Jack. I believe she wishes to check on your moral fortitude and suitability for marriage.'

Jack cursed under his breath. 'And I suppose Gregory Holt has offered to escort Sally,' he said tightly, fighting down the wave of possessive fury that gripped him.

Sally merely smiled placidly and his jealousy tightened a notch. 'How clever of you to guess!' Charley said admiringly. 'That is exactly what he suggested!'

'Lord Holt has always behaved as a perfect gentleman to me,' Sally said, her tone reminding Jack pointedly that he had not. 'I am sure I shall be perfectly safe with him.'

'His reputation is worse than mine,' Jack said grimly, and saw her smile in mock-disbelief.

'Surely that is impossible?' she said sweetly.

Jack caught Sally's hand just as they entered the drawing room. 'Don't forget that for tonight you are engaged to *me*,' he whispered, 'or I may be obliged to remind you.'

Sally's beautiful hazel eyes opened very wide. 'And how might you do that, Jack?' she enquired, in an even sweeter tone.

'By kissing you in front of everyone,' Jack said, and watched with pleasure as the pink colour came into her cheeks.

'You dare,' she hissed.

'Don't tempt me…'

They stared at one another, captured in both the fierce mutual attraction and the equally fierce mutual hostility they could see in each other's eyes and only broke apart when Stephen Harrington came up, cleared his throat loudly, and drew them into the room to introduce them to the other dinner guests who had come to Dauntsey for the evening.

Between fending off his aunt's enquiries into his moral character, being polite to Stephen and Charley's neighbours when he did not feel like it, and watching Gregory Holt flirt with his fiancée, Jack was in a vile mood by the end of dinner. The whole meal seemed interminable: consommé, oysters, champagne sorbet, trout, venison, trifle, cheese... Each course was more elaborate than the last and seemed to take hours to serve and even longer to consume. And through it all Jack could do nothing but glower at Gregory Holt as he chatted easily and with the greatest of pleasure to Sally.

'Drown your sorrows in a glass of Tokay, old man,' Stephen Harrington said in his ear as the ladies rose to leave the men to their drink. 'Must say, you have got it bad. You've been watching Miss Bowes all through dinner. Never thought to see you brought so low!'

'Holt annoys me,' Jack said, through his teeth, watching as Gregory Holt took Sally's hand and placed a kiss on the back of it in a gesture of laughing gallantry. 'He has a damned nerve to do that to my fiancée!'

'Oh, Greg's harmless,' Stephen said calmly. 'He's only doing it to spite you, old fellow, and because he has always held a candle for Miss Bowes. He was a protégé of her father, you know, and I understand he wanted Miss Bowes to run away with him when matters became particularly grim between herself and her late husband. Not,' he added hastily, seeing Jack's glare, 'that she gave him the least encouragement.'

'She didn't tell me,' Jack said. He could feel the shreds of his control slipping. So Gregory Holt was an old flame of Sally's. Their situation was uncannily close to his elopement with Merle all those years ago. Except that Sally had had the good sense not to run away and provoke the desperate kind of situation that he and Merle had found themselves in. He took a deep breath. At least he knew they could not have been lovers, though probably not for want of trying on Holt's part. He wanted to go straight over and confront the man about it but bearing in mind that Greg was some distant cousin of Stephen, they had known each other for years, and it was bad form to cause an affray at a country house party, that was probably not a good idea. What the hell was the matter with him? he wondered. Where had his self-control gone? He'd been a friend of Greg Holt since their schooldays and never had the slightest inclination to ram the other man's teeth down his throat before now.

'Well,' Stephen said, giving him a sympathetic smile, 'I understood from Charley that—strictly on the quiet—there is some doubt over whether Miss Bowes really *is* your fiancée, old man, so perhaps she did not see the need to tell you. Seems to me,' he added, 'that you could do with sorting out your romantic life properly, Jack, before you explode with frustration. Always thought you had a reputation for conquest, but you seem to be making a dashed mull of everything at the moment.'

'Thank you,' Jack said ruefully, reflecting that Stephen had hit the nail on the head. Before he had met Sally Bowes he had had no problem controlling his frustrations or ordering his romantic life successfully.

He looked up as Greg Holt put his hand on his shoulder. 'A word, Kestrel?'

The smile faded from Jack's eyes as he took in the other man's demeanour. Greg had always struck him as being the most easy-going of fellows, rather like Stephen himself, but now there was no good humour in his eyes. Holt looked as though he was itching to take Jack by the throat and throttle the life out of him.

'With the licence of an old friend,' Greg said, his

mouth a thin line, 'I have warned Miss Bowes against marrying you, Kestrel. You would make the devil of a husband.'

Jack was already half out of his seat when Stephen grabbed his arm to restrain him.

'Easy,' Stephen muttered, and Jack allowed himself to relax infinitesimally.

'It's none of his damned business,' he said, through gritted teeth.

Holt inclined his head ironically. 'Miss Bowes is unprotected. It is my business when I stand in the place of a brother to her.'

'Brother!' Jack exploded with disbelief.

'Just so,' Greg said. 'I hope for your sake that you will be an exemplary fiancé, Kestrel, because I would hate to ruin our long friendship by putting a bullet through you.'

And with a curt bow he walked away.

Jack let out the breath that he realised he had been holding for the whole encounter.

'Damn it, he was in earnest,' Stephen said, staring after Holt, his glass of Tokay suspended halfway to his lips.

'In deadly earnest,' Jack agreed. He realised that Gregory Holt must have been in love with Sally for a very long time. He wondered why she had turned him down. Holt was rich, titled, the perfect catch for a good-time girl on the make. Even if she had run off with him and had to weather the scandal of divorce, they could have been married by now.

Jack was accustomed in business to weighing evidence, making quick decisions, trusting his own judgement. He looked at Gregory Holt's ramrod-straight back and furious demeanour and wondered what it was about Sally Bowes that seemed to command the loyalty of all the people whose lives she touched. It did not square with the evidence that he had uncovered about her. Perhaps it was time to confront her.

'Come on,' he said, knocking back the rest of his Tokay in one gulp, 'it's time to join the ladies. I want to talk to Sally.'

'Wait a moment, old chap!' Stephen protested. 'It's only ten minutes since dinner! They won't want to see you yet. And that's no way to treat my best wine—'

But it was too late. Jack had gone.

'So, my dear,' Lady Ottoline said to Sally, patting the seat beside her, 'come and sit with me.' She gestured to the deck of cards on the table. 'Do you play?'

'A little,' Sally said, thinking ruefully of the gaming

tables at the Blue Parrot. She wondered how Dan was getting on in her absence. She trusted him completely, but with the opening of the Crimson Salon a mere few days away she was extremely nervous.

'Then perhaps we may have a game of bezique later,' Lady Ottoline said. 'But first I want to talk about you—and about Jack. He tells me that you met at the Wallace Collection.'

'Indeed we did,' Sally said, wondering how much truth and how many lies Jack had mixed together to describe their relationship.

'Well, at least you must be a cultured gel,' Lady Ottoline said. 'Buffy, the current Duke, is an utter philistine, but Jack has the making of a good custodian of the Kestrel collection as long as his cousin don't sell it off before Jack inherits.'

'The Duke has no children of his own?' Sally said.

'No.' Lady Ottoline gave her a sharp look. 'Buffy don't like the girls. Robert, Jack's father, is heir to the dukedom of Kestrel and Jack after him.'

'I see,' Sally said, thinking that Jack Kestrel really was a great catch for any woman prepared to put up with his vile temper and inability to love her.

'I hope,' Lady Ottoline said disagreeably, 'that you

are not going to pretend you did not know you had caught the heir to a dukedom?'

'I do not really care,' Sally said, with extreme frankness. 'When I choose to wed, Lady Ottoline, it is the man that matters to me, not his title or his money.'

Lady Ottoline's plucked brows shot up towards her diamond headdress. 'Well, upon my word!'

'Having been married once before,' Sally continued, 'I have to be extremely careful in my next choice.' Suddenly she felt reckless. If she could shock Lady Ottoline into repudiating her, it would serve Jack right for his machinations. 'I do not wish to make as ghastly a mistake second time around as I did the first time,' she said. 'So the selection of a new husband is of paramount importance to me. He must have integrity and wit and be faithful, honourable and never, ever bore me. That is all I ask.'

There was a long silence. Sally selected a bonbon from the dish on the table in front of her and popped it into her mouth, before daring to steal a look under her lashes at Lady Ottoline. Her ladyship was regarding her with a very shrewd expression in her dark eyes.

'I see,' Lady Ottoline said. She frowned slightly. 'Your name is familiar to me, Miss Bowes. Now, why would that be?'

Sally glanced at Jack across the room. He and Stephen had rejoined the ladies a scandalously short ten minutes after dinner was finished, having certainly not had time to consume a leisurely glass of port or luxuriate in a cigar, but when he had shown every sign of wanting to speak with her, Lady Ottoline had told him curtly to take himself off.

'*I* wish to talk to your fiancée, Jack,' she had said imperiously. '*You* may speak to her later.'

And so Jack had been obliged to make small talk with the other guests, but Sally was very conscious of his gaze resting on her from time to time, dark and serious but without the edge of anger that she had become accustomed to seeing there since their terrible confrontation that morning.

'Miss Bowes?' Lady Ottoline's tone was sharp, but with a betraying edge of indulgence. 'It is all very well to stare at one's own fiancé, but I would like an answer as well, if you please.'

'I beg your pardon, my lady,' Sally said, hastily dragging her gaze away from Jack. 'Perhaps you recognise my name because you have heard that I own the Blue Parrot, which is a nightclub on the Strand in London?'

There was another silence whilst she waited for Lady Ottoline to explode with shock. Surely, this time, she had overstepped the mark. No respectable great-aunt could contemplate such an alliance for her nephew. But Lady Ottoline was made of sterner stuff. She pursed her lips and shook her head. There was a steely light in her eye now as though she had realised just what Sally was about and was determined to thwart her.

'No, that wasn't it,' she said. Her dark eyes brightened. 'Do you, though? How marvellous to own a nightclub! You must tell me all about it, Miss Bowes. I do admire a gel with a bit of spirit, having been one myself.'

'Thank you, ma'am,' Sally said, realising she had underestimated the opposition. 'I am sure that you were.'

'You were married to Jonathan Hayward, were you not?' Lady Ottoline said abruptly. 'He was a dreadful cad, a total rotter. My late brother always said that it made him feel quite nauseous to think of him.'

Sally laughed. She was starting to like Lady Ottoline rather a lot. 'Thank you, my lady. He had much the same effect on me.'

'We have much in common,' Lady Ottoline said drily. 'I suppose Jack thought I'd cut up rough if I knew all about your history?' Her eyes gleamed with suppressed amusement. 'Silly boy, just because I never married he must think I am as cosseted as a baby!'

'I imagine he might have been a little wary of telling you,' Sally said, smiling. She was enjoying this conversation a lot now. 'After all, owning a nightclub is scarcely respectable, and nor is potential divorce.'

'Well, who cares a fig about that?' Lady Ottoline demanded. 'Sometimes it is more fun to be scandalous. I remember my mama telling me that being respectable all the time was a dashed dull deal. She worked as a spy for the British government, you know, and eloped with her husband. She was quite a woman.'

'I saw her picture at the Collection,' Sally said. 'She was stunningly beautiful.' She smiled. 'You were a very pretty child yourself, Lady Ottoline.'

Lady Ottoline gave a spontaneous chuckle. 'Changed a bit since then, eh!'

'Not so much, I imagine,' Sally said, smiling.

Briefly Lady Ottoline's beringed hand clasped Sally's own. 'I like you, Miss Bowes. I'm glad your experiences didn't put you off men.' She looked across at Jack. 'Jack's a good boy. You mustn't listen to all the gossip about his past.'

'He hasn't told me much about that,' Sally said truthfully.

'Terrible scandal,' Lady Ottoline said gruffly. 'Ran off with a married woman when he was barely out of his teens. Robert banished him abroad, the fool. Not that I didn't think Jack needed to grow up, but it was a terrible tragedy to cast him out like that. Broke his mother's heart and Charlotte's too.'

'I am sorry for that,' Sally said. 'Charley is a lovely person.'

'Well, she's got him back now,' Lady Ottoline said. She squeezed Sally's hand. 'You'll be good for him, my dear. I can tell. And as I say, don't listen to any gossip. He'll tell you everything in his own good time.'

Sally doubted it. Whatever had happened between Jack and his mistress was part of the dark secrets that he kept locked inside. There was a lump in her throat as she though how little she and Jack deserved Lady Ottoline's good opinion.

'What will I tell her?'

Both Sally and Lady Ottoline jumped as Jack spoke from right beside them.

'Shouldn't go creeping up on deaf old ladies, nephew,' Lady Ottoline said crossly, 'or you'll be enjoying my fortune before you know it.' Her eyes gleamed. 'Perhaps that's the plan, eh! Scare me into my grave and take the money!'

'I'd prefer to enjoy your company rather than your money, Aunt Otto,' Jack said, and Lady Ottoline looked pleased, although she did not say anything.

'I thought,' Sally said, 'that it was Mr Basset who was your heir, ma'am, not Jack?' She smiled challengingly at him. 'Surely he has enough money of his own?'

'I've decided that I don't want to leave my money to that silly widgeon Bertie Basset,' Lady Ottoline said astringently. 'My money—I can do as I please with it. He would only spend it on gambling and loose women.'

Jack caught Sally's eye. A faint smile curled his firm mouth as though to remind her that Bertie had already done precisely that.

'I've remembered!' Lady Ottoline said triumphantly. 'Knew I'd heard the Bowes name before. I heard your father speak once at the Sheldonian in Oxford. He was a fascinating speaker and a most talented architect.' She glanced around. 'I believe Gregory Holt was a pupil of his.'

'He was.' Sally could feel Jack's gaze on her and was annoyed to feel herself blushing when she had nothing to blush about.

'If you will excuse us, Aunt Otto,' Jack said, 'I

wondered if I might take Sally for a short stroll on the terrace.'

Lady Ottoline smiled. 'Oh, very well. I suppose you may steal Miss Bowes away now.' She looked up at him. 'Seems you have more sense than I gave you credit for, nephew. I like your fiancée. The only miracle is that she likes *you*.'

Sally avoided Jack's gaze. He offered her his arm and she put her hand on it gingerly, as though it might burn her. She wished she were not so shockingly conscious of Jack's physical presence. Her awareness of him always undermined her defences.

'How the hell did you do that?' Jack asked abruptly as they stepped through the door on to the darkened terrace. 'She likes you more than she likes me!'

'I answered her questions honestly,' Sally said. She saw his look of patent disbelief and added, 'That may surprise you, Mr Kestrel, given your opinion of me, but your great-aunt is a good judge of character by my estimation, and she liked me.'

She expected Jack to make some cutting remark, but he was silent; glancing at his face, she saw he looked pensive. They walked along the terrace to where the moat opened out into a broad lake fringed with reeds.

'Gregory Holt warned me off a little while ago,' Jack

said, after a moment. 'He told me that he was standing as your brother and if I hurt you he would kill me.'

Sally shot him a look of surprise. She was not sure whether she was annoyed or amused at Greg's interference.

'He should mind his own business,' she said. 'He knows I can look after myself.'

'So I thought,' Jack said. He paused. 'He is in love with you,' he added, and there was an odd tone in his voice.

'Yes,' Sally said after a moment. 'I suppose he is.'

'Has he asked you to marry him?'

'Now *you* should mind your own business,' Sally said.

Jack laughed and put a hand over hers where it rested on his arm. 'It is my business. I am your fiancé.'

'My *temporary* fiancé,' Sally said. 'Until tomorrow only.'

'So my guess is that he proposed and you refused him,' Jack said. 'Why?'

'Must you be so persistent?' Sally let her breath out on a sigh. 'I do not like you, Mr Kestrel, and I do not particularly wish to speak with you.'

'Indulge me,' Jack said. 'I want to know.'

Sally freed herself and went to stand on the edge

of the terrace, looking out over the darkened garden where the topiary shapes were silhouetted against the deep blue of the summer night sky. She was very conscious of Jack, still and waiting, behind her.

'I refused him because it would not be fair to make so unequal a match,' she said, after a moment.

'In terms of wealth and status?' Jack sounded incredulous. 'But you are a baronet's daughter.'

'I was speaking in terms of affection,' Sally said. 'Not everything can be measured in pounds and pennies, Mr Kestrel.'

'Not a philosophy I would expect to hear you supporting, Miss Bowes.'

'Probably not,' Sally said. She rubbed her fingers over the cool mossy stone of the terrace wall. 'I care for Greg,' she said. She wondered why she was even trying to explain to Jack Kestrel, who thought that her motivated by nothing but avarice. 'I have known him a long time and he has never played me false. I owe it to him not to take his affection for me and use it badly or take advantage.'

Again she expected Jack to make some kind of cynical reply, but he was silent, and in the darkness she could not read his expression.

'Whilst you are engaged to me,' he said, after a moment, 'you will have nothing to do with him.'

Sally shook her head. 'You cannot tell me what to do, Mr Kestrel. We are not really betrothed and you have no claim on me.'

She saw Jack make a sharp movement, full of repressed anger, and she backed a step away from him. 'If you value Holt as you say you do,' he said, 'it would wise to agree.'

'In case you decide to challenge him?'

'Quite.'

Sally tapped her fingers irritably on the balustrade. 'You are both as bad as each other,' she said. 'I do not think that your aunt would appreciate your attempts to rid Stephen of his relatives.'

'Probably not,' Jack conceded. He looked at her thoughtfully. 'I noticed you attempting to persuade her not to cut Bertie out of her will in my favour. Thank you for that.'

'I am sure that you have enough money,' Sally said.

'And Bertie does not—particularly if he is to keep your sister in the style you are hoping for.'

Sally shrugged. She might have known that he would interpret her intervention as an attempt to gain everything for Connie when all she was concerned about was that Lady Ottoline should not change her will on the basis of an engagement that was a sham.

'Tomorrow,' she said, 'unless you have a better plan, we shall travel on to Gretna and then we shall see if it is too late to save your cousin from my sister.'

'What was it that Aunt Otto said I would tell you about?' Jack asked, as they started to walk along the terrace towards the lavender-scented beds of the parterre.

'She said that I should not listen to any gossip about you,' Sally said. She smiled. 'I imagine she wished to reassure me, believing as she does that I am genuinely betrothed to you.'

'And have you heard any gossip about me?'

'Yes, of course,' Sally said. 'I have heard plenty relating to your elopement with Merle Jameson, but I do not require reassurance since I am only betrothed to you for the duration of this one night.' She shivered in the breeze off the lake. No matter how much she professed not to care, she knew she was shamefully jealous of the other woman—the only one that Jack had ever loved.

'Let's go back inside,' she said.

Jack smiled. 'A moment,' he said. 'If this night is all we have, we had better make it worth every moment.'

He put a hand out and caught her wrist, drawing her closer to the warmth of his body. He smelled of cologne and fresh night air and the longing caught at the back of Sally's throat and made it ache.

She put a hand against the crisp white of his shirt-front and held him off. 'Mr Kestrel, it may have escaped your notice, but, as I said, I do not like you very much. Nor do you care for me. Only a man with supreme arrogance would assume that I would fall into his arms again after what has happened between us.'

Jack put up a hand and brushed the strands of hair back from her face. His touch made her skin tingle. She turned her head aside in an attempt to deny the way he made her feel.

'In a moment,' he said, 'we are going to go back through those doors into the drawing room. In order to persuade everyone that we are indeed betrothed, you must look like someone who has been thoroughly kissed in the moonlight, Miss Bowes, rather than someone indignant after an acrimonious discussion.'

Panic caught at Sally's heart. If he kissed her, she was not sure that she could resist the feelings that coursed through her. Once again she wondered, helplessly, how it was possible to dislike a man so much and yet hunger for his touch. It felt like a betrayal of her principles and yet she wanted him.

'I could pretend—' she started to say, but Jack slid a hand into her hair and turned her face up to his.

'The reality,' he said, as he leaned down very slowly to kiss her, 'is far, far better than the pretence.'

It was not like his kisses earlier, when he had been asserting his possession and his mastery over her. Now he courted a response from her, the kiss gentle and persuasive, teasing her, tempting her to open her lips beneath his and return the kiss. Sally relaxed, feeling the warmth in her veins turn her body soft and willing. It was so seductive that she let her hands slide over Jack's shoulders, drew him closer to her and kissed him back. Immediately Jack slid his arms about her, deepened the kiss, and the feeling flared between them like wildfire. They were both breathing hard when he let her go.

'Jack…' Charley's voice floated across the terrace to them '…Aunt Otto says that you have been out there quite long enough and that Sally promised to play bezique with her.'

Jack swore under his breath. 'It's like having a nursemaid again. You had best go in and humour her.'

'Gladly,' Sally said, smoothing her gown. 'I enjoy her company very much.' She took a deep breath to steady herself. Her hands were still trembling slightly from the residual excitement tingling in her blood.

'Try not to take too much money off her,' Jack said. 'I know you will be tempted to fleece her but I will make up any shortfall.'

His words touched Sally on the raw. It seemed that every time she permitted herself to forget he thought her a money-grabbing charlatan, he would remind her.

'I'll take her for every penny I can,' she said recklessly, seared by his scorn. 'What else would you expect from me, Mr Kestrel?'

'Nothing, I suppose,' Jack said.

Sally paused with her hand on the door. 'Incidentally, Mr Kestrel,' she added, 'I have requested a room as far distant from your own as possible. I shall be removing my name from the panel by the door. And anyone creeping in there in the dead of night will be met with a chamber pot to the head, two hundred pounds or not. Do I make myself clear?'

'As crystal,' Jack said. 'Good night, Miss Bowes.'

Chapter Seven

Jack was up early the following morning. He had slept poorly, tantalised by the knowledge that Sally's room was just down the corridor from his own, so near and yet so far. More disturbing than his sexual frustration was the fact that he actually missed sleeping with her; he missed her warmth and her scent and the confiding way that her body curled closely with his, bringing a deep sense of peace and comfort to him. It was not a feeling that was familiar to him and it irritated him profoundly.

He wished he had not provoked her when they had parted the previous night. She had spoken so convincingly about her reasons for refusing Gregory Holt that he had almost believed her. Then he had kissed her and once again he had been swept by the need to have her, to hold her, to keep her close. He wanted to believe in her. He was hesitating on the edge of a precipice and it infuriated him that Sally could get under his skin like this because he knew he was losing control; after Merle, he had no wish to let a woman get that close to him ever again. It was impossible. He would not permit it. He would keep Sally with him on his own terms, but keep his heart locked against her. She *had* to be the corrupt and venal adventuress Churchward had shown him.

He took one of Stephen's specially ironed newspapers and made his way to the library. It was quiet and the early morning sunshine dappled the carpet. One of the Labradors was dozing in a patch of warmth and raised its head when he walked past only to sink back down with a grunt again as Jack sat down. In the parlour the servants were laying out a gargantuan breakfast, but no one could eat until Lady Ottoline decided to put in an appearance and she was probably still in bed enjoying hot chocolate and toast. Jack wondered how anyone could eat as much as his great-aunt and still remain stick thin. She had an appetite like a Labrador and he was beginning to think that her much-vaunted frailty was merely a cunning trick to get her own way. It worked, he thought ruefully. He could imagine Sally being like that in fifty years' time, still as beautiful, still as strong-willed and busy terrorising a younger generation. He realised he was smiling indulgently at the thought and stopped abruptly. His wits were definitely going begging that morning. He had never thought of any relationship in terms of such longevity before, not even his affair with Merle.

He paused. When had he started to think of his hastily arranged false engagement to Sally in terms of something more enduring? He had almost forgotten that it was meant to be a short-lived ruse. Even more disturbing was the fact that his family had warmed to Sally and taken her to their hearts, even Aunt Otto, who was notoriously hard to please. Sally had Gregory Holt's loyalty too—Jack gritted his teeth—no, she had Holt's love to the point he was prepared to stand as her brother to protect her when he clearly wanted a very different relationship with her. Yet she refused to take advantage of Holt's devotion. But perhaps she was after a better catch, someone who would one day inherit a dukedom. The test would come if she sued Jack for breach of promise when they broke the false engagement. Then she would reveal her true colours.

He could imagine that happening. It would be another logical step in the Bowes sisters' financial plan.

Yet still his doubts persisted.

Jack unfolded the paper and tried to distract himself with the news.

His business acquaintance Robert Pelterie had made a mile-long flight in a monoplane. Jack, who had financed some of Pelterie's work in aviation, was impressed. There was much news on the last-minute preparations for the Olympic Games, which were opening at the White City stadium in London the following month. And at the bottom of the third page there was a not particularly sympathetic account of the miseries experienced by the suffragette campaigners in Holloway jail:

'All the hours seem very long in prison. The sun can never get in...and every day so changeless and uninteresting. One grows almost too tired to go through to the exercise yard and yet one has a yearning for the open air...' There was also a list of other suffragists who had been arrested trying to enter the House of Commons by concealing themselves in a furniture van. Jack perused the list casually, his interest sharpening when he saw the name of Petronella Bowes. He remembered Sally mentioning her other sister when they had taken

dinner together and saying that Nell's life was made miserable by lack of money for food and medicines and how the constant threat of imprisonment and the need to pay fines seemed sometimes to overwhelm her.

The breakfast gong sounded. Jack finished the article he was reading before casting the newspaper aside and striding out of the library. The others were already in the breakfast room; as he approached he could hear the sound of voices and his great-aunt's cut-glass tones as she requested kedgeree and lamented the lack of properly brewed coffee.

'Good morning, nephew,' she said sharply, as Jack appeared in the doorway. 'Late again, I see.' Her gaze swept from him to Sally's demurely bent head. 'I trust that you slept well?'

'Never better,' Jack said untruthfully. He smiled a greeting at Charley and Stephen, managed a civil nod for Gregory Holt, then went to Sally and took her hand, pressing a kiss on the back of it. He was rewarded with a slight blush and a flicker of her eyelashes as she cast one, quick look at his face. Astonishingly, she seemed shy. It made Jack feel protective. He reached for his customary cynicism. She must be no more than an extremely accomplished actress, as he had always suspected.

'Good morning, my love,' he said, and saw Lady Ottoline, if not Sally, smile with approval.

Sally was dressed very plainly today in a blue blouse and panelled skirt, and if she had slept as badly as he it certainly did not show. She looked fresh and, to Jack's eyes, exceedingly pretty.

'Miss Bowes tells me that you are both to leave today for a pressing engagement,' Lady Ottoline said, her smile fading into a look of disagreement. 'That does not suit me *at all*. In fact, I absolutely forbid it, nephew. Tonight is my birthday dinner and if my own nephew and his fiancée cannot be present, then it is a sad day for the family. As it is, neither your papa nor Buffy can join us, which I consider shows a deplorable lack of respect. That boy does not deserve to be a duke.'

Jack was saved from replying by a sudden rapping at the main door. Patterson, the butler, who had been overseeing the breakfast arrangements, hurried out, adjusting his livery as he went and wearing a faintly disapproving expression. Visitors were not expected to have the bad manners to arrive at ten when the family was still at table. It was the height of discourtesy.

There was a commotion in the hallway with the butler's voice raised in surprised greeting and then a cacophony of voices. Jack looked at Charley and raised his brows. She got to her feet and hurried out, closely followed by Stephen.

'You had better run along too, Jack,' Lady Ottoline said, digging her knife bad-temperedly into the lime marmalade. 'I would hate any of you to preserve good manners and remain at table with me.'

'That sounds like Connie's voice,' Sally said. She sounded suddenly nervous. She put down her napkin. 'Excuse me, Lady Ottoline.'

Jack followed her out into the hall. The familiar dapper figure of his cousin Bertie Basset was crossing the marble floor towards him. There was a blonde woman with him, achingly fashionable in a suit of cerise with a wide-brimmed hat framing her china-doll face. She was speaking in a light, drawling voice to one of the hapless footmen who was attempting to bring in what looked like vast quantities of luggage.

'Be careful with that bandbox, you oaf! No, don't hold it like that—you will squash my hat! And mind little Herman the Dachshund. He does not care for motorcar journeys and may well be sick on you…'

'Connie!' Sally said, in failing tones. 'What are you doing here? Where have you been?' She flashed Jack a look. 'We thought—'

'Sally darling!' Connie wafted towards her sister on a cloud of expensive perfume. 'What fun to find you here! We looked for you at the club yesterday, but Matty said that you had gone with Mr Kestrel.' Her perfectly arched eyebrows rose in a look of wide enquiry. 'I thought it most odd since I understood that you barely know one another.' She pouted. 'Indeed, it was most thoughtless of you not to be there to greet us when we were newly wed and simply *aching* to share the good news with you!'

'I am sorry that I missed you,' Sally said politely.

Connie waved a dismissive hand. 'No matter. We saw Nell instead, and she was very happy for us.' She frowned. 'She was at the club. Apparently she had come to find you to thank you for the money you sent her.'

Jack's stomach dropped. He looked sharply at Sally. She met his eyes for a brief, guilty moment and then looked away with a studiously feigned lack of interest, fidgeting with the cuff of her blouse before glancing quickly back at him again. Jack raised his brows and smiled at her and she blushed. She looked the picture of guilt. Some of the tight, angry feeling inside Jack eased. He knew now where his two hundred pounds had gone the previous morning. He knew what Sally had wanted the money for. He knew that his original instincts about her had very probably been sound. He felt an overpowering urge to confront her there and then, but unfortunately his new cousin was still holding the floor.

'I thought Nell looked quite frightful,' Connie was saying, blithely ignoring everyone else as she gossiped to her embarrassed sister. 'She was all ragged and thin, but perhaps now that I am Mrs Basset I may be able to help her. It is good to be in a position where one can be charitable… Yes, what is it, Bertie?' She spoke to her husband in tones of extreme irritation.

'Sorry to interrupt you, darling,' Bertie said uncomfortably, 'but I wanted to introduce my cousin Charlotte Harrington and her husband Stephen, and also my cousin Jack Kestrel—'

'Mr Kestrel!' Connie ignored Charley and Stephen completely, but held out a hand to Jack upon which glittered the largest diamond he had ever seen. She was smiling winsomely at him, but it left Jack singularly unmoved. Looking from her little painted face to Sally's, seeing them together for the first time, he was struck by how very different the two of them appeared. Connie, with her vapid airs and sharp tongue, was

exactly how he had imagined her. He thought his cousin an even bigger fool than previously.

'How do you do, Mrs Basset,' he said, and Connie preened herself.

'Connie,' Sally intervened, 'what are you doing here? This is Mrs Harrington's home, you know, and everyone is here for a family party.'

'Great-Aunt Ottoline's birthday,' Jack said helpfully, turning to Bertie. 'You will have remembered that it is her party, of course, Bertie? She will be delighted to meet your new bride, I am sure.' He had the pleasure of seeing his cousin turn a gratifying colour of white.

'I had no notion Aunt Ottoline would be here,' Bertie choked. 'Came to see Charley, to ask that she might help smooth our way into the family, don't you know.' He looked askance at Jack. 'Didn't know you would be here either, Jack, for that matter.'

'No,' Jack said. 'I dare say that if you had you would have thought twice about coming. I have been looking for you on your father's behalf for the past week.'

Bertie gulped. 'Deed's done now,' he said, 'signed and sealed. We were married yesterday.'

Connie skipped up to Sally and thrust her hand under her nose. 'Look at my diamond! Is it not tremendous!'

'It is extraordinary,' Sally said. 'We thought that you might have headed for Gretna Green for your runaway match, Connie.'

'Gracious, no!' Connie wrinkled up her nose. 'I could not possibly get married in such a hole-in-the-corner way! We had a special licence. Bertie bought it weeks ago.' She caught Sally's arm, smiling beguilingly. 'I am sorry to have deceived you about my intentions, Sal, but it was the only way to keep the whole matter secret. I know you would have tried to dissuade me with your tiresome scruples.'

Jack looked at Sally again. She was pale and her face was set. 'My tiresome scruples,' she said. 'Yes, they have always been such a trial to you, have they not, Connie?' Again, she met Jack's eyes for a brief moment, but there was no triumph in her own to have been vindicated. She looked hurt and regretful, and Jack felt a sudden fury that Sally could care so much for other people when Connie clearly cared nothing at all for her sister's feelings.

'Well, you cannot help yourself, I suppose,' Connie said, smiling blithely. 'You always were prim and principled. It was fortunate that I had Bertie to conspire with instead!'

Bertie flushed bright red. 'I say, old thing,' he protested, 'it was not really like that! All we did was plan to raise a bit of cash.'

Jack turned to his cousin.

'Congratulations on a stunning piece of duplicity,' he said icily, and watched Bertie wither beneath his contempt. 'You have nearly driven your own father to his grave with your blackmail, leaving aside the anxiety you have both caused Miss Bowes.'

'Only wanted enough money to get married, what,' Bertie said plaintively. 'Papa wouldn't countenance it, don't you know, so Con and I had to think of something.'

'I'm glad to see that in the end a shortage of funds didn't stand in the way of true love,' Jack said bitingly.

'Papa will probably stop my allowance now it's happened,' Bertie said gloomily, 'but he can't disinherit me because of the entail.'

'And his health is poor—' Connie started to say, then stopped as Bertie shot her a look and Jack realised that even Connie Bowes did not quite have the brass neck to come out with the bald statement that she was merely waiting for her father-in-law to die.

'I do apologise,' Sally said, turning to Charley and Stephen, who had been standing watching the exchange in fascinated horror. Jack was not sure whether she was apologising for her sister's behaviour or Connie's very existence.

Charley shook her head and gave Sally a squeeze of the hand, which seemed to convey sympathy and support together, then stepped forward hospitably to smooth things over, offering breakfast and to show the newcomers to their room.

'For if you have travelled from London this morning you must have set off extremely early and be very hungry...'

'Oh, we stayed in Oxford last night,' Connie said airily, 'at the Randolph, you know. Nothing but the best.'

'She'll ruin you within a month,' Jack said to his cousin in an undertone.

Lady Ottoline's querulous tones, floating from the breakfast room and demanding to know what was going on, put an end to further discussion. Connie picked up a small bag from the floor and thrust it into Sally's arms. From inside peeped the smallest and most bad-tempered-looking dog that Jack had ever seen.

'You are far better with dogs that I am, Sally darling,' she said. 'Could you take him to the kitchens and feed him? And whilst you are there, would you secure me the services of a personal maid as well? I simply cannot manage on my own.' Her face brightened. 'Oh! But since you are here, perhaps you could attend to me yourself?'

Jack felt his temper snap comprehensively. 'Out of the question,' he said. He grabbed the bag with the dog in it and handed it to the butler, who recoiled with a look of horror on his face. 'Keep him away from the Labradors,' Jack said. 'They'll think he is a rabbit.' He took Sally's hand in his.

'Your sister is here as my fiancée, Mrs Basset,' he said, 'so you will have to make shift for yourself.' And he pulled Sally's hand through his arm and marched her back into the breakfast parlour, with Connie's indignant voice rising and falling like a siren behind him.

Sally's head was aching by the time that breakfast was over. Connie had chattered non-stop about her wedding and about how utterly marvellous it was to be Mrs Bertie Basset now. Lady Ottoline had sat in ominous silence, her sharp gaze going from Connie's animated face to Bertie's embarrassed one and back again. After the meal she had announced that she wished to speak with Bertie and when Connie had tried to accompany them into the drawing room had uttered the chilling words, 'Alone, if you please!'

Connie had looked mutinous, but Charley had persuaded her to go and inspect her bedchamber instead and they had disappeared upstairs with Connie's fluting tones floating back down to Sally as she commented on the dowdiness of Charley's colour schemes.

'You didn't tell me,' Jack said in her ear, 'just how unlike you your sister is.'

'Connie was not always this way,' Sally said, sighing. 'Before her broken love affair with John Pettifer she was a sweet girl.' She looked at him. 'I did try to tell you about that, Mr Kestrel, but, as I recall, you were not interested in listening.'

'Touché,' Jack said. 'I think we have rather a lot to talk about, Miss Bowes.' He gestured towards the door. 'Shall we walk for a little?'

'I do not wish to discuss matters with you,' Sally said coldly. She wanted nothing more than a bit of peace and a corner in which to hide away from Connie's presence. She supposed dully that she should be grateful to her sister, whose artless prattle had confirmed so comprehensively that all the things she had told Jack were true, but she was too heart sore and too miserable to appreciate it.

Jack tucked her hand through his arm and steered her

out on to the terrace. 'Too bad, my love,' he drawled, 'for I need to talk to you urgently.'

They did not speak again until they were well away from the house, across the moat and in the arboretum, where the huge pines and redwoods spread their shade and the sharp and sweet scent of the pine needles was all around them. It was warm and tranquil, but Sally did not feel very peaceful. Connie was no doubt wreaking havoc even as they spoke, Lady Ottoline would probably have a heart attack and Jack was looking so unyielding that she quailed to see it.

'I think,' he said mildly, 'that you owe me an explanation.'

Sally's overtaxed nerves snapped. 'Oh, do you!' she said. 'Well, I think that *you* owe *me* an apology!'

Jack nodded. 'That too,' he said pleasantly. He drove both hands into the pockets of his trousers and faced her directly. Sally's heart started to pound.

'First,' he said, 'I want to know why you did not tell me that you wanted the two hundred pounds for your sister Nell. You let me think you were selling your own virtue—'

'I let you think nothing,' Sally interrupted. She was incensed that instead of a polite apology he was trying to blame her for his own misjudgements. 'You *chose* to think that I was venal and grasping because you had already decided to believe it,' she said. 'I tried hard enough to tell you that you had your facts wrong, but you chose not to listen.'

Jack raked his hand through his hair. 'But if you had told me the truth I could have helped you.'

'You were in no mood to help,' Sally said. 'Have you forgotten how severely we had quarrelled, Mr Kestrel? Besides, I barely knew you. I was not going to ask for a loan from a man I had met only two days before.'

'You knew me well enough to sleep with me when we had met only two days before,' Jack said. His gaze was hard and narrow. 'So instead of requesting a loan you let me think you a grasping harpy who had sold her virginity.'

Sally shrugged, trying to pretend she did not care. 'You offered the money.'

'So you took it.'

'I did not think it would make a whit of difference to your opinion of me, given that it was already so low.'

Jack shook his head in exasperation. 'What did Nell need two hundred pounds for?'

Sally turned away to hide the naked emotion in her face. She had been hurt too badly by him to want to reveal the depth of her feelings and explain how desperately she had needed to help her sister.

'She needed food and rent and money for medicine,' she said. 'The fines have crippled her financially and many of her friends are in gaol so she cares for their children too. They are all sick with a fever—' Her voice broke and she put her hands up briefly to her face, letting them fall so she could look at him with defiant eyes. 'That is why.'

'So you sent the money to her directly before we left London?' Jack asked.

'I…' Sally hesitated, but she knew there was no point in further prevarication. 'Yes, I did.'

Jack cursed softly. 'I knew it! I saw you give it to Alfred to deliver. But when I asked you and you denied it, I thought…' he shrugged '…well, I assumed it was for some pressing debt.'

'Nell's debts were pressing. As I said, her children were sick and near starving.'

'And once again,' Jack said, 'you took responsibility for helping your sisters.'

Sally did not answer. Taking care of Nell and Connie was something she had always done.

There was a silence. 'And Connie,' Jack said. 'She

plotted this whole elopement scheme with Bertie's help, not yours, didn't she?'

'It seems so,' Sally said. 'I did not realise that Bertie was involved.'

'I am sorry that I doubted you,' Jack said.

Sally smiled bitterly. He sounded as though the words were sticking in his throat, but she knew that any sort of apology was a major concession from Jack. Perhaps in time she would be able to accept it, when her feelings were not so raw.

'Thank you,' she said politely.

'The evidence about Chavenage and Pettifer seemed so strong,' Jack continued. 'I read the court papers.'

'It is true that the Chavenage family tried to pay me off, but I would not accept a penny,' Sally said. 'Whoever gave you that information had their facts quite wrong, Mr Kestrel. As for John Pettifer, Connie loved him. You may find that hard to believe—I do myself when I see her now—but I think he was the only man she has ever truly loved. He used her very badly and when he jilted her it seemed only fair to sue him for breach of promise, to make the world see what a cad he was rather than to extract any money from him.'

'The judge agreed with you,' Jack said.

'Yes. But in the end it was a hollow victory because

Connie had been badly let down,' Sally said. 'I am sure it was then that she turned cynical towards men. She had always been flighty, but there was an innocence in her too. Now, though…' Sally sighed '…she is as hard as nails.'

'Your sister,' Jack said grimly, 'is the most conniving little piece it has ever been my misfortune to meet and she does not deserve your love and support.'

Sally shot him a startled look. He sounded so grim, and his mouth was set in an angry line. She supposed that his fury was no great surprise. He had maintained all along that Connie was an adventuress and now they had all seen and heard the proof of it. Connie had been out to make an advantageous match and had no respect for Bertie, who had only been the means to an ambitious end.

'At least we are saved the trouble of travelling to Gretna,' Sally said, sighing. 'I might have known that we would be too late.' She shook her head slightly. 'It always was too late to talk sense into Connie. She always did do exactly want she wanted.'

'And now,' Jack said, 'they are married—'

'Thereby removing the necessity for us to be engaged,' Sally said. This, she thought, was the end between them, and it had come sooner than she had thought. 'I think I shall go back to London,' she said. She looked at him. 'If you would be so good as to convey me to the nearest station, Mr Kestrel? I think it is the least that you could do under the circumstances.'

Jack did not answer immediately. 'I am not really minded to let you go so easily,' he said.

Sally stared at him, her thoughts in a sudden spin. 'Whatever do you mean by that?' she demanded.

'Exactly what I say.' Jack sounded maddeningly arrogant. 'I wish to keep you here at Dauntsey with me as my fiancée.'

'Well,' Sally said, her temper flaring abruptly again at this further display of high-handedness, 'I do not think that you are in a position to make any further demands upon me, Mr Kestrel.'

'I accept that you have a right to be angry with me—' Jack conceded, but Sally did not let him finish. It felt good to let all her indignation and anger and pain at last have free rein.

'Oh, you accept that, do you?' she said. She put her hands on her hips. 'You drag me here on what turns out to be a wild goose chase, you insult me by suggesting I am in league with my sister to fleece your family, you calmly announce that we are engaged, and you think I have a right to be angry with you! Well, thank you for that!'

'I have said that the fleecing accusation was a mistake,' Jack said. Infuriatingly, he looked amused rather than annoyed at her show of temper and Sally realised with a sudden pang that it was because he was still supremely confident, still utterly sure that he could persuade her to his point of view. She wished desperately that she were not so vulnerable to him. But she was strong too. She had no intention of succumbing to his practised charm ever again, not when it was accompanied by no deep emotion.

'It is handsome of you to admit it,' she said, her eyes flashing. 'You can trust your own judgement, but you cannot trust my word! And what did your "evidence" amount to anyway? Some trumped-up report from your lawyer? You did not even give me a chance to defend myself!'

'No,' Jack said slowly, 'I did not.'

Sally's temper flickered again. She warmed to her theme. 'You have been intolerably rude to me, you tried to break the bank at my casino, you threatened to destroy my business, you *seduced* me—'

'Please, Sally…' Jack put out a hand towards her as a nervous-looking gardener's boy came through the trees pushing a wheelbarrow and went swiftly into reverse on hearing the word 'seduced'.

'And now you decide that you are not minded to let me go!' Sally finished. 'You are intolerable!'

'Given the disparity in our experience, as a gentleman I must take responsibility for what has happened between us,' Jack said. 'Therefore you remain as my fiancée.'

'Oh, no, I don't!' Sally said furiously. 'Just because you have exonerated me of blame you do not need to take responsibility for my actions! I knew what I was doing even if—' She stopped, embarrassed, as the heated memories swamped her mind again.

'Even if you were a virgin,' Jack said softly. 'Which we both know that you were.' He took her hand and drew her into the shelter of one of the trees. His touch was warm and insistent. She could feel her resistance to him melting and tried desperately not to weaken. He was standing close to her and she could smell the fresh scent of his cologne. She felt a little light-headed.

'I… This…' Sally struggled to regain her self-control. 'This is nothing to the purpose,' she said. 'The point is that now Connie and Bertie are married we no longer need to pretend to be engaged and, as I said, I would like to go back to London.'

'I cannot allow it,' Jack said, with every appearance of regret. 'I want you to stay here with me.'

Sally stared at him. 'You *want* me to stay here? Just what is it that you are suggesting, Mr Kestrel?'

'I am proposing marriage.' Jack thrust his hands moodily into his pockets. 'I dislike the idea of your silly little sister having precedence over you just because she is married and you are not.'

Despite herself, Sally laughed. 'A lamentably bad reason for marriage, Mr Kestrel. I assure you that even if Connie insists on entering every drawing room in London before me, which no doubt she shall, I can still deal with her.' She shook her head. 'And I have to say that that is without a doubt the worst proposal of marriage that I have every heard.'

'No doubt you have heard a few.' Now Jack sounded even more bad-tempered.

'Certainly enough to know that yours was extraordinarily inept.'

'I suppose that Gregory Holt was more proficient?'

'He said some very pretty things,' Sally conceded, 'but I still refused him. As I do you, Mr Kestrel. The idea is absurd.'

'If we call off our engagement now, Aunt Ottoline will be extremely disappointed,' Jack said.

Sally raised her brows. She found that in spite of everything, she was starting to enjoy this litany of the worst possible reasons to wed. 'Another poor basis for marriage,' she said. 'I like your aunt, but I am not tying the knot with you simply to oblige her.'

'If you go now, I will sue you for breach of contract.'

'That,' Sally said ruefully, 'sounds much more like you, Mr Kestrel.'

Jack smiled at her. 'Have you noticed,' he said conversationally, 'that when you are trying to keep me at arm's length, you always call me Mr Kestrel?'

Sally's heart skipped a beat at the intimacy of his tone. 'You are at arm's length,' she said. 'You are practically a stranger to me.'

'Rubbish.' Jack straightened. 'You have met my family. You have *slept* with me.'

'Yet another bad reason for marriage.'

Jack took her hand and pulled her to him. 'Sally,' he said, 'we were both a little carried away these past two nights, and as a result I have a need to protect you and your reputation—'

'Nonsense!' Sally said. She spoke abruptly to quell the little quiver of feeling that his words aroused in her. 'I can look after myself.' She took a deep breath. 'You said it yourself, Mr Kestrel. I am a widow, I was almost a divorcée, I own a nightclub, and I have a scandal-ous reputation already. It was one of the reasons why you—' She stopped.

'Why I took you to bed,' Jack said helpfully.

The gardener's boy, who had stuck his head around the tree again to see if the coast was clear, disappeared with a strangled squeak.

The colour flooded Sally's face. 'You thought me experienced,' she whispered.

'I did. And now I know you are not. So—'

'No,' Sally said, before he could finish. 'No one knows what happened. No one will know, least of all your strait-laced great-aunt. And even if they did, my reputation, such as it is, could stand it. It is the height of hypocrisy only to propose when you have it proved to you that I am virtuous.'

'Could your reputation stand having a child out of wedlock?' Jack asked softly.

Sally caught her breath. It was not that she had not acknowledged the possibility to herself already, but she was not ready to talk to Jack about it. She gritted her teeth.

'That will not happen,' she said.

'Do you know that,' Jack enquired, 'or are you just

burying your head in the sand and hoping that you are right?'

Sally looked at him. She wanted a child. She had wanted one for a long time, with a desperate ache that she had sublimated in her work. But she did not want one like this. She thought of little Lucy Harrington and the love and happiness that surrounded her and the fact that Jack was so indulgent and adoring an uncle and her throat ached with tears at the thought of what might have been. He would be a good father. But she wanted him to be a good husband first and she was not sure he had it in him to give her that, not when he could not love her because his heart was already long given to another woman.

'That must be at least the fifth bad reason you have given me for marriage,' she said.

Jack sighed. 'Sally—'

'No,' Sally said. 'You do not love me.'

Jack did not contradict her. 'I want you,' he said. 'I need you. It is enough.'

'It is not enough for me,' Sally said stubbornly.

'It will have to be because I will not let you go.'

Sally shook her head.

'I will court you.'

'You make it sound like a threat,' Sally complained.

'Jack, be sensible. You have loved only one woman in your life. Perhaps you are still in love with her and, because she is dead, she is untouchable. How do you think I would feel as your wife, knowing that I was competing with a ghost? I have made one bad marriage in my life and I do not intend to make a second. And when the physical passion between us dies, as it surely will, we would have nothing left.'

'Very well,' Jack said. He loosed her and stood back, still holding her hands. There was a bright, challenging light in his eyes, the same light Sally had seen there that night at the Blue Parrot when he had been on a winning streak. She looked at him with misgiving.

'Give me this weekend to court you,' Jack said. 'Don't reject me outright. Give me two days in which to make you change your mind. Give me your answer on Monday.'

'Two days!' Sally said incredulously. 'You think you can win my consent in only two days?'

'Yes,' Jack said. He did not smile. The intensity of his regard rocked her to the soul.

'And if I do not succumb?' Sally questioned. 'Then will you accept defeat and not press me to wed you?'

'I will.' The touch of his hand gave her a different answer.

'You lie,' Sally accused.

Jack laughed. 'All right. I will continue to try to persuade you, Sally, for the need I have for you burns me up. But I swear I shall not press you.' He raised one of her hands and kissed the tips of her fingers. 'It is your call now.'

They had the whole day together. They went riding in the park and took a picnic luncheon. It was scandalous, of course, because they went out without servants or chaperonage, but even Lady Ottoline smiled indulgently. They spread a blanket beneath the broad oaks of the park and ate their fill of cold ham and chicken pie and cream pastries with strawberries, washed down with champagne. The drink and the warmth made Sally sleepy and she lay back in the dappled sunshine and watched the shadows of the leaves dancing over her head.

'It is nice to experience an English summer again,' Jack said. He was lying beside her, his body relaxed, hands behind his head as he too looked up at the trees silhouetted against the sky. 'I had almost forgotten what it was like, so fresh and cool after the heat of southern France.'

'Tell me about what happened when you left England

all those years ago,' Sally said sleepily. She turned her head to look at Jack. His face seemed tranquil enough, but there was some tension now in the long lines of his body. She knew he hated talking about the past, but she thought that if he was not prepared to let her into even a small part of his history then there really was no hope for them. She could not marry a man who kept his innermost thoughts locked away.

'I was twenty-one when I left,' Jack said, after a moment. A rueful smile twisted his lips. 'Until the business with Merle I had thought myself so much a man, but when my father banished me I felt no more than a lost boy, though I would have fought with my last breath to keep that weakness hidden.'

'You had not expected him to send you away,' Sally said.

'No.' Jack shifted a little. 'Oh, I could see that I had let my family down monstrously, but in my youthful arrogance I had thought that I could have it all—a glittering future, the support of my family, and…Merle.' His voice fell. 'And then I lost it all. Merle died and I was disgraced and my privileged and golden future disappeared.'

Sally shifted so that she could look at him properly. His gaze was thoughtful and dark with memories.

'I heard,' she said, 'that you joined the army.'

'I fought against the Boers,' Jack said. 'I tried to get myself killed in a glorious way that would make my father proud, but all I succeeded in doing was living when I wanted to die.'

His voice was devoid of expression, but his face was grim. Sally's heart ached for him. After a moment she slipped her hand into his and felt his fingers, long and strong, close about hers. His touch brought a sense of relief and peace to her. If she could only reach him, she sensed she could thaw some of the bitter chill in his heart.

'Life has an inconvenient habit of thwarting you,' she said, and saw him smile.

'Yes. After the war, when I realised that I was not only going to live, but needed to make a living, I went into the aviation business. The rest you know. I came home at the end of last year.'

'Did you never come back before?' Sally asked. When he shook his head, she protested, 'But Charley must have missed you terribly! And you would not have seen Lucy when she was a baby, and when your mother died...'

Jack's fingers tightened cruelly on hers for a second

before he let her go. 'I could not return until I had wiped out the shame of what I had done.'

Sally shook her head slightly, trying to understand the demons that drove this complex man. There was something here that he was not telling her. It had been a long and bitter struggle for him to come to terms with the past; even now, she suspected there were matters he still could not forgive himself for.

'They have welcomed you back with open arms,' she said. 'Both Charley and Lucy dote on you, and I think Lady Ottoline probably likes you much more than she pretends.'

'Oh, everyone has treated me like the prodigal son,' Jack said, and once again Sally heard the thread of bitterness in his voice.

'You do not feel that you deserve it,' Sally said.

Jack shook his head, but he did not speak and after a second Sally leaned over to kiss him, wanting to comfort him in the only way she could. For a moment he was still beneath her and then his mouth moved on hers and his hand came up to clasp the back of her head to hold her still so that he could kiss her more deeply. He tumbled her over on to the rug beside him and raised himself on one elbow to look down into her face. There was a hard glitter of desire in his eyes, barely leashed, and it lit an excitement like wildfire in her blood.

'Jack,' she whispered.

His expression was dark. 'This was not how I had planned my courtship of you to be.'

'I don't care,' Sally said recklessly. 'I want you.'

Somewhere deep within her she did care; she loved him and wanted his love in return, wanted it to wash away all the doubts between them and the pain of the past. But this was all that Jack could give her, this intense, sensual need that could not be denied, but threatened always to rule her.

'When I am with you I feel alive,' she said. 'I want that, Jack. Make me feel alive.'

He was on her in an instant, kissing her deeply, his hand buried in her hair. His tongue thrust, demanding a response as though he owned her and wanted to taste every inch of her. Her body felt hot and heavy as though they had been apart a long time and she could not wait to welcome him back. The champagne fizzed through her veins and the sunlight danced against her closed eyes, hot on her skin. Jack's hair felt warm and silky beneath her fingers. She felt him shift, his hand coming up to clasp her breast and tease her nipple beneath the material of her riding habit. She writhed against him, desperate to be free of the constriction of her clothes, and he started to unbutton the bodice of her gown and unlace the chemise beneath. The summer air played across her heated skin and Sally moaned with pleasure.

Then, suddenly, shocking her, Jack stood up and bent to lift her in his arms. Her head spun and the green darkness of the tree cover closed about them.

'What—?' she began, but Jack silenced her with another searing kiss that stole her very soul. He placed her gently on her feet, giving her a gentle push so that her back came up against the warm, rough bark of a tree. Understanding came to her then and she gasped, but he silenced the sound with another searching kiss, his mouth moving over hers, then dipping to taste the hollow above her collarbone and the sensitive skin at the base of her throat. Sally leaned back and felt the bark score the palms of her hands. Jack pulled open the bodice of her habit and dipped a hand inside, warm against the silk of her chemise. Her nipple hardened against his palm and he pushed the silk aside. Her bodice fell down, leaving her naked to the waist.

'Thank goodness,' he murmured, 'that you wear no corset for riding.'

'I protest,' Sally said weakly, 'that I am losing my clothes and you are still fully dressed.'

'And that is the way that it is going to be,' Jack said. He bent his mouth to hers again, stifling her protests, his kiss deep and hungry. His hands moved. Sally heard something give. Her legs felt weak and she leaned back against the tree for support, held there by the press of Jack's body against hers. When he released her mouth abruptly, she swayed, her body hot and melting, her mind dark with wanting.

Jack moved a little away from her and she looked down to see that he had caught hold of the hem of her riding habit, looping it over his arm. Beneath the habit she wore only her bloomers, which were no protection as they were designed to be open. Jack lifted her, then slid her down so that he held her by the hips, forcing her back against the tree trunk even as his erection pushed just inside her. Sally screamed at the unbearable and pleasurable tension within her.

'Hush, my sweet.' Jack's tone was laced with wickedness. He thrust lightly. 'You would not wish the gardeners to hear you, I am sure.'

Sally sobbed as he bent his head to her breasts and slid inside her a few inches further. She squirmed against his body, needing nothing now other than the intense satisfaction of being impaled on him. He continued to tease her breasts, nipping and biting gently whilst she writhed desperately, seeking release. And when he finally buried himself within her, thrusting deep again and again, the pleasure overwhelmed her and she gave another choking cry and hung limp in his arms.

When she could breathe again, and move, and look at him, she found that she was lying once more on the rug beneath the trees, her body boneless with bliss. Jack wrapped his arms about her and drew her close to his body and she listened to his breathing slowing and felt the gentleness in his hands and a part of her felt exultant to be so close to him. But even in her physical satiation a small part of her felt lonely too, because she knew that Jack had given everything that he could and she still wanted his love, but perhaps he would never be able to give it to her.

It was Lady Ottoline's birthday dinner that night and because they were a small family group they were seated at a round table exquisitely decorated with pale pink and old gold roses amongst asparagus fern and ivy. The main course of pheasant was decorated with its tail feathers and Connie laughed herself into a fit at the fact that Lady Ottoline was wearing osprey feathers in her hair.

'Two old birds together that are well past their best,' she whispered to Sally.

There was dancing after the meal. Jack behaved with impeccable propriety, the attentive fiancé, always at Sally's side, his attention on her alone. But for all his surface decorum the touch of his hands would remind her of their encounter in the park and her whole body would flush with the heat of remembered desire as she wondered if he might come to her room that night.

Connie was in her element, so full of her own importance as Mrs Bertie Basset that Sally could see even the kind-hearted Charlotte was rueing the day Bertie and Connie had decided to come to Dauntsey. Connie flaunted herself in a dashing gown of purple silk, draped herself all over Bertie in a very public display of affection and insisted loudly on taking precedence over her sister as a married woman, just as Jack had predicted. Lady Ottoline, who had greeted her godson and his new wife that night with a cool civility that, Sally thought, had fooled Connie into thinking she was an insignificant old relative, was watching Connie very sharply with her shrewd dark gaze.

It was late that night when the dancing was over that Connie sought Sally out as she was on her way to bed and fitted yet another cigarette into her mother-of-pearl holder.

'I suppose Mr Kestrel is very handsome,' Connie said, drawing daintily on her cigarette as she tripped up the stair beside her sister, 'and he is rich, of course. I can see why you might wish to marry him.' She sighed. 'But really, Sally, I could kill you for causing such a scandal! *I* wanted to be the centre of attention.'

'Well,' Sally said, her borrowed shoes pinching and her irritation just as sharp, 'I do not think you need to fear that, Connie. You have managed to make a profound impression on everyone in a very short space of time. Besides,' she added, 'this weekend party is to celebrate Lady Ottoline's birthday and it is for neither of us to steal her thunder.'

Connie brightened. 'Yes, and Bertie has just told me that he is the old lady's heir! Why he chose to keep that piece of information from me until now is a mystery, for I have wasted a whole day when I could have been making up to her, but never mind.' She caught Sally's arm, dropping cigarette ash on to the sleeve of the gown Sally had borrowed from Charley. 'But you must tell me what she is like, Sal, and how best I can get into her favour.'

'I cannot help you,' Sally said. She felt furious at this further example of her sister's barefaced greed. 'Lady Ottoline will make her own judgements.'

Connie's face was working like boiling milk. 'Well, upon my word! You have become very high and mighty all of a sudden! I suppose this is because you are engaged to Mr Kestrel. Well, I shall become a lady long before you are a duchess!' She looked down the stairwell to where Jack and Stephen Harrington were standing chatting in the hall. 'You know, Sally darling, I think I am happier with my Bertie than you will be with Jack.' She fidgeted a little with the cigarette. 'Bertie made me promise not to say anything, but I think you should know...'

'Know what?' Sally said. Her attention was half-distracted because Jack had just looked up and smiled at her and her heart turned over in her chest in the sweet and poignant way to which she was becoming accustomed.

'That Jack Kestrel murdered his mistress, of course,' Connie said. She looked with satisfaction at Sally's shocked, horrified face. 'There! I told Bertie that you would not know. It is scarcely the thing a man tells his new fiancée, is it?' And, having delivered her barbs, she slipped past Sally with a sinuous little slither of silk.

Chapter Eight

Sally was not sure how she got outside. She vaguely remembered running back down the staircase and seeing Jack's and Stephen's startled faces as she rushed past them. Jack put a hand out to her and called her name, but Sally brushed him aside and slammed the door open. She hurried across the terrace and stood with her palms resting on the flat top of the wall that bounded the moat, and breathed in deep breaths of the fresh night air in an attempt to still the whirling, giddy spin of sickness within her.

You mustn't listen to all the gossip about his past, Lady Ottoline had said to her only the night before, but it was difficult not to listen to fiction when Jack himself refused to speak of his first love and Sally knew nothing beyond the fact that he had loved her and they had run away together and that she had been shot. To think that it might have been Jack who had killed Merle was shattering, impossible, even if it had been a tragic accident.

An icy trickle of despair ran down Sally's spine. She could not believe it of Jack. She simply could not. It was not just because she loved him. She did not think she was so blinded to his faults because of that. She knew Jack could be ruthless. She knew that his mistress had died. But the rest…

It would explain the scale of the scandal, a little voice whispered inside her. *It would explain why he was banished abroad. It would explain Jack's silence…*

'Sally?'

With a start Sally realised that Jack had come to stand beside her. The night wind was ruffling his dark hair and he raised an absentminded hand to smooth it down in one of the gestures that she was coming to love. He was looking at her with concern and Sally realised that she was gripping the masonry so tightly that her knuckles were white and the stone was scoring her hands.

'Sally?' he said again. 'What is the matter? What has happened? Did Connie say something to upset you?'

'Yes,' Sally said. She did not think of lying to him.

She could not see a way of pretending that there was nothing the matter when suddenly there was this ugly, monstrous secret between them.

'Yes,' she said again. 'She told me that Bertie had told her—' She stopped and cleared her throat. 'She told me that Bertie had told her you killed Merle Jameson,' she said. 'She said that you murdered her.'

There was a silence. Behind them the fountain in the courtyard splashed softly. A swan floated past on the smooth waters of the moat, its head tucked beneath its wing as it slept.

'And did you believe her?' Jack asked quietly.

Sally looked at him. 'You told me yourself that she had died,' she said slowly, knowing that it was no answer.

Jack took a step closer to her. 'You don't trust me,' he said, and his voice was hard.

'I don't know!' Sally spun around on him. Her heart felt torn. 'God knows, I don't want to believe you capable of murder. I cannot believe it! I cannot even imagine that you might hurt her by accident. But you have never told me the truth, Jack. You told me Merle died, but you never told me what happened.'

'And because of my reticence you think I may be guilty?' Jack's icy tone flayed her to the bone.

'No!' Sally spoke, once again on instinct, and when

he turned away from her she felt sick and dizzy all over again. She did not want to believe it, could *not* believe it was true...

'Connie was right.' Jack drove his hands into his trouser pockets and stood braced, staring out into the darkness. 'I did kill Merle.'

'No,' Sally said again, but this time it came out as a whisper. She felt cold with shock.

'I did not pull the trigger myself,' Jack went on, as though she had not spoken. 'But that does not matter. I was guilty. Her death was my fault. And I have carried that guilt ever since.' He turned slightly towards Sally, but when she reached out a hand to touch his arm he drew back as though he could not bear it.

'It was my fault,' he repeated. His tone was violent. 'You wanted to know the truth and now you have it.'

'What happened?' Sally felt cold through and through. She had thought she wanted to know the truth, but now she was desperately unsure. 'Was there an accident?'

Jack folded his arms. 'I told you before that I was young and foolish. I fell madly in love with Merle and was desperate for her to leave her husband and run away with me. When she agreed I thought I was the happiest man on earth. Merle wasn't happy, though. She was afraid. She was afraid of what her husband would do when he found out. And I…' he sighed '…I laughed off her fears. Jameson was frail and I was young and strong and arrogant and thought I could protect her.'

His face was bleak.

'When Jameson caught up with us he had a gun. I thought he was going to challenge me—kill me, even. That would have been just. I never thought that he would kill Merle instead. Up until the last moment, his attention, his hatred, was focused entirely on me. I was afraid too by this point. I thought I was going to die. But he shot Merle, not me, and it was my fault. Her death was my responsibility.'

'No,' Sally said. Her lips shaped the word, but made no sound. 'It was not your fault,' she said. 'You did not pull the trigger.'

'As good as,' Jack said. 'I was the one who persuaded Merle to elope. I was the one who swore to protect her. I was the one who failed.'

'She chose to go with you,' Sally argued. 'It was her decision, just as it was Jameson's decision to pull the trigger. You cannot bear that blame, Jack.'

Jack's expression was blank and Sally despaired of her words ever reaching him. He had kept his guilt and his misery locked away inside for ten years. At last she understood that part of him that was unreachable; the bitter part that had abandoned the idea of love. She felt hopeless of being able to change that now.

But she had to try.

'You told me you loved Merle sincerely,' she said, ashamed that even at a time like this she could feel jealousy over Jack's deep love for the other woman. 'You loved her and you wanted her to be happy. You thought that happiness could be achieved if the two of you ran away together. And who knows—you could have been right if matters had fallen out differently.' She fixed her gaze on the dark trees etched against the night sky. 'You knew that Michael Jameson was a dangerous and violent man. That was one of the things that you wanted to save Merle from, because you loved her. So you did what you thought was right. You asked her to elope with you and she agreed. She chose to go with you.'

Jack did not speak, but she sensed that his dark eyes were fixed on her face. 'Neither of you could have foreseen what would happen,' Sally said. 'Neither of you knew what Michael Jameson would do. Merle's death was *his* responsibility, Jack. It was his fault.'

'You did not go with Gregory Holt,' Jack said.

'That was different,' Sally said. 'I did not love him. But if I had, I would have chosen to run away with him exactly as Merle did with you.' She smiled at him, but his face was set hard in the moonlight. 'I think that you could love again,' she said softly, 'though I expect it will be different from your feelings for Merle. But it need not be less profound.'

She took a deep breath. This was the hardest part. 'Which is why,' she said, 'you should not marry, Jack, until you find someone you can love. Least of all should you marry me.' She stopped, her voice threatening to break. She wished she had guarded her heart more carefully when they had first met instead of tumbling into love with him like a young girl fresh from the schoolroom. But it was too late for those regrets now. She loved Jack Kestrel, but he could not love her in return and, foolish as she might have been, she would not be so unwise as to marry him and then watch him fall in love with someone else when his heart had healed.

'Good night, Jack,' she said. 'Think about what I have said. It was not your fault. Let it go.'

She heard him call her name, but she did not wait. She knew she had to get back inside the house and into the privacy of her room before she was tempted to reveal her most secret feelings. She could not tell Jack that she loved him and expose the deepest vulnerability of all.

* * *

Jack stood on the darkened terrace for a long time after Sally had gone. He could smell the faintest, most elusive hint of her fragrance still in the air and for a shocking moment he felt so bereft without her presence that he was hollow with longing. For the first time in ten years he felt at a loss, unsure of himself in his relationship with a woman. He had told her more of his feelings for Merle than he had ever told another living person. He had locked that pain and that grief away for all those long years, but Sally had gently brought him right to the edge of the precipice. He was so close to opening his heart to her and revealing his true feelings. Except that now he was not sure what those feelings were.

A few days ago it had all seemed so easy. He had desired Sally Bowes. He had felt so powerful a passion for her, but he had thought it no more than lust. He had told himself that he could manage his lusts. He had always done so before. His emotions had never been involved.

But one night with Sally had made him realise that he needed her as well as wanted her. Yet still he had not seen his danger. He had assumed that because he had kept the memory of Merle preserved so perfectly, because he had loved her with a youthful and idealistic first passion, that nothing and no one could ever match that. Now he was not so sure. He did not feel for Sally what he had felt for Merle. His first love had had an innocence about it, despite the circumstances. It had been rash, idealistic and magical. What he felt for Sally was deep; his desire for her was the least complicated part of his feelings. He had tried to pretend that they were his only feelings, but he knew now that he needed her. He wanted to spend his life with her. He wanted to grow old with her and for her to have his children.

He did not want to have to live without her.

He admitted to himself that he was afraid. He, who had fought for his country in the cause of freedom and justice, who had shown extreme physical bravery and made difficult decisions of life and death, did not have the moral courage to confront his fears of love.

'You should not marry, Jack, until you find someone you can love. Least of all should you marry me.'

Sally's words seemed to hang on the night air. She had been generous, just as she had been to Gregory Holt when she had refused to take advantage of his love for her. Jack had misjudged her and insulted her, yet now she was generous enough to try to help him and to prevent him from making an error that could conceivably lead him to repeating the mistakes of the past. She had thought that he might marry her and then fall in love with another woman and be trapped.

Except that he could not imagine wanting to be with anyone other than Sally...

Jack swore softly under his breath and started to walk slowly back towards the house. He knew where his thoughts were leading him and he did not like it. He did not like it because he was not in control. Sally had the power in their relationship now. He thought about the power that she had over him because of his emerging feelings for her. He was afraid to confront them.

They terrified him.

Sally slept badly and awoke to a bright, sunny Sunday morning that seemed an ill match for her feelings. They rode to church by horse-drawn carriage—Lady Ottoline would not dream of permitting anyone to be conveyed to the service in a motorcar—and immediately the difficulties of precedence raised their head again when Connie insisted on riding in the first barouche with Lady Ottoline and Charlotte, leaving no space for Sally.

'As a widow woman,' Connie said to her sister, 'you must become accustomed to taking a step back, Sally.'

'I am a *spinster*, Mrs Basset,' Lady Ottoline said sharply, her bright gaze fixed on Connie's petulant little face, 'not even a widow, and I have never been accustomed to taking a step back *in my life*.'

'Oh, but it is different for you, ma'am,' Connie said blithely, 'for you are the daughter of a duke.'

'And Miss Bowes is your elder sister,' Lady Ottoline said, 'and, for reasons that I cannot quite fathom but that do her great credit, she has wanted the best for you all your life. The least that you can do is show her a little respect.' And she patted the seat in the barouche beside her and gestured to Sally to join her.

Not even Connie's elephant hide was proof against such a set-down and she rode in the second carriage with Bertie and the Harringtons, all the while shooting venomous glances at Sally and Lady Ottoline and waving her hand in ostentatious display at the villagers so that everyone could see her enormous diamond ring.

'Truly, Sally, I do not know how you tolerate her,' Charley whispered to Sally as they slipped into the family box pew in the little fifteenth-century church and Connie's complaining tones bounced off the rafters as she sent the hapless Bertie off to find her extra cushions. 'I am afraid that I would have strangled her long since if she was my sister!'

'I know,' Sally whispered. 'I am sorry. She has become much worse since the wedding. I think that her status has gone to her head.'

Charley snorted. 'Bertie is no great catch! Not like Jack. And it is not for you to apologise for her, Sally. It's not your fault! Besides—' she shot Sally a mischievous look from her dark eyes '—I think that Aunt Otto will utterly crush her. I know Aunt Otto, and I am not taken in by her quietness. She is working up to something tremendous!'

Sally did not have a great deal of spare energy to worry about Connie and her discourtesy. She was far more concerned about Jack. The pleasure that they had taken in each other's company the previous day had vanished. Jack had sat across from her in the barouche, moody and withdrawn, and once again Sally had felt a helplessness that she could not reach him and barely knew him at all. Charley had also noticed Jack's bad mood and had sought to reassure her:

'It is just a way that men have, you know,' she confided. 'I have observed that if Stephen is wrestling with a problem he barely speaks to me *at all* until the matter is solved.' She opened her eyes wide. 'Such silence is quite incomprehensible to me and it used to worry me dreadfully in the early days of our marriage, until I realised that it was just his way. Jack is the same.'

Sally smiled, but was not reassured. She knew the nature of the problem that must be troubling Jack. It was the same matter that had kept her tossing and turning all night. Their engagement was surely at an end now. She had finished it the previous night when she had told Jack he should not marry until he had found love again. When they travelled back to London the following morning they would go their separate ways.

'Thank goodness that Greg Holt has gone,' Charley added irrepressibly as the choir procession heralded the start of the service. 'I think his continued compliments to you would have made Jack intolerably bad-tempered!'

It did not help Sally that the vicar preached on the benefits of a happy marriage and Connie beamed and sat with her wedding and engagement bands on prominent display. Lady Ottoline nodded sagely at various points in the sermon and when the vicar quoted that the value of a good woman was above that of rubies, she shot Connie a very hard look indeed.

Jack excused himself immediately after Sunday lunch and he and Stephen went off to look at the hedge-laying work on the home farm, whilst Connie and Bertie set out to look at properties for sale in the neighbouring villages. Charlotte had turned pale at the news that she might have Connie as a neighbour and had sworn to bribe anyone with property on the market not to sell. She and Sally and Lady Ottoline took their parasols and took afternoon tea on the terrace overlooking the lake.

'It is entirely delightful,' Lady Ottoline opined, as she watched Lucy playing by the lake, 'to see children enjoying themselves here at Dauntsey. When you and Jack are married, you must encourage your sister Petronella to bring her children here. Jack is very good with children.'

'I have observed it,' Sally said. The sadness clutched at her heart.

'Perhaps,' Lady Ottoline continued, 'you have talked about setting up your own nursery?'

'Great-Aunt Otto!' Charley said, laughing. 'Sally and Jack are but recently engaged!'

'I am only asking,' Lady Ottoline said mildly. She turned her bright stare on Charlotte. 'If Sally were to become *enceinte*, it might even encourage you to increase your nursery, Charlotte!'

Charley laughed again. 'Stephen and I have only

been married for four years, Aunt Otto, and we have already produced Lucy. Give us time.'

'You could have had at least three children in that time,' Lady Ottoline observed. 'I cannot think why you delay.'

'Perhaps,' Charley said, her mouth full of sultana scones and jam, 'because we are simply enjoying one another's company, Aunt.'

Lady Ottoline sniffed. 'If you enjoy each other's company that much, Charlotte, you would *definitely* have more children by now!'

Charley caught Sally's eye and rolled her eyes. Sally hid her smile in her teacup. It was pleasant sitting here by the lake in the afternoon sunshine—so soothing that she could almost forget that her engagement to Jack was a sham that would shortly be at an end and there would certainly be no children for them, not now, not ever. It was even more pleasant to be wearing one of Charley's tea gowns, blessedly free of the constraints of the corset beneath. Its loose and flowing lines were cool on such a hot day and made her feel relaxed and sleepy.

'I expect that Jack will be purchasing a country estate for the pair of you shortly,' Lady Ottoline said, turning her observant dark gaze on Sally. 'Of course,

he will have both Saltires and Kestrel Court in Suffolk one day, but a man cannot have too much land, I
always say, and at least he has the income to support
it.'

'We have not discussed it, your ladyship,' Sally said
truthfully, wishing that Lady Ottoline would leave all
questions relating to their imaginary future.

Lady Ottoline snorted. 'You seem to have discussed
nothing! Young people today are remarkably lax in
their planning!'

Charley opened her mouth to spring to Sally's de-
fence again, but there was a sudden scream from the
lake where the nursemaid was supervising Lucy's
games. They all turned to see what was going on. The
maid was shrieking ineffectually and running along
the edge of the water. Of Lucy there was no sign other
than her bonnet floating out on the lake.

'Lucy!' Charlotte said in a horrified whisper. She
was half-out of her seat, the china cup falling from her
hand to smash on the terrace. 'She's fallen off the jetty
into the deep water! What can we do? I can't swim.'

Sally did not hesitate. She ran down from the terrace towards the lake. All she could see was a hot day
in June on the River Isis so many years ago, and her
father losing his footing in the punt and toppling backwards, oh so slowly, into the water. She had waited

then, waited for him to surface and swim to the bank, but as several frantic moments had passed there had been no sign of him. She had never seen him alive again.

That had been her mistake, to take no action, to wait. She had blamed herself for failing him and she had been terrified of water ever since. But she could not afford to let that fear rule her now.

Sally could feel the planks of the wooden jetty hot underneath the soles of her thin slippers. The maid had stopped screaming now and was running back up the slope of the grass towards the house. Charlotte had already disappeared around the corner of the stables to get help.

Sally ran to the end of the jetty and jumped. The water was deeper than she had imagined, closing over her head for one brief, terrifying moment before she broke the surface, gasping for air. It was shockingly cold and thick with weed and sludge. The beautiful lacy tea gown was immediately soaked and wrapped around her legs, weighing her down.

Gulping a breath of air, she dived under the water and felt a mixture of inexpressible relief and abject fear as she saw Lucy's frighteningly inert body floating beside the jetty uprights. She swam over and grabbed the child, hoping and praying that Lucy had not swallowed too much water or hit her head on the wooden frame of the jetty when she fell. The little girl's body felt heavy, weighed down by water, threatening to slip from her grasp. Sally's arms ached as she tried to hold her up.

People were running down the lawn now; one of the grooms with a ladder, another with a rope, and Jack in front of them all, ripping off his jacket as he ran and dropping it on the grass so that he could dive straight in and catch hold of Lucy from Sally's arms, passing the little girl up into the eager grasp of the grooms.

Sally felt her skirts hitch on something under the water and struggled ineffectually to free herself, gulping a mouthful of clammy weed-filled water in the process. Her limbs suddenly felt weighted with lead, her shoulders aching, and the drag of her skirts pulling her down. She thrashed about, reaching for the rope that snaked into the water beside her, missing it and going under again. For a second she had a terrifying vision of what it must have been like for her father as the water closed over his head, and then Jack was beside her, his arm hard about her waist, dragging her up into the daylight again and she could feel his strength and knew that she was safe. He scooped her up in his arms and her sodden skirts ripped and then she was rolling over and over on the warm wood of the jetty and someone was wrapping a blanket about her and the heat of the sun started to penetrate her chill and she began to shiver and shiver with reaction.

Charlotte was holding Lucy in her arms and rubbing her chilled body with the blanket. Lucy had recovered her consciousness and been violently sick, which Sally could only think was a good thing. Lady Ottoline was marshalling the servants, sending a groom to Dauntsey village for a doctor, despatching housemaids to warm some water for baths and to fetch fresh towels and blankets. Stephen had just arrived, pale and distraught, to support his wife and daughter back up to the house.

'Come on.' Jack swept Sally up into his arms. 'We need to get you out of those wet clothes and into a warm bath.'

'Thank goodness,' Sally said, through chattering teeth. 'Thank goodness you came, Jack. I was so afraid I was going to let her go. I thought she was dead!' Her voice broke on the word and she turned her face into the warmth of Jack's neck and breathed in the reassuring scent of his skin. For a second she thought she felt his lips brush her cheek in utter tenderness although his arms were as strong as steel about her.

'You did very well,' he whispered. 'You saved Lucy's life.'

Sally closed her eyes as he carried her up to the terrace, into the house and directly up the stairs to her bedroom, ignoring the ineffectual fluttering of the servants and shutting the bedroom door in their faces.

'Take those wet clothes off,' he ordered, as he put Sally gently on her feet in the black-and-white tiled bathroom and turned on the taps so that the water gushed into the bath.

Sally blushed. 'I will do no such thing with you in the room! You can send one of the maids to attend to me.'

Jack shook his head. 'They are all at sixes and sevens and would be no use at all. You will have to make do with me. I'm going to fetch some hot water to top up the bath; by the time I get back, I expect you to be naked and in the water.'

The hot colour deepened in Sally's face even as she shivered in the wet folds of the tea gown. She heard the door slam behind Jack and started to struggle with the buttons and laces of the dress, but her fingers felt cold and were shaking so much that the fastenings slipped from her grip. When Jack returned, what seemed like a mere few minutes later, he found her half-out of the gown and struggling helplessly while the material dripped a puddle onto the floor.

'One of these days,' he said thoughtfully, 'I will get you out of your clothes without destroying them in the process.'

He ripped the sodden shreds of the tea gown from Sally's body and dropped them on the floor.

Sally gave a gasp. 'Charley's dress!'

'You surely don't think that it would be fit to wear ever again, do you?' Jack countered. He looked at her. 'Do you want me to take off your chemise as well?'

'No!' Sally said. 'Go away!'

Jack grinned. 'I'll wait for you in the bedroom.'

After he had gone out, Sally managed to struggle out of the clinging remnants of her underwear and slid into the scented waters of the bath with a little sigh of relief. She lay back, eyes closed, whilst the hot water lapped about her shoulders and soothed her cold body. But the little shivers that racked her would not go away. Unbidden, the image of her father's lifeless body came into her mind. His face had been grey when they had finally dragged him from the river, the weed clinging to his body, sodden and unmoving. She shuddered, remembering the weight of Lucy in her arms and the terrible conviction she had that the child would slip from her grasp and be lost to her for ever, just as Sir Peter had been…

'Sally?'

She had not heard Jack's voice through the tormenting images in her mind, but now she realised with a pang of shock that she must have been sitting there a long time; the bath water was cooling and he had come into the bathroom to find her and once again she was shaking and shaking as though she could not stop. Jack gave an oath, grabbed a towel and plucked her bodily from the water, wrapping the material around her and holding her close as he carried her into the bedroom and dropped her on to the bed. A second later he was back at her side with a glass of brandy in his hands. He held it to her lips.

'You're in shock,' he said harshly. 'I should have realised.'

Sally shook her head. 'No—'

'Drink this, then we'll talk.'

The spirit burned Sally's throat and helped her to pull her thoughts back from the brink. She put the glass down and drew the towel more closely and protectively about her, reaching for the eiderdown and drawing it up to her chin.

'I am sorry,' she said. 'I think I am more shaken than

I realised. It is true that the accident reminded me of my father. He died of drowning.'

Jack swore again. 'I did not realise. I am sorry.'

'I do not speak of it,' Sally said, burrowing beneath the covers and feeling the warmth gradually banish the chill in her bones. 'It was a long time ago now. We were punting on the river and he lost his footing and fell. I thought he would swim ashore and I tried to grab his hand, but he disappeared. I waited and waited— and only realised too late that there was something dreadfully wrong.'

'What happened?' Jack asked. He sat down on the edge of the bed and sought her hand beneath the covers, holding it in a comforting grasp.

'When I realised he had not come up to the surface again, I screamed and screamed,' Sally said. 'Some of the other boatmen came then and helped me search, but it was too late. The police recovered his body from the river that evening. He had hit his head on the edge of the punt as he fell and sank like a stone.' Another shudder racked her. 'I have been terrified of water ever since.'

'And yet you jumped in without hesitation to rescue Lucy,' Jack said, his grip tightening on her hand.

'I could not let it happen again,' Sally said. 'It was

my fault that Papa died. I learned to swim after that, in case I ever needed it.'

Jack was very still. 'What do you mean when you say that it was your fault your father died?'

Sally freed herself from his grip and fidgeted a little with the edge of the eiderdown. She avoided his eyes.

'I could have saved him,' she said.

'And then Nell and Connie would not have had to fend for themselves?' Jack suggested. 'I had wondered at your determination to take care of them.'

Sally was shocked by his perception. She had not intended to say so much. She had not wanted to reveal her innermost fear and guilt.

'I am the eldest,' she excused.

'But that is not why you struggle so hard to defend them,' Jack said. Sally saw something change in his face. 'You feel guilt for something that is not your fault.' Abruptly, Jack stood up. He walked across to the window before turning back to look at her.

'Do you remember telling me last night that I should not take the blame for something that was not my fault?' he said conversationally.

'That was different,' Sally said.

Jack smiled. 'Was it? Strange how it is always easier to see the beam in someone else's eye. Think about it.'

His smile broadened. 'And at the least you need not worry about taking care of Connie any longer. That is Bertie's responsibility now.'

He came back to her and bent to kiss her, a kiss for once that was gentle and devoid of the tempestuous passion that had characterised their relationship.

'Oh, Sally Bowes,' he said, against her lips, 'don't let the past haunt you. You are too sweet and generous for that to happen.'

The tenderness of his kiss undermined Sally's defences completely. She felt a sudden, huge and surprising rush of relief because the fear had gone and with Jack she felt safe. She drew him to her, sliding her hands over his shoulders and it was only then that she realised his shirt was still damp and clinging to his body. In his hurry to care for her he had certainly neglected his own comfort.

'You'll catch a chill!' she protested, drawing back, and he smiled at her and pulled the shirt over his head in one fluid movement before joining her on the bed again.

His skin was warm beneath her fingertips and he felt so vital and alive that Sally drank in the scent and the taste and the strength of him, giving him back kiss for gentle kiss, wanting to feel closer still. Their tongues tangled, delicate at first, then bold and searching. Both of them were too intent on each other to hear the commotion in the bedroom doorway until Charlotte gave a muffled squeak.

'We did knock!' she said.

'Are you lost to all sense of propriety, nephew?' Lady Ottoline demanded, bustling into the bedroom and thrusting Jack's wet shirt towards him.

'Absolutely, Aunt Ottoline,' Jack said. 'Utterly and completely.'

For a second even Lady Ottoline was silenced. 'When I spoke to you of setting up your nursery,' she said, with a ferocious glare in Sally's direction, 'I did not mean for you to start immediately. I shall call the bishop and arrange a special licence *at once*!'

'That,' Jack said pleasantly, pulling his shirt on, 'is Sally's decision, Aunt, not yours.' He bent to place a final kiss on her lips. 'I will see you later, darling. For now I think I should leave you to rest.' He paused, his eyes still very close to hers. 'Despite our conversation last night,' he said in a low voice, 'I would like you to reconsider, Sally. Please do not reject me out of hand.'

'Out!' Lady Ottoline ordered, shooing him through the door and closing it firmly behind them.

Charley gave a giggle and sat down on the end of the

bed. 'I only came to thank you, Sally, and to make sure that in saving Lucy you did not take hurt yourself,' she said, 'but now I see that you are in such good health I shall have no more concerns on that score!'

'I hope,' Sally said hastily, 'that Lucy is recovering?'

'Oh, yes,' Charley said. 'The doctor thinks there is no real harm done and she is sleeping now. Stephen is sitting with her.' She looked at Sally. 'But for your prompt actions though, Sally…' She shuddered. 'Well, I do not like to think what might have happened. What a blessing that you can swim!' A frown puckered her forehead. 'One thing puzzles me though.' She made a slight, embarrassed gesture with her hands. 'When we came in and you and Jack were…well, you know…'

'Kissing,' Sally said helpfully.

'Yes!' Charley said. 'And sort of lying on the bed together and—'

'Yes,' Sally said, 'anyway…'

'Well…' Charley blushed. 'I am a little confused as I am sure that when you arrived on Friday your engagement was only a ruse and yet now…' Her voice tailed away uncertainly.

'Yes, of course.' Sally had forgotten that Charley had been party to the original deception. 'I am sorry to give you concern, Charley. The truth is that your brother has proposed to me in earnest, and—'

She was unable to say anything else as Charley launched herself at her and gave her a bear hug.

'How marvellous!' Charley gasped. 'I knew it! I knew that Jack was in love with you. All that posturing around over Greg Holt's attentions to you, and pretending that he did not care. I knew from the start that you were meant to be together.'

Sally extracted herself carefully from the hug. 'I haven't said yes yet,' she warned.

Charley's face fell ludicrously. 'But you will! Oh, Sally, please say you will!'

'I don't know,' Sally said honestly. 'I know you think that Jack loves me, Charley…' she put a hand out to halt Charley's rush of affirmative words '…but the truth is that I think he is still in love with Merle Jameson and maybe he always will be.'

Charley's face stilled and she was uncharacteristically silent for several moments. 'I was only sixteen when Jack eloped with Merle,' she said thoughtfully, 'and it is true that he did love her desperately.' She saw Sally's expression and shook her head slightly. 'I am sorry, Sally, but you yourself have said that it was the case. I didn't understand Jack's feelings at the time, but now that I am older I can see that it was a mad, passionate, sort of love. He put her on a pedestal and wanted to take her away from her cruel husband. But it was also a very young and naïve kind of a love. I do not know if their feelings would have survived had Merle lived. But…' she hesitated '…I think Jack loves you in a way that is no less profound, just different.'

The door flew open without a knock and Connie bustled in. Behind her in the doorway Sally could see Lady Ottoline lurking with a face like thunder, and Bertie, looking distressed.

'Not now, old thing—' he started to say, but Connie ignored him and wafted towards her sister on a wave of overpowering scent.

'Sally darling!' Connie said dramatically. 'We just got back and heard what happened. How utterly ghastly! Such a good thing that I wasn't here—I am terrified of water and might have damaged my new blue tussore gown in all the excitement!' She turned to Charley. 'I hope the child was not injured?'

Charley was, for once, completely silenced, and it was left to Lady Ottoline to sweep magnificently into the room and deal with the interloper. 'It might help, Mrs Basset,' she said icily, 'if you knew the name of

Charlotte and Stephen's daughter and actually cared about her welfare into the bargain.'

'I beg your pardon!' Connie spluttered. 'I am here to enquire into my sister's health—'

'As though you care a ha'pence for that either!' Lady Ottoline snapped. She looked from Connie to Bertie, who was trying to efface himself against the velvet wall hangings. 'Sadly it does not take a towering intellect to work out why my nephew chose to marry you, Mrs Basset,' she said, 'and I realise that it cannot be for your conversation. If he wishes to sit and look at a spiteful and empty-headed little doll for the rest of his life, then that is his choice. But I do not care to, so you will remove yourselves from this house forthwith and make sure that you are not within twenty miles of me at any time in the future. That is all.' And she swept out again.

'Well, upon my word,' Connie spluttered, a bright spot of colour burning in her cheeks. 'Who does she think she is?'

'She *was* the person who was going to leave her fortune to me,' Bertie said gloomily. He grabbed Connie's arm. 'Come along, old girl. Time to make a swift exit, I think. What do you say to another night at the Randolph?'

Chapter Nine

It was raining when Sally got back to London, big fat summer raindrops that spattered the dry cobbles and made the air smell of dust. Jack had wanted to drive her back, but Sally had insisted on taking the railway; she needed time alone to think. She had told Jack that she would give him an answer to his proposal that night, after the opening of the new Crimson Salon at the Blue Parrot, which meant that her whirlwind affair had lasted precisely a week. It seemed a perilously short space of time on which to make a decision that would affect the rest of her life so profoundly. Yet even if she turned Jack down, she could see that things would not be the same; he had come into her life and changed everything.

The club was reassuringly calm and quiet. Dan took her through everything that had happened in her absence and assured her that they were ready for the opening. Keeping her eye on the clock so that she would have plenty of time to get dressed for the evening, Sally worked her way through the pile of papers and correspondence on her desk. It was at about five o'clock, when she was thinking of going upstairs to get changed, that there was a knock at the door and Greg Holt came in and closed the door behind him.

'May I speak with you, Sally?' he asked.

Sally smiled. 'Of course! It is good to see you again, Greg. Are you coming to the opening of the Crimson Salon tonight?'

Greg nodded. He rubbed his chin a little uneasily. 'I wondered… That is, I thought I might bring Nell with me as my guest.'

Sally was so surprised she almost upset the inkpot. 'Nell? My sister?'

'The same,' Greg said, with a faint grin. His eyes were nervous. 'I looked her up when I got back to London.'

'That must have caused a stir in Blakelock Street,' Sally said drily.

'Yes.' Greg pulled a face. 'I will move them out of

there as soon as I can. I am sure the children would be happier in the country and Nell would look so much better with colour in her cheeks. It's no place for them to be—' He broke off as he saw Sally's expression. 'What?' he said, a little defensively.

Sally was laughing. 'Oh, Greg, that was quick! I always said that you were a managing sort of a man!'

'And you never needed me to manage you,' Greg said ruefully, 'but Nell is different. And I have known her for years. It is not as though this is sudden.'

'No,' Sally said. She gave him a sharp look. 'But Nell is not like me. She is a person in her own right, Greg.'

'I know,' Greg said. 'I do know that, Sal. I can only hope that with her political convictions Nell can be persuaded to look kindly upon me.'

'As long as you support the right of women to have the vote, then I am sure there shall be no problem,' Sally said, smiling.

'I try,' Greg said, 'but then I think of your sister Connie having the right of suffrage…'

'Well,' Sally said, 'if it comes to that, I need only think of the likes of Bertie deciding the future of the country…'

'A fair point,' Greg conceded. 'You have my support. Were they unbearable after I left?'

'Intolerable,' Sally agreed. 'But Lady Ottoline gave Connie a piece of her mind and they retired to the Randolph and left us alone.'

'You do not seem too concerned,' Greg observed. 'Not long ago you would have blamed yourself for the entire episode.'

Sally fidgeted with her pen. 'I suppose so. But Jack made me see that Connie and Nell are not my responsibility any longer.'

'I've been telling you that for years,' Greg said drily.

'I know.' Sally avoided his eyes. 'I am sorry, Greg.' She smiled. 'But if you came for my permission and blessing for you and Nell, then you have it anyway. Dear Greg. I am happy for you.'

Greg smiled slightly too, but the smile faded from his eyes quickly. 'I wish I could say the same for you,' he said. 'I understand from Charley that you do intend to go through with it?'

Sally sighed. 'Greg, we have had this conversation already.'

'You are going to marry a man who cannot love you.' Greg said. He shook his head. 'You deserve better than that, Sal.'

'I have not given Jack my final decision—' Sally started to say, but Greg stopped her with a look.

'You *have* decided, Sal. You know you have. You have made the first reckless and ill-considered decision of your life.'

'The second one,' Sally said, thinking back to her first night with Jack.

Greg did not smile. 'There is something I haven't told you. I wondered whether I should interfere or not...' He cleared his throat. 'Damn it, Sal...'

'If it is something to do with Jack's past,' Sally said feelingly, 'then I do not want to know. I have no desire to spend my married life with people coming up to me and whispering maliciously in my ear that there's something I should know about my husband. There is always going to be someone talking scandal.'

'It's not that,' Greg said.

Sally raised her brows. 'Then what is it?'

'You must accept that I am telling you this for your own good—' Greg began, but Sally shook her head sharply.

'All you are doing is making me nervous. Well?'

'Whilst we were at Dauntsey,' Greg said, 'my agent had an approach from someone acting on behalf of an anonymous buyer. They wanted to buy my stake in the Blue Parrot, Sal.'

Sally felt a chill tiptoe down her neck.

'Why would anyone want a stake in the club?' she asked.

'I don't know,' Greg said, 'but they wanted it badly. They offered twice the value of my investment. I told Montgomery that I would not sell under any circumstances and I asked him to try to discover the identity of the mystery buyer, but all he could find was that the agent was Churchward, who acts on behalf of the Kestrel family, and that he had approached all the other investors as well. They all sold, Sal. I am sorry.'

The chill in Sally's blood intensified. She toyed with a pen, trying to concentrate and succeeding only in getting ink stains all over her fingers.

'Not everyone is as loyal as you are, Greg,' she said lightly. 'So you think that Mr Churchward's mysterious buyer is intent on controlling the Blue Parrot?' She put the pen down. 'And indeed if he has already bought up all my other investors, he owns the club now, for your share and mine come only to forty percent.'

Greg nodded. 'Churchward represents many other clients in addition to Jack Kestrel, of course.'

'Of course,' Sally echoed. She looked up and met

Greg's eyes. 'But I think we both know that it must be Jack who is behind this. Who else would be interested in buying the Blue Parrot?'

Greg shook his head. 'I do not know. But why would Jack seek control of the Club, unless…?'

Unless…

Sally thought back to the very first night that she had met Jack. It was only a week ago, but it felt like an age. So much had happened. Despite the shortness of their acquaintance she had even fooled herself into thinking she knew him, understood him. But what did she *really* know of Jack Kestrel, the man she had fallen helplessly in love with, but who could not love her in return?

She had been careless when they first met, she acknowledged, telling him that her business situation was precarious and dependent on the investors in the club. Such information would be crucial for a man looking to buy a stake… Or looking for revenge…

'Montgomery said that the offer arrived whilst we were at Dauntsey?' she asked carefully.

'On the Friday,' Greg confirmed.

The Friday. That had been two days after she and Jack had met. The very day that Jack had come to the Blue Parrot to accuse her of conspiring with Connie to fleece his family.

'And Churchward's client was still interested when you came back to London yesterday?' Sally questioned.

Greg nodded sombrely. 'He pressed me for an answer immediately even though it was a Sunday,' he said. 'Montgomery said that Churchward was most insistent. I am sorry, Sal.'

'I will see you tonight,' Jack had said, when he had put her on the train at Oxford and given her a brief, hard kiss in parting. Tonight, with the King present and the unveiling of the Crimson Salon, Jack Kestrel would walk in not only as her fiancé, but also as the man with a controlling share in the Blue Parrot. If Greg had sold, he would have owned almost everything. Everything that Sally had worked for, everything that she had struggled to achieve over the last seven years, belonged to Jack. He had taken her body and he had taken her heart and now he had almost succeeded in taking her business. She was ruined. It was the perfect revenge.

Yet some stubborn instinct in her told her that Jack would never do that to her. Even while the doubts whispered in her mind, reminding her that Jack was ruthless and she barely knew him at all, an obstinate loyalty and the deep conviction she had that she *did* know him, made her cling tenaciously to the idea that he would never hurt her like that.

'I don't believe it,' she whispered.

Greg was looking at her with pity. She knew he thought she was denying the truth because she could not face the idea of Jack's betrayal.

'Don't say you are sorry again,' Sally said, as Greg opened his mouth to speak. He shrugged, but kept silent.

'Jack would not do that,' Sally said, but she wondered if she was trying to convince herself.

'Whatever happens tonight,' Greg said, standing up, 'I shall be there for you, Sal.'

He went out. Sally heard him say goodbye to Mary, heard the sound of the door closing behind him, and then she sat in silence, she did not know for how long, with the thoughts and fears, dreams and nightmares jostling in her head, until she finally admitted to herself that she did not know what to believe.

'Matty! Matty!' Sally tumbled through the door of her bedroom to find Mrs Matson knitting placidly in the chair beside the fireplace.

'Here's a to-do!' Mrs Matson said, laying her work aside and getting stiffly to her feet. 'Wondered what had happened to you, Miss Sally. Isn't the King due in an hour and a half?'

Sally threw a harassed look at the clock. 'He is! Why did no one come to find me?'

'Didn't want to disturb you,' Mrs Matson said, pursing her lips. 'Remember what happened last time I walked in—?' She stopped, peering. 'You've been crying, pet. You never cry. What's the matter?'

'Nothing,' Sally said. 'Everything.' She dashed the back of her hand across her cheeks. 'Oh, Matty, some-one has bought up the Blue Parrot and I think it is Mr Kestrel and I can't help but worry he has done it for revenge! He will take everything, Matty, everything I have worked for, and I can't bear it!'

'Can't bear for him to take it or can't bear that he might have betrayed you?' Mrs Matson asked shrewdly.

'Both!' Sally gulped. 'How *could* I have been so stupid to have fallen in love with him, Matty? I barely know him! And it hurts so much to think he might have done this.'

Mrs Matson caught Sally's cold hands in hers. 'Wait, wait! You don't know what he has done. You won't know until you ask him.'

'No,' Sally said, 'but I cannot speak to him when the King is here and all my guests... Oh!' She ran a hand through her hair, dislodging the pins. 'How monstrously stupid I have been!'

'Can't help who you fall in love with,' Mrs Matson said comfortably, going over to the wardrobe and taking out a glittering silver gown that tumbled like a waterfall over her arm. 'Knew the moment I saw Matson that he was the man for me.'

'Did you?' Sally said, staring. She had never known that.

'Didn't marry him for nine years, mind,' Matty said. 'We had to save up.' She looked at Sally. 'One week, nine years… Sometimes it doesn't make any difference to how you feel. I'll draw you a bath, Miss Sally. You'll feel better after that.'

An hour later, dressed in the beautiful Worth silver gown, with her hair in diamond pins and all traces of tears removed from her face, Sally hurried down the stairs at the Blue Parrot.

Dan met her as soon as she reached the bottom step.

'There's trouble,' he said.

Sally shot him a look. Her nerves, already fluttering as tight as butterflies in her stomach, tightened further.

'The King is here,' Dan said.

'Already?' Sally was horrified. She checked the marble clock in the hall. 'He is not due for another half-hour and he is always late! Why did you not come to tell me?'

'I was on my way,' Dan said plaintively. 'He only arrived five minutes ago—with Mr Kestrel.'

Sally felt a flash of panic. So Jack had arrived, too—and he had not come to find her. All the fears and doubts she had tried so hard to suppress came rushing back. Was he going to use this night, of all nights, to announce that he now owned the Blue Parrot and had ruined her business and her reputation? She pushed the terrifying thought out of her mind and tried to concentrate.

'Where are they now?' she enquired.

'In the Crimson Salon. They thought they would be the first to use the new gaming tables for a game of *chemin de fer.*'

Sally swore softly. 'Very well.' She might have known that Jack Kestrel and King Edward between them would create havoc with her carefully planned evening. First she was supposed to greet the King and make a little speech welcoming her guests, then she was going to declare the new Salon open and send around the champagne... But of course Jack and King Edward had had to arrive early and ruin all her plans. The guests were streaming in now, the ladies elegant in rainbow silks, the gentlemen stark in black-and-white evening dress. All looked horrified when they heard the whisper that the King was already there. Sally hurried towards the Crimson Salon, her heels snapping over the marble floor.

Dan threw open the door and Sally paused on the threshold. For a moment it felt as though time had unrolled and she was standing there on the night a week before when Jack had almost broken the bank. Tonight he had observed the dress code and was looked devastatingly handsome in black and pristine white. In other ways the picture was the same as it had been the previous time; Jack was sprawled in his chair, a lock of dark hair falling across his forehead, his cards held in one careless hand. He had discarded his jacket and the pure whiteness of his shirt looked stark against the darkness of his tanned skin. He looked arrogant and dangerous and so shockingly attractive that Sally's heart beat violently against her ribs before she took a deep breath and schooled herself to calm.

Jack looked up as Sally started to walk towards the *chemin de fer* table. His gaze, intense and black, seemed to devour her. His concentration was on her alone. Sally was vaguely aware of all her guests hurrying into the Salon behind her, whispering and jostling. They could feel the tension in the air. They knew something unexpected was going to happen.

As Sally approached the table, both King Edward and Jack Kestrel rose to their feet.

'Your Majesty.' By sheer force of will, Sally kept her gaze from Jack and smiled demurely at the King as she dropped her curtsy. The light from the diamond chandelier was dazzling. The King, already wreathed in cigar smoke and with a champagne glass at his elbow, smiled expansively.

'Evening, Sal.' Edward planted a gallant kiss on the back of Sally's hand. He did not apologise for arriving early and throwing all her plans into confusion. He knew he could do as he liked. 'You look stunning tonight, my dear,' he said, 'does she not, Kestrel?'

'Exquisite,' Jack said, and the look in his eyes made Sally burn inside.

'I am sorry,' she said, 'that I kept you waiting, your Majesty.'

'No matter.' Edward beamed broadly. 'Jack here thought to keep me entertained with a game of *chemin de fer*. I fear he is already winning though, my dear. Five hundred up against the house.'

Sally grimaced. 'Mr Kestrel has the devil's own luck, sir, as you have observed yourself.'

Jack laughed. There was a wicked spark in his eyes. 'I'll wager all my winnings tonight against one night with you, Miss Bowes,' he said, as he had once before.

There was a ripple of scandalous shock around the room.

Sally took a deep breath. 'Mr Kestrel,' she said, meeting the challenge in his gaze, 'for all your prowess at the gaming tables, you are a slow learner. I told you once before that the Blue Parrot is not that sort of establishment and I am not that sort of woman.' She raised her brows. 'Besides, you are playing against your own bank now, are you not, Mr Kestrel? Now that you own a controlling stake in the Blue Parrot?'

Jack's eyes narrowed. He masked his surprise well, Sally thought. It was no wonder that he was so successful at cards. But she could also tell that he had not known she was aware of his plans. In that one respect she held the upper hand. His gaze was fixed on hers and for the briefest second Sally saw uncertainty in his eyes, vulnerability even. He hesitated. Sally had never thought to see vulnerability in Jack Kestrel. It caught at her heart and it puzzled her as well.

Suddenly there was a silence in the room so acute that Sally could hear her own breathing.

'What's this?' King Edward spoke sharply and both

Sally and Jack jumped. Sally had forgotten he was even there. 'You have bought up the Blue Parrot, Kestrel?'

'I… Yes.' Jack cleared his throat. 'It was intended to be a surprise for Miss Bowes.'

'It certainly was that,' Sally said.

The King was looking from one to the other. 'To what end?'

Jack was silent. The King was frowning. The crowd shifted and shimmered under the dazzling white lights of the chandeliers as everyone strained to hear what was going on. Even the waiters, busy dispensing champagne, had frozen where they stood.

'I think I can answer that question, your Majesty,' Sally said. She did not take her gaze from Jack for a single second. She could feel that she was shaking. She was about to take a huge risk, to let go of her doubts and show publicly all the love she had for Jack and the faith she had in him. And if he chose to use that to humiliate her then she would be finished.

'I think Mr Kestrel bought the Blue Parrot for me as an engagement present,' she said. 'I think he intended to give the deeds to me tonight.'

Something shifted in Jack's expression and suddenly she saw all the love and fear and doubt in him that was a mirror image for her own anxieties, and then she saw it swamped by a blazing joy as he grabbed her in his arms and kissed her so fiercely she lost her breath. Her heart leapt and she gave a gasp of mingled disbelief and elation.

'Sally Bowes,' Jack said, against her lips, 'you are the sweetest and most generous and loving of women and I do not deserve you, but I love you so much…'

The King, as an amused onlooker, started to applaud. He had a wide smile on his face. After a shocked second everyone else in the Crimson Salon joined in.

'Well,' Sally said, emerging ruffled and breathless from Jack's embrace, 'that was neither the speech nor the spectacle I was planning, but I think it has got the evening off to a fine start.'

Everyone was coming up to congratulate them now. Gregory Holt shouldered his way through the crowd and offered Jack his hand.

'You could have had my stake as well if you had only told me what it was for, old fellow,' he said. He smiled at Sally. 'I will make my shares over to you tomorrow, Sal.'

Jack looked rueful. 'I am sorry,' he said. 'I have a bad habit of secrecy. But I am sure Sally will cure me of it.'

Some enterprising musician struck up a celebratory dance and Jack caught Sally's hand.

'If you will permit, your Majesty?' he said.

'Of course.' Edward kissed Sally soundly. 'Spirit your fiancée away with my blessing, Kestrel. I shall come to the wedding of course,' he added, much to Sally's secret horror. 'But for now, more cards—and more champagne!'

All those who had been present at the Blue Parrot that night later agreed that it was the event of the Season. The King won at *chemin de fer*, the champagne flowed like a river, the dancing continued until morning and that most unobtainable bachelor, Jack Kestrel, was so besotted with his fiancée that he refused to leave her side for a second, a sight which many people had thought never to live to see.

'You were right, of course,' Jack said. Dawn was breaking and he and Sally were sitting alone in the rose arbour in the garden of the Blue Parrot. The morning scent of dew on the grass filled the air and the birds were starting to sing. Jack held Sally's hand as though it was a lifeline. He could still not quite believe that she was truly, publicly his. He still could not believe he could love her so much.

'When I first bought up all the stakeholders in the Blue Parrot, I had no intention of giving the club to you,' he said. 'I was so angry and disillusioned that

I wanted to take everything away from you and ruin you. I am so sorry, Sally.'

Sally's head was against his shoulder. Her hair tickled his face. 'It doesn't matter,' she said serenely. 'I guessed that was what you planned. Greg came to warn me, and I was very fearful, but some instinct told me you would never hurt me like that. So I took the risk.'

'You showed me how much you trusted me,' Jack said, turning his face into her hair and inhaling the scent of her, wanting to feel her deep in his bones. 'You are braver than I. I was humbled.'

'Hmm,' Sally said. 'That cannot happen very often.'

'I love you,' Jack said. He slid an arm about her and drew her closer against him, where it felt as though she belonged. 'I loved you from the first moment we met, though I utterly failed to realise it. I was so accustomed to thinking that the only woman I could ever love was Merle.'

'I understand,' Sally said. 'She was your first love.'

'It was madness,' Jack said, 'like a drug. From the moment she and I met I was entirely swept away, in love with the idea of love, as well as with her. But with you...' he paused, then kissed her '...I feel so much more—love and acceptance and peace as well as excitement at the prospect of the future.' He stopped. 'I am not so good with words,' he said gruffly, 'but I love you so much I can scarce believe it.'

'You could show me,' Sally said, tilting her face up to his in the most innocently provocative way he had ever seen, 'if you would like to.'

Astonishingly, Jack found himself hesitating for a second. It seemed extraordinary that he, the greatest rake in London, should be reluctant to make love to his own fiancée, and yet he felt unsure. He felt hesitant about almost everything in the newly discovered world of his where Sally held his future in her hands.

'If you are absolutely certain—' he began, stopping abruptly as Sally put a hand around his neck and brought his lips down to hers. She tasted sweet and desirable and his head spun. He relaxed into the feeling, recognising now that there was so much more here than lust, so much of warmth and generosity and love, and that it was his for the taking.

'I think,' Sally said, as their lips parted, 'that once we set a wedding date your Great-Aunt Ottoline will insist on an inordinate amount of propriety from us, so it is perhaps best that we should be totally improper now.'

Jack grabbed her hand and was about to hurry her back inside the club, but she stopped him. 'No,' she whispered. 'There are too many people there. Come with me…'

Like a wraith in her silver gown, she led him into the green depths of the garden to where a topiary arch led to an enclosed garden with a sunken pool and a little wooden pagoda. The dawn light glittered on the water and the air was full of the scent of roses. Sally let go of him only for long enough to go into the pagoda and emerge with a heavy rag-rug seat cover the same red-and-gold colour as the roses. She laid it down on the grass in the shadow on the hedge.

'Here,' she said, with a bewitching smile. She lowered her lashes. 'I must confess,' she continued, 'that our last encounter gave me a taste for fresh air.'

Jack's mouth went dry. 'Here?'

She looked at him a little quizzically. 'I am beginning to think that your reputation is decidedly unde-served, Mr Kestrel.'

Jack was beside her in one stride, covering her mouth with his, pulling her into his arms. 'We'll see,' he said.

'This is a Worth gown,' she said, when he released her. Her voice was a little unsteady.

Jack laughed. 'Darling, I'll buy you twenty of them.'

Sally, whose busy fingers had been working on the fastenings of his shirt, paused for a moment. 'Could you?'

'Yes,' Jack said, obliging her by shrugging himself out of the shirt, and pulling her down to sit with him on the rug. 'So far you seem to have given little real thought to my financial circumstances—despite my shameful suspicions that you were a fortune hunter—but I am accounted extremely wealthy, you know.'

'How delightful,' Sally said. Her hands were sliding over his bare chest in distracting circles. She pressed a kiss against his collarbone and the ripples of sensation shivered across his skin. He tried to concentrate, before it was too late.

'You will want to continue working after we are wed,' he said huskily. 'I understand that.'

'I thought that you must,' Sally said, trailing kisses haphazardly down his chest, 'when you gave me the deeds to the Club.'

'But we may have a house in the country—'

'Where I may design a garden even bigger and more exciting than this one,' Sally finished. Her fingers had reached the waistband of his trousers now. 'Must I do this all myself?' she complained.

'No,' Jack said. He tumbled her over beneath him so that she lay looking up at him, ethereal in her silver gown, her hair spread out about her on the rug. He slid the gown from her shoulders. 'Mmn. I like this one.'

Her skin was creamy white, bathed in the dawn light. He lowered his head to kiss her brow softly and to trace the curve of her cheek with his lips, nuzzling lower to her neck and the vulnerable skin beneath her ear. He heard her breathing catch and felt her shiver as he eased the gown down over her body to pool in a silver heap on the rug beside them.

'No damage done,' he said. He ran his hands down her tightly laced body, lingering over the curve of her breasts, delving into the satin softness of the bloomers, finding the gap that left her completely defenceless to his touch. 'Odd,' he said reflectively, 'that a corset is as effective as a suit of armour above, and yet below...' Slyly, his fingers stroked her inner thigh, then slipped deeper to caress her intimately. Sally gave a little gasp and arched to the touch of his hand.

'Jack...' Her voice broke on his name.

'Have patience, sweetheart.' He dropped a lush kiss on her mouth. He found the contrast of her tight lacing above and flagrant exposure below intensely arousing. It was something, he thought, that he would need to explore at length in future. But for now, he needed her naked. He wanted to devour every last inch of her cool, sweet body and know that it was his entirely, freely given.

'I need to unlace you,' he whispered.

Through a combination of luck, force and willpower Jack managed to relieve Sally of her underwear and himself of the remainder of his own clothes, and managed to keep his sanity intact as well. He was so hard now that he was desperate for her, but he was not going to hurry. He covered her pale body with his own, worshipping her with his hands and his mouth, branding her with kisses over her breasts and the sweet curve of her stomach. His tongue traced the line of her hip and again she arched against him with a gasp of pure need. With a groan he dragged her body against him. She tasted hot and sweet and smelled of summer and roses and it drugged his senses until they spun. She gave him back each eager kiss and caress, generous and open as ever, and his heart swelled with love and peace and the last dark corners of his mind were flooded with light.

'This time it is with love,' he whispered, 'and it always will be.'

Her eyes were wide and dark, dazed with passion, brilliant with tears. His fingers brushed her cheek tenderly. She clung to him, drawing him down, and he took her mouth with leashed passion, pressing gently within her, feeling her tighten around him and his body catch fire from hers. He was aware of nothing then but her sweet, fevered response and the whirling, painful spiral of his own desire until he tumbled over the edge, gave all of himself without reservation for the first time in his life, and lay spent and dazzled with Sally clasped tightly in his arms and against his heart.

'Sally?'

Sally woke reluctantly to the sound of Jack's voice and realised that she was still lying naked in his arms on the rag rug and that a drift of rose petals had fallen from the tree about them and dusted their bodies with pink and gold. Her skin felt a little chilled from the fresh morning air and she shivered and burrowed closer to Jack's warmth. His arms tightened about her in response.

'Sally?' he repeated.

'Mmm?' She was so happy and at peace that she did not wish to have to move or think, but Jack persisted.

'You do realise,' he said, his breath stirring her hair, 'that you have not told me that you love me.'

Sally gave a little spurt of laughter. It seemed extraordinary that she had never told him when she had known almost from the start that she had fallen in love with him.

'Well…' she said, thoughtfully, rubbing her fingers

in gentle circles over his chest. 'I do like you a great deal, Jack. I enjoy your company. You have a delightful family. And although such matters do not weigh with me, I am thrilled that you are so rich—'

She broke off with a muffled gasp as he stopped her words with a kiss.

'Minx!' But there was a note of anxiety in his voice that she was quick to hear and she realised with surprise that he was nervous. Jack Kestrel, the last rake in London, was anxious because he loved her so much that he would not be able to bear it if she did not love him equally. Sally's heart ached as she realised how much he needed her.

'Oh, Jack,' she said, 'I love you very much.' She hesitated. 'Although I have known you but a short time, I feel as though I have loved you for a very long time.'

Jack made a sound of satisfaction and wrapped her closer still in his arms. Sally thought fleetingly then of Merle Jameson and of her father and of all the shadows that had haunted the past for both her and for Jack. She opened her mind like a flower opening to the sun and let the regrets and the jealousy and the guilt drift away for the last time, then turned her face up to Jack's and kissed him until they lost themselves again in one another.

Epilogue

They were married in the church at Dauntsey a month later. Charley and Nell were the bride's attendants and Lucy made an adorable flower child. The King and Queen were the guests of honour, which gratified Lady Ottoline exceedingly. Gregory Holt was groomsman.

Connie and Bertie did not attend. They were on an extended honeymoon in Scotland. Connie, forgetting that she was writing to congratulate her sister, instead wrote that she detested Scotland; that most of the time it rained and when it did not she was eaten by the midges, that Bertie spent all his time fishing or shooting things and she was bored to death.

After the wedding reception was over Sally, Jack and Lady Ottoline stood in the hall beneath a portrait of Sally, Duchess of Kestrel, and Lady Ottoline took Sally's hand in hers.

'One day,' she said gruffly, 'you will be Duchess in my mother's place and in her own image. I know she would have approved of you.'

Sally, looking up at the Duchess's piquant face and smiling green eyes, thought that she was perhaps right.

Jack's arm tightened about Sally's waist. 'She will be magnificent,' he prophesied and Sally could see all the love he felt for her in his eyes.

Lady Ottoline smiled. 'And as for you, nephew,' she said, 'I am glad that you have come home at last.'

Jack looked up at the picture of Justin, Duke of Kestrel, on the opposite wall to his wife.

'The last rake in London is caught,' he said, an irresistible smile on his lips. 'He is home and he is very happy with his fate.'

* * * * *

Read all about it...

MORE ABOUT THIS BOOK

MORE ABOUT THE AUTHOR

2

Read all about it...

NICOLA CORNICK ON *Dauntsey Park: The Last Rake in London*

As an author who has set most of her books in the Regency period, I found writing a book with a background of the Edwardian era quite a challenge! Yet the more I researched the Edwardian period, the more struck I was by the similarities with the Regency. There was the same glitter and decadence in High Society, there was the gambling and the balls and the country house parties, the fabulous fashions and the contrast between the self-indulgent lifestyle of the rich élite and the poverty of the rest of the population. And somewhere in the process of planning the book, I thought it would be nice to link *Dauntsey Park: The Last Rake in London* with my Regency writing because the comparisons were so strong that this felt the natural thing to do.

Jack Kestrel is the last rake in London, a man whose behaviour harks back to an earlier era when his ancestors, the Dukes of Kestrel, were renowned for their gambling and womanising. I wrote the stories of Justin Kestrel, his brothers Richard and Lucas and their friend Cory Newlyn in my **Bluestocking Brides** trilogy and I thought it would be wonderful if Jack was a man cut from the same cloth, not simply in terms of his ancestry but also in the way that he had inherited all the vices—and virtues!—of his rakish forbears!

For me, Jack Kestrel epitomises all the fascination of the Edwardian era. He is born into the aristocracy but is also a self-made man deeply involved in the scientific advances of his day. He is a rake who needs a strong self-made woman to tame him! Like his ancestors he thinks he will never fall in love. Like them he finds his destiny.

Fashion

Edwardian etiquette demanded several changes of clothing for both men and women throughout the day, depending on the social event they were attending.

The fuchsia pink silk dress worn by Sally in **Dauntsey Park: The Last Rake in London** was at the cutting edge of fashion in 1908. Whilst gowns by designers such as Worth were made for a more traditional clientele, the tea gowns designed by Mariano Fortuny and evening gowns by Paul Poiret freed women from the constraints of the old-fashioned corset.

The corset was designed to produce an S-shaped figure and was laced as tightly as possible. This placed restrictions on breathing and movement that were dangerous to health. In 1906 *Woman's Life* magazine criticised tight lacing for causing "more ruined digestions, more red noses, more weak hearts, more agonies of pain…than anything else." It must have been a huge relief when fashion moved on!

Poiret established his own fashion house in 1903. He designed flamboyant window displays and threw legendary parties to draw attention to his work; his instinct for marketing and branding was unmatched by any previous designer. In 1909, he was so famous that the wife of HH Asquith, the Prime Minister, invited him to show his designs at 10 Downing Street. The cheapest garment at his exhibition cost thirty guineas, double the annual salary of a scullery maid.

Men's fashions were also changing at this time. In **Dauntsey Park: The Last Rake in London**, Jack borrows a tuxedo to wear for a formal dinner. Whilst these were increasing in popularity during the period they were not considered com-

Read all about it...

pletely acceptable for formal events!

The Age of Science and Invention

Renowned for its golden days of aristocratic indulgence, the Edwardian period was also the age of science and invention, with the first motor cars taking to the streets, the first developments in aviation and the London Underground Railway spreading out into the city suburbs.

Nowhere were the inventions and developments of the age more spectacularly displayed than at the Franco-British Exhibition of 1908. This was the largest fair of its kind and the first international exhibition that was sponsored jointly by two countries. It was organised to celebrate the Entente Cordiale of 1904 and to display and promote the industrial achievements of both countries. On 14th May, 1908, the Prince of Wales, the future George V, declared the exhibition open, and Madame Albani sang the national anthem in the pouring rain. On 26th May "The Marseillaise" and the national anthem were played for the visit of President Fallières of France and Edward VII. As the exhibition buildings were all painted white the event and the site soon gained the nickname, "The Great White City," a name that was to be preserved for history when the Central Line opened a station there in the 1950s.

Besides the "serious" exhibitions of machinery and products, there was a wide range of novelty attractions and sideshows such as toboggan rides, slides, helter-skelters and the Flip-Flap. This was a fairground ride consisting of two one-hundred-and-fifty-foot counterpoised iron arms, with carriages holding fifty people, which went up to two hundred feet, passing each other. By the end of the exhibition over a million people had paid £27,000 to go on it. The attraction also inspired the White City hit song, Darewski and Willmott's "Take Me on the Flip-Flap" which was performed in the music halls to great acclaim. The 1908 Olympic Games also took place in London and the stadium was built on the same site.

In the words of the song:

"Good old London's in a maze
With its very latest craze
And every day in crowds we fight and push
On a motorbus to climb
Twenty-seven at a time,
Or take a good old tube to Shepherd's Bush.
It's an exhibition rare that is drawing
thousands there
Every nation gaining in the grand display…"

It must have been quite an experience!

Read all about it...

FURTHER RECOMMENDED READING

The Edwardian Country House by Juliet Gardiner—A book that gives a fascinating insight into the romance and reality of Edwardian society and evokes the "golden" years before the First World War.

Victorian and Edwardian London by AR Hope Moncrieff—First published in 1910, this book, written by a Victorian gentleman about town, takes the reader on a tour of central London and describes the customs of the times.

The Edwardians: Biography of the Edwardian Age by Roy Hattersley—A vivid picture of Edwardian Britain, covering everything from the class system to the indulgences of the aristocracy, to the invention of the motor car and aeroplane.

The Edwardians by Vita Sackville-West—Written in 1930, this fictional account of the Edwardian aristocracy is a riveting read! Vita Sackville-West was the daughter of the third Baron Sackville, was born at Knole House in Kent, and drew on all her personal experience to recreate the age of her youth.

Victorian and Edwardian Fashion: A Photographic Survey by Alison Gernsheim—A must for those interested in costume design and fashion. Lavish photographs illustrate the fashions of the era.

NICOLA CORNICK – Biography

For the first eighteen years of her life Nicola lived in Yorkshire, within a stone's throw of the moors that had inspired the Brontë sisters to write *Jane Eyre* and *Wuthering Heights*. One of her grandfathers was a poet, and her family contained teachers and avid readers who filled the house with books. With such a background it was impossible for Nicola not to become a bookworm.

Nicola went to school in a historic building that had originally been the dower house of a stately home. Studying in an ancient building helped her to develop her love of history and literature, and she is grateful for the inspiration she was given by some exceptional teachers.

Whilst at school, Nicola spent her evenings reading piles of romances and historical novels and watching costume dramas with her grandmother. Her grandparents, who were a huge inspiration to her, also taught her canasta, ballroom dancing and how to grow rhubarb.

Nicola studied history at London University and during her holidays did a variety of jobs, from sticking price tags on shoes in a factory to serving refreshments on a steam railway. When she left college she worked in university administration, combining her work as a Deputy Registrar during the day with writing historical romance in the evenings. She met her future husband in London and married after a wonderfully old-fashioned courtship based on letter writing. They moved to Somerset and lived for seven years in a cottage haunted by the ghost of a cavalier.

It took Nicola a while to realise that she was meant to be a writer. She wrote bits and pieces of novels in her spare time, but never finished any of them. Eventually she sent in the first three

Read all about it...

chapters of a Regency romance to Mills & Boon and, although they were rejected, she found she had become so addicted to writing that she could not stop. Happily, her third attempt was accepted and she has never looked back. She has now written twenty-five historical romances and has been short-listed for the Romance Writers of America RITA® Award, nominated twice for the Romantic Novelists' Association Romance Prize and *Romantic Times* Reviewer's Choice awards, and has won the LORIES Award of Excellence.

Nicola lives in Oxfordshire with her husband, two lazy cats and an adorable Labrador. She works part-time as a guide at a historic house and also in a second-hand bookshop, which she says is like letting a chocolate addict loose in a sweet shop! In 2006 she was awarded a Master's degree with distinction from Ruskin College, Oxford, where she wrote her dissertation on heroes.

Nicola loves to hear from her readers, and can be contacted by e-mail at ncornick@madasafish.com or via her website, www.nicolacornick.com

Read all about it...

NICOLA CORNICK ON Writing

What do you love most about being a writer?

I feel very happy to be able to do a job that I love. I love creating characters and sharing their world. And the feeling I get when the writing is going well and I'm on a roll fills me with elation.

Where do you go for inspiration?

I go to several different places for inspiration. If I'm feeling studious I will turn to my history books for ideas and stimulation. If I need to think I will go out for a walk on the hills to clear my head. And if I want to soak up some historical inspiration I will visit a castle or ancient site and just absorb the atmosphere.

Where do your characters come from and do they ever surprise you as you write?

My characters surprise me all the time because I can never predict in advance what they are going to do. As the story progresses they will take on a mind and a will of their own and react to the developments in the plot in their own way, and that's just how it should be. They become very real to me. Sometimes they spring from a story idea I have had, sometimes they are a mixture of qualities and behaviours that I have observed in real people, but mostly they are individuals whose needs and motivations develop naturally.

Do you have a favourite character that you've created and what is it that you like about that character?

Asking me to choose a favourite character is like asking me to choose between my cats! I love them all. In *Dauntsey Park: The Last Rake in London* I loved Jack's aunt, Lady Ottoline Kestrel. I have a soft spot for outspoken old ladies, probably because my grandmother is one! She'll tell you exactly what she thinks and never mince her words but, like Lady

Ottoline, she has a kind heart underneath.

When did you start writing?

I started to write stories when I was at school and I still have the reports praising my imagination but telling me to cut down the number of adjectives and adverbs! I started my first book, *True Colours*, when I was about eighteen and used to read passages out to my college friends over a late-night coffee. I was writing the same book for fourteen years. The difficulty was fitting in my writing between the demands of my family and day job, but I never gave up on it and when it was finally accepted for publication I was over the moon. Before that I hadn't even considered a career as a writer.

What one piece of advice would you give to a writer wanting to start a career?

Believe in yourself and your writing. Believe that you will be successful even if you are trying to juggle your writing with a job, family and a hundred and one other responsibilities. Don't give up. Writers need to be determined to succeed!

Read on for an exclusive extract from Nicola Cornick's
upcoming novel

NOTORIOUS

CHAPTER ONE

"He who does not burn with desire grows cold."
—Seventeenth Century Proverb

JAMES DEVLIN WAS twenty-seven years old and he had everything that he had ever wanted. He had a place in society, he had a beautiful, rich fiancée and he had a title of his own. Yet on the night that his former wife walked back into his life after nine years absence he was bored; as bored as it was possible for a gentleman to be at a ton ball at the height of the London season.

It was another night of lavish excess and hollow entertainment. The Duke and Duchess of Alton threw the best parties in the ton, opulent, tasteful and frightfully exclusive. For Dev it was also another night of fetching lemonade for Emma when she became thirsty, of finding her fan when she misplaced it and of fawning on Emma's mama, who could not stand him and probably did not even know his name although he had been betrothed to her daughter for two years. Once upon a time Dev had had to brave the elements on the rain-lashed deck of a ship of the line, scramble up rigging and fight for his life. Each day had brought new dangers, new excitement. It had only been two years but it felt like a century ago. These days he did nothing more dangerous than check the set of his coat and pass Emma her reticule.

"Jealous, Dev?" His sister Francesca put a hand on his sleeve and Dev realized that he had been frowning at Emma across the dance floor, glaring at her as she twirled through the steps of the waltz in the arms of her cousin Frederick Walters. Chessie was not the only one who had noticed his grim stance. He saw the sideways glances and covert amusement. Everyone thought that he was possessive, resentful of the time that Emma, a consummate flirt, lavished on other men. If he had been the jealous type he would have spent his days on the dueling field but the fact was that one had to care in order to be jealous and Dev had long ago realized that he did not care a jot if Emma flirted with every man in London.

He straightened up and smoothed the frown from his brow. "I'm not jealous in the least," he said.

Chessie's blue gaze appraised his face, looking for signs that he was trying to fool her. "It is no secret that the Earl and Countess of Brooke prefer Fred as a suitor for Emma," she said.

Dev shrugged. "The Earl and Countess would prefer a distempered hound as a suitor for Emma but I am the one that Emma wants."

"And Emma always gets what she wants." There was the very faintest edge to Chessie's voice now.

Dev shot his sister a look. Chessie had not yet got what she wanted and she had been waiting a long time. Fitzwilliam Alton, only son and heir to the Duke and Duchess, had been paying Chessie marked attention for some months. Such public notice could only end respectably in a proposal of marriage but so far Fitz had not declared himself and now the ton was starting to gossip. Society, Dev thought, had not been kind, talking scandal about him and Chessie in particular from the first. They had breeding of sorts, but precious little of it and no money. He had at least carved out something of a Navy career for himself before he had resorted to hunting a fortune. Chessie had had to make an impression through her beauty and her vivacious personality alone. It was always harder for a woman.

"You don't like Emma," Dev said now.

He felt rather than saw his sister's scornful glance. "I don't like what she has done to you," she said. "You've become one of Emma's pets, like that fluffy white dog or her bad-tempered monkey."

Ouch.

"It's a small price to pay for what I want," Dev said.

Wealth. Status. He had hunted them for the last ten years. Born with nothing, he had no intention of going back to the poverty of his youth. Now everything was within his grasp and if that meant he had to be Emma's lapdog for the rest of his life there were worse fates. Or so he told himself.

"You are no better," he said to his sister, aware that he sounded perilously close to the tit for tat banter of their childhood. "You have caught yourself a marquis."

Chessie flicked her fan in a gesture that conveyed total disdain. "Don't be so vulgar, Dev. I am completely different from you. I may be a fortune hunter but at least I love Fitz. And anyway—" a tiny frown marred her brow "—I have not caught him yet."

"He'll propose soon," Dev said. He had heard the trace of uncertainty in Chessie's voice that revealed how wafer thin was her confidence. He wanted to reassure her, even though he thought Fitzwilliam Alton nowhere near good enough for his sister. "Fitz loves you, too," he said, hoping he was right. "He is only waiting for the right moment to tell his parents the news."

"That will never happen," Chessie said dryly.

"You must love Fitz very much to be prepared to endure the Duchess of Alton as a mother-in-law," Dev said.

"And you must love Emma's money very much to be prepared to endure the Countess of Brooke," Chessie said.

"I do," Dev said.

Chessie shook her head slightly. "It will not serve, Dev," she said. "In the end you will hate her."

"I'm sure you are right," Dev said. "I already dislike her very much."

"I meant Emma," Chessie said, her eyes on the shifting patterns of the dance, "not her mother. Though if Emma becomes more like her mother as she grows older that will be hard to bear."

Dev could not deny that it was not an appealing prospect.

"If Fitz becomes more like his mother you will have to squeeze money out of him like a lemon," he said. The Duchess of Alton had a sour disposition and a mouth like the tightly drawn drawstring of a purse. It gave fair warning as to her character.

Chessie gave a spontaneous giggle. "Fitz will not become like his parents." The laughter faded from her face and she fidgeted with the struts of her fan, her gloved fingers pulling at the lace. Lately, Dev thought, she seemed to have lost some of her sparkle. Now he could see her searching the crowded room for Fitz. She was wearing her heart on her sleeve. He felt a rush of protective concern. Chessie was pinning everything on the prospect of this betrothal and Fitz, genial enough, but arrogant and spoiled in equal measure, was aware of her regard and was toying with her reputation. Chessie deserved better than that. Dev clenched his fists at his side. One step out of line and he would ram that silver spoon Fitz had been born with right down his throat.

"You look very fierce," Chessie said, squeezing his arm.

"Sorry," Dev said, smoothing out his expression again. He smiled at her. "We haven't done badly," he said, "for two penniless orphans from County Galway."

Chessie did not reply and he saw that her gaze had returned to the waltz, which was now spinning to a triumphant climax. Fitz, tall, dark, distinguished, was at the far end of the room, almost lost in the shift and sway of the dancers. He was partnering a woman in a shimmering silver gauze gown, a woman who was also tall and dark. They looked magnificent together. Fitz had always had a weakness for a pretty face, just as his cousin Emma wanted a handsome trophy of a husband. But this woman was different from Fitz's usual flirts and there was something about the way that she moved, the lilt and cadence of her steps that shot Dev through with recognition even though he could not see her face.

"Who is that?" he said, and his voice sounded a little hoarse. Something strange—premonition—was edging up his spine. He was the least superstitious of men yet he felt the cold air breathe gooseflesh along his skin even though the Duke and Duchess of Alton's ballroom was stiflingly hot.

He could see that Chessie felt something, too. She was strung as tight as violin, her face pale now. He saw a shiver rack her body.

"Someone rich," she said bitterly. "Someone beautiful and eligible whom Fitz's parents will have introduced to him tonight in order to distract him from me."

"Nonsense," Dev said bracingly. "She will be yet another horse-faced, inbred poor relation—"

"Dev," Chessie reproved, as a dowager rustled past them on a wave of disapproval.

The music finished on a resounding flourish. There was a ripple of applause about the room. The pattern of dancers broke up. Fitz was escorting his partner across the floor toward them. Evidently he intended to introduce her to Chessie. Dev was not sure whether that reassured him or worried him.

"Dev!" Emma had also arrived, breathless and flushed by his side, dragging Freddie Walters with her by the hand. "Come and dance with me!"

For the first time in as long as he could remember, Dev did not respond immediately to Emma's imperious demand. Instead he was watching the woman at Fitz's side. She was not in the first flush of youth, closer perhaps to his age than Chessie's. Age, or experience, or both, gave her an unconscious confidence. She walked with the same elegance that Dev had seen in her in the waltz, a fluid grace that was accentuated by the sinuous swirl of the silver gauze gown. It caressed her breasts and hips, wrapping itself about her like a lover's kiss. There was not a man in the room, Dev thought, who was not staring at her, his mouth drying with lust, his mind a rampage of images as to what it would be like to unwrap that gown from those curves.

Or perhaps those were just his fantasies.

She was very pale with the kind of translucent skin dusted with freckles that was a feature of the Celtic races. The contrast between her vivid green eyes and her black hair was shocking, exhilarating. It made her look fragile and fey, like a kelpie or dryad, too exotic to be human. Her black curls were piled up on her head in a tumble of ringlets held by a dazzling diamond comb. Matching jewels sparkled about her slender neck and adorned her wrists. Not a poor relation then. She looked magnificent.

She also looked familiar.

Dev's heart missed a beat then started to race. For a moment it felt as though everything had stopped; the music, the chatter, the breath in his body. For one long moment he could neither think nor speak.

It was almost ten years since he had seen Susanna Burney. His last memory of her was not one he was likely ever to forget; Susanna gloriously naked and fast asleep in the bed that they had shared for their brief, passionate wedding night. As he had blown out the guttering candle he had had no notion that he would never see her again.

In the morning she was gone, and with her his marriage. She had left him a note—it had all been a terrible mistake, she had said. She had begged him not to come after her, had said that she would sue for an annulment. Young and full of pride, angry, hurt and betrayed, he had let her go.

It had been two years later when he had returned

from his first full tour of duty with the Royal Navy that he had reconsidered his abandonment of his wayward wife and had traveled to Scotland to find her again. He had told himself that it had been for curiosity's sake alone and to ensure that their annulment had indeed been granted. He had plans for the future, ambitious ideas, and they did not involve the girl he had seduced, married on impulse and let go. Sweat broke out over his body now as he recalled knocking on the door of the rectory and confronting Susanna's uncle and aunt. They had told him that Susanna was dead. He could recall the fierce punch of shock that had made a mockery of his bravado. He had cared for Susanna a great deal more than he had pretended.

Susanna Burney looked very much alive to him.

One whisper of scandal and
a reputation dies...

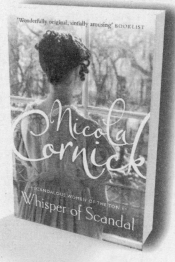

'Wonderfully original, sinfully amusing' BOOKLIST

Nicola Cornick

SCANDALOUS WOMEN OF THE TON

Whisper of Scandal

London, May 1811

Widow Lady Joanna Ware has no desire to wed again
but that doesn't stop the flurry of suitors knocking on
her door. Desperate to thwart another proposal, Joanna
brazenly kisses Arctic explorer Alex, Lord Grant.   But
matters are complicated when she learns her deceased
husband has bequeathed his illegitimate child to her and
his friend Alex; and they must travel to the Arctic to
claim the orphan. Battling blizzards, dangerous wild life,
and a treacherous plot, Alex must protect Joanna but
not before he wickedly seduces her...

Scandalous Women of the Ton continues in
One Wicked Sin and *Mistress by Midnight*

www.mirabooks.co.uk

"I hired you as a novelty, an attraction, the most notorious woman in London..."

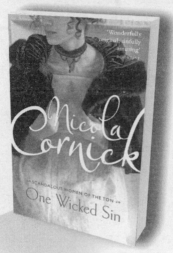

London, July 1813

Once the toast of the *ton*, Lottie Cummings is now divorced—and penniless. Shunned by society, the destitute beauty is forced to become a courtesan. Refusing to oblige her customers, Lottie's about to be turned out on to the streets. Until a dangerous rake saves her with a scandalous offer.

The illegitimate son of a duke, Ethan Ryder rose to the ranks of Napoleon's most trusted officer—until his capture landed him in England as prisoner of war. Now Ethan is planning his most audacious coup yet. But he needs to create a spectacular diversion. And having the infamous Lottie as his mistress will certainly do that...

*For a reputation compromised,
there are but two options:
marriage—or infamy...*

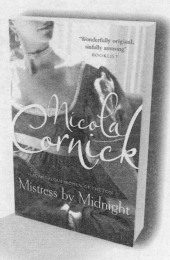

London, May 1811

After her family name was tarnished at his hands,
Merryn has waited ten years to satisfy her revenge
against sensual, mysterious Garrick Northesk,
Duke of Farne.

Yet when a disaster traps Merryn and Garrick
together, white-hot desire stirs between the two
sworn enemies. Her reputation utterly compromised,
Merryn is forced to do the one thing she cannot
bear: accept the scandalous marriage proposal
of the man she has vowed to ruin.

www.mirabooks.co.uk

"I promise that I will release you tomorrow – when the hour of the wedding is past."

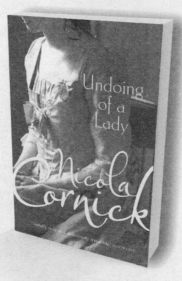

Nat Waterhouse must marry an heiress.
Lady Elizabeth Scarlet vows there is just one way
to save her childhood friend from a loveless
marriage: kidnap him!

When her inexperienced attempt flares into intense
passion, Lizzie is ruined…and hopelessly in love!
Now the wild and wilful Lizzie must convince Nat
that they are a perfect match – in every way.

www.mirabooks.co.uk

"Blackmail is such an ugly word, Miss Lister. It is essential that I marry you. So let us call it a bargain."

When a law requires all unmarried ladies to wed or surrender half their wealth, maid-turned-heiress Miss Alice Lister is a prize to be won!

Now the insufferably attractive Lord Miles Vickery is certain he can gain her fortune by blackmailing her into marriage. Of course, he doesn't yet know he's falling hopelessly in love with this formidable innocent…

www.mirabooks.co.uk

"The arrogance! To think that they can come here with their town bronze and sweep some heiress or other to the altar."

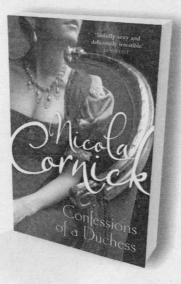

When a feudal law requires all unmarried ladies to wed or surrender half their wealth, the quiet village of Fortune's Folly becomes England's greatest Marriage Market.

Laura, the dowager duchess, is determined to resist the flattery of fortune hunters. Young, handsome and scandalously tempting Dexter Anstruther suspects Laura has a hidden motive for resisting his charms…and he intends to discover it.

www.mirabooks.co.uk